ST. MARTIN'S

MINOTAUR

MYSTERIES

"The sleuthing is fun, but what makes *The Twylight Tower* comparable to the fine works of Allison Weir is the strong writing of the author."
                                        —*Midwest Book Review*

"Exciting . . . and as cleverly crafted as only Karen Harper can be . . . [A] hugely appealing and fast-paced tale that keeps the reader satisfied and yearning for more."
                                        —Romancereviewstoday.com

THE TIDAL POOLE
"A nice mix of historical and fictional characters, deft twists and a plucky, engaging young heroine enhance this welcome sequel."
                                        —*Publishers Weekly*

"Harper delivers high drama and deadly intrigue . . . [S]he masterfully captures the Elizabethan tone in both language and setting . . . Elizabethan history has never been this appealing."
                                        —*Newsday*

THE POYSON GARDEN
"Impressively researched . . . the author has her poisons and her historical details down pat."   —*Los Angeles Times*

"Intoxicating . . . [W]hether you love history, romance, adventure, or mystery, you will be intrigued by this view of Elizabeth as queen and as a brilliant detective."
                                        —*Romantic Times*

"A walk side by side with one of history's most dynamic characters."   —Anne Perry, author of *Half Moon Street*

AN ELIZABETH I MYSTERY

The Thorne Maze

KAREN HARPER

St. Martin's Paperbacks

THE THORNE MAZE

Copyright © 2003 by Karen Harper.
Excerpt from *The Queene's Christmas* © 2003 by Karen Harper.

Cover photograph of the Old Palace © Hatfield House, Hertfordshire, UK / Bridgeman Art Library.

Image of Queen Elizabeth I, by Nicholas Hillard © Fitzwilliam Museum, University of Cambridge, UK / Bridgeman Art Library.

Photograph of maze © Romilly Lockyer / Getty Images.

ISBN: 0-312-99349-8

Printed in the United States of America

St. Martin's Press hardcover edition / February 2003
St. Martin's Paperbacks edition / October 2003

St. Martin's Paperbacks are published by St. Martin's Press, 175 Fifth Avenue, New York, NY 10010.

10 9 8 7 6 5 4 3 2 1

*Our special thanks and much love
to Jayne Harper Black
for her gracious Sunshine State hospitality*

*And, as ever,
to Don.*

Earlier Events in Elizabeth's Life

1533 Henry VIII marries Anne Boleyn, January 25. Elizabeth born September 7.

1536 Anne Boleyn executed. Elizabeth disinherited from crown. Henry marries Jane Seymour.

1537 Prince Edward born. Queen Jane dies of childbed fever.

1544 Act of succession and Henry VIII's will establish Mary and Elizabeth in line of succession.

1547 Henry VII dies. Edward VI crowned.

1553 Catholic Mary Tudor crowned Queen Mary I.

1554 Protestant Wyatt Rebellion fails, but Elizabeth implicated. She is sent to Tower, accompanied by Kat Ashley.

1558 Queen Mary dies; Elizabeth succeeds to throne, November 17. Elizabeth appoints William Cecil Secretary of State. Robert Dudley made master of the Queen's Horse.

1559 Elizabeth crowned in Westminster Abbey, January 15. Mary, Queen of Scots becomes Queen of France at accession of her young husband, Francis II, July.

1560 Death of Francis II of France makes his young Catholic widow, Mary Queen of Scots, a danger as Elizabeth's unwanted heir.

1561 Mary, Queen of Scots, returns to Scotland, August 19.

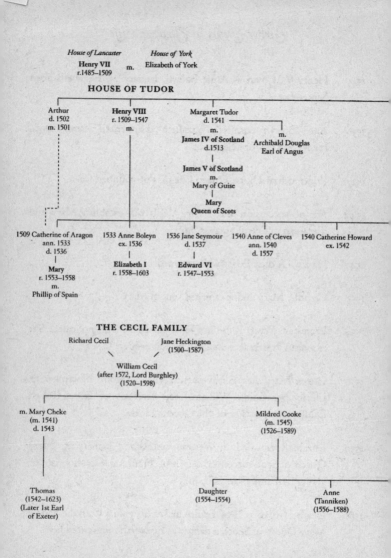

House of Lancaster   *House of York*
Henry VII   m.   Elizabeth of York
r.1485–1509

HOUSE OF TUDOR

Arthur   **Henry VIII**   Margaret Tudor
d. 1502   r. 1509–1547   d. 1541
m. 1501   m.

                        James IV of Scotland   m.
                        d.1513   **Archibald Douglas**
                                                   Earl of Angus

                        James V of Scotland
                        m.
                        Mary of Guise

                        Mary
                        Queen of Scots

1509 Catherine of Aragon   1533 Anne Boleyn   1536 Jane Seymour   1540 Anne of Cleves   1540 Catherine Howard
     ann. 1533   ex. 1536   d. 1537   ann. 1540   ex. 1542
     d. 1536   d. 1557

     Mary   **Elizabeth I**   **Edward VI**
     r. 1553–1558   r. 1558–1603   r. 1547–1553
     m.

Phillip of Spain

THE CECIL FAMILY

Richard Cecil   Jane Heckington
                       (1500–1587)

          William Cecil
          (after 1572, Lord Burghley)
          (1520–1598)

m. Mary Cheke   Mildred Cooke
(m. 1541)   (m. 1545)
d. 1543   (1526–1589)

Thomas   Daughter   Anne
(1542–1623)   (1554–1554)   (Tanniken)
(Later 1st Earl   (1556–1588)
of Exeter)

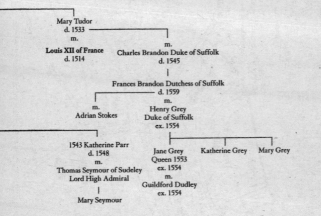

Mary Tudor
d. 1533
m.

Louis XII of France   m.
d. 1514   Charles Brandon Duke of Suffolk
d. 1545

Frances Brandon Dutchess of Suffolk
d. 1559

m.   m.
Adrian Stokes   Henry Grey
Duke of Suffolk
ex. 1554

1543 Katherine Parr   Jane Grey   Katherine Grey   Mary Grey
d. 1548   Queen 1553
m.   ex. 1554
Thomas Seymour of Sudeley   m.
Lord High Admiral   Guildford Dudley
ex. 1554

Mary Seymour

William   Robert   Elizabeth
(1561–1562)   (1563–1612)   (1564–1588)
(Later 1st Earl
of Salisbury)

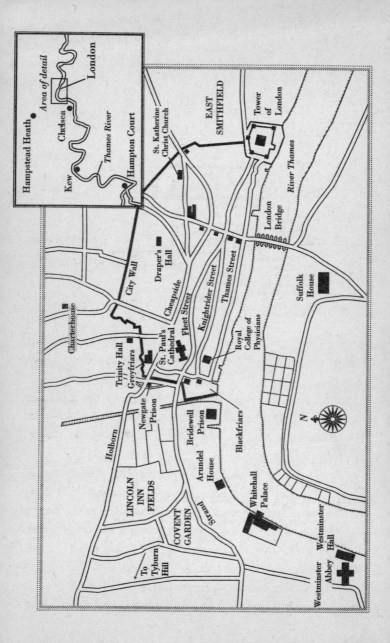

The Prologue

In such a manner of labyrinth am I placed...

—QUEEN ELIZABETH TO WILLIAM CECIL

IN A LETTER, 1564

JULY 7, 1564
CONVENT GARDENS, LONDON

 "EVEN ON THIS DAY, DAMNED DEATH SO NEAR..."
William Cecil whispered to himself, but the queen
overheard him as she walked just ahead.

Squinting into the late morning sun, Elizabeth
of England looked back at her closest advisor. He said naught
else, shaking his head as if to scold himself before he noticed
her sharp stare.

"Your meaning for such mutterings, my lord?" she inquired.

"Forgive me, Your Grace. I warrant we should not have
walked back from the church this way, but since it was only a
half-furlong to my house..." His voice faded, and he shrugged.

"The walk is fine," she assured him. "You know I favor
constitutionals in good country air." Despite the joyous occasion, she had sensed her principal secretary had been of melancholy mind today. His usually careworn countenance had

become solemn, and he seemed older than his forty-four years. It was not like him to leave thoughts half-spoken, especially morbid ones. Elizabeth's unease increased as their small, guarded party wended their way from the church along the fringe of the Convent Garden orchards toward the brick-and-timber facade of Cecil House.

It was hardly the rural view which had riled Cecil, the queen surmised, so perchance it was the old cemetery clinging to the stony skirts of the church. She surveyed the warren of tilted gravestones guarded by the low wall of St. Clements Dane where she had just attended the christening ceremony of Cecil's week-old daughter, Elizabeth, named in honor of the Tudor monarch.

Her Majesty had stood as one of the three godparents for the child. The customary second sponsor of the same sex as the child was Elizabeth's half-Scottish cousin, Margaret Stewart, Countess of Lennox, the person of second royal rank in the realm. Templar Sutton, the brilliant law lecturer and Cecil's mentor and friend from his law school days, was the traditional single sponsor of the opposite sex of the newborn. The father and godparents always attended the service while the mother remained at home until she had her own churching ceremony at a later date.

Elizabeth's scrutiny of the graveyard finally yielded what could have caused Cecil's outburst. "Within lies your son's grave, the child who died two years ago," she said and motioned he should walk with her apace. She rested a hand on his arm. "Yet you have another daughter and last year Mildred bore you little Robert, so surely all will be well with this new babe, too. But that grave is of the boy who was your namesake and Mildred's first hope for a son after nine years of marriage."

"Your wits are sharp as ever, Your Grace, and I meant not to be morose," Cecil said, his usually clear voice rough with emotion. "Yes, William's loss as well as my care for my lady wife has laid me low of late. Truth be told, Mildred's been distressed since Robert's birth, though you've seen the best of her when she's come to court. She'll be fine for a while, then lose herself in the depths of despair. She can become someone I hardly know. I fear baby William's death and little Robert's slightly crooked back and frailty are only part of it . . ."

His voice broke and faded to nothing again. Cecil silent— now that was momentous and ominous.

"You are also worried because your first wife died in child-bed? Mildred cannot have childbed fever. It's been a week since the birth."

"Your Grace, I meant not to burden you with this, nor to be ungrateful for God's bounty." He glanced back at the wet nurse who carried the sleeping, swaddled infant in her arms. As if he would address the commons or the queen's privy council, he cleared his throat. "I fear Mildred compares my hearty, hand-some nineteen-year-old Tom by my first wife—hell-raiser that he is," he added, "to the lack of robustness of baby Robert, the firstborn surviving son she bore."

"I charge you to tell Mildred she must count her blessings she has an heir. I would tell her so myself today, if it weren't deemed bad luck for the mother to attend any of these festiv-ities."

"Mildred greatly admires your womanly wisdom. I'll tell her, Your Grace. And all this was for your ears only because the last thing I need is for your cousin Margaret to be privy to my affairs, though I make it my business to know hers."

"I also, or I would not even have the smug harpy about the court. I trust her and her scheming Papist Scottish husband and her eldest son Lord Darnley as much as I do my 'dear, devoted cousin Mary of Scots,' who is the most rapacious schemer out to get my throne I've ever known. But I have held it firm through twists and turns these six years, and I shall hold it for my people's charge and care yet many more. I am but thirty and shall rule even longer than my father did!"

"Of course, you shall, Your Grace. By the way, Templar also knows Mildred's state of mind," he added, with a nod toward his friend, who, with his sprightly wife, brought up the rear of the procession as they neared Cecil House. Templar was somewhat unsteady of step, so by now their party was a bit strung out.

"You told him before you told me—and I had to nearly pry it from you?" she asked, tapping his arm with her fan, hoping he took her words as banter and not rebuke. "Then you two are closer than I realized," she mused when he did not defend himself.

Strangely, Cecil now looked pained, as if she'd accused him of some dire deed. Under the portals of his London home, he glanced back with a frown at his dignified fellow lawyer while they waited for the others to catch up with them.

"I understand your concern for Mildred's being out of sorts," the queen assured him. She spoke quickly, wanting to get this out before they went inside for a light repast. "As unhinged as my dear Kat's become, I surely know why you don't want the word out. People presume to gossip, to stare and poke and pry—in my case to whisper that I'll replace her as First Lady of the Bedchamber or Mistress of the Robes—or even put her away somewhere. But, God as my witness, I never shall, not Kat."

"She's been almost—forgive my bluntness, Your Grace—a mother to you."

"She has indeed, and I will take that from you, Cecil, when another dare not say such. So we both have those dearest to us in sad straits and shall search out ways to best treat these malaises of the mind, shall we not?"

Cecil had no time to answer as Margaret Stewart pressed close to be certain she would be directly behind the queen to enter the doors of Cecil House. Inside the threshold, liveried servants scurried to take hats and gloves and proffered trays of cooled Rhenish and sweetmeats. In the bustle, Elizabeth studied the distinguished-looked Templar Sutton and his buxom wife Bettina, for she had never met them before the ceremony. She guessed the silver-haired and -bearded Templar was a good two decades older than his wife.

"Master Sutton," Elizabeth said as everyone strolled into the dim, wood-paneled parlor, "you and your wife must come to court, and we shall discuss the state of law and lawyers in my realm."

" 'Tis a fiercely litigious society we live in, Your Gracious Majesty, though lawyers, necessary and sought after as they may be, are much abused in tales and jests these days. I shall be honored to come at any summons from my queen."

He inclined his head and splayed a hand on his chest as if he would declaim a fervid closing argument even now. "And, I must admit," Templar added, "it has long been a dream of mine to see your great vintage hornbeam maze at Hampton Court."

"Then consider the invitation for Hampton. Indeed, my

court moves there on the morrow as there have been rumors the dreaded plague will return to the city."

"Pray God not, but for today's occasion, I shall strike a happier note," Templar said as Cecil came closer. "I must show you what I brought for my new godchild."

"As we have no children, Your Majesty," the dark-eyed Bettina put in, "my husband's former law students like Lord Cecil and others at your court have been his heirs. Beyond the law, mazes have ever been his passion, and I believe he's interested more than one student in them, too." The petite woman spoke with a hint of continental accent, one the queen recognized was, blessedly, neither Spanish nor French, but Italian.

Templar Sutton produced from a black velvet drawstring bag a handkerchief-sized wooden puzzle, open on top, that resembled an intricate maze. He dropped a wooden ball into its opening, then tipped the piece so that the ball clicked into turns and out of dead ends as it rolled toward the center, which sported an elaborately carved *E*.

"Charming and clever, too," the queen proclaimed. "*E* for the newborn Elizabeth or the royal one?"

"For both," Templar declared, beaming.

"He gives these to his law students," Bettina explained, "with a *J* in the center for *Justitia* to demonstrate that the law is like a labyrinth."

"Or like life, since—" Elizabeth began, then noted with alarm that Mildred Cecil suddenly stood in the doorway of the room.

She looked like a ghost loosed from limbo. Though Mildred Cooke Cecil was a respected and learned woman, one with strict

Puritan leanings, she looked as if she'd been on an all-night debauch. Her hair could have nested birds, her nightrail and gown were pulled awry, and she looked feverish and frenzied. So much, the queen thought, for tradition and ill luck at christenings.

"Cecil . . ." the queen murmured, gesturing only with her eyes and the tilt of her head. He turned and gasped to see his wife.

"If you are going to give Tom the lands at Stamford, what will you give Robert then?" Mildred cried as if they had been in the midst of a deep, privy conversation.

Cecil moved instantly toward her, but she tried to shake him off. "Robert shall inherit the new property," Cecil said, his voice low and restrained, "and the grand house yet to be built. Come, Mildred, back to your bed."

She leaned far out to nearly topple the spare Cecil as he tried to steer her from the room. Her loosed hair swinging wildly, half covering her face, Mildred looked past his shoulder at the queen.

"Are you taking him away again—back to court?" she cried. "I cannot be without him, cannot lose him!"

"Do not fear, my lady," Elizabeth said as everyone else gawked. "You have borne your lord a lovely child, and your family needs you."

"It is you who needs a lord and child, Your Majesty!" Mildred shouted, then pulled free of Cecil and ran from the room with him in quick pursuit.

Everyone stood silent and still. Elizabeth felt her face flush. "It's some sort of fever talking," she said, turning away to look out the window as if naught were amiss. But she was astounded by the behavior of the tormented woman, as bewildering as the convoluted dementia which oft possessed her dear Kat. And sometimes, if God's truth be told, she thought, even Elizabeth of England, the calm and courageous, the grand and great, floundered in the dark turns and dead-end agonies of her own fears.

Chapter the First

 "I'M ECSTATIC TO HAVE MY DEAR MARY BACK AT court," Elizabeth said as Kat helped her fasten on her sleeve a mermaid pin that her friend Mary Sidney had given her long ago.

"Too many Marys about you to keep straight anymore," Kat groused. "It's a good thing you call Mary Radcliffe Rosie."

Kat's head seemed to be quite clear today and that lifted the queen's spirits even more. The older woman often had trouble recalling recent events and slipped back into the past, too often a painful past. But it was only recently Elizabeth had nicknamed her young maid of honor Rosie, partly because her surname meant "red cliff" and partly for her blushing complexion.

"I hope you don't include Mary, Queen of Scots among my Marys," Elizabeth told her long-time companion. She patted Kat's arm, longing to be able to command her to be young and strong again, despite the increasingly frail form, graying hair, and web of wrinkles.

Kat, First Lady of the Bedchamber and Mistress of the Robes, walked the customary two steps back and a single yeoman of the guard brought up the rear as the three of them left the privy chambers of the queen. Chatting, nodding, Elizabeth and Kat wended their way through the public rooms, stuffed with chatting courtiers. With the guard still in their wake, they turned into the library and walked out the other side into a back hallway to leave the others behind. Immediately, Elizabeth slowed her steps and linked her arm in Kat's as they strolled companionably toward Mary's rooms in the wing near the Chapel Royal.

Mary Sidney, sister to Elizabeth's former favorite, Robert Dudley, had once been her closest friend at court. But the busy wife, mother, and lady of the bedchamber had been stricken with smallpox when Mary and Kat nursed Elizabeth through her nearly fatal battle with that dread disease. Although the queen bore few pock marks, Mary's case had been more virulent, and the once beautiful woman was dreadfully disfigured with pits and scars.

Though Elizabeth could not bear to part with her, Mary had begged that she be able to retire from court to her rural home of Penshurst in Kent. Elizabeth missed her greatly and visited when her busy schedule allowed it. Even at home, Mary went veiled and, the few times she came to court, remained a recluse, seeing only Elizabeth, Kat, her own family members, and servants.

"No, I don't include Mary, Queen of Scots," Kat said, when the queen, this time, had quite forgotten their conversation. "She wants your crown, and she'll not have it, not have anything of yours, lovey."

"Not even my candidate for whom she would marry, though she pretends to ask me for my advice on that. But to keep her from wedding a Catholic to breed dangerous rivals to my throne, I shall suggest someone I know will be faithful to *me*."

"Not Lord Darnley?" Kat asked. "Oh, he's handsome enough for Mary's tastes, I credit, and his mix of noble Scots and royal Tudor blood must make him a tasty morsel for her."

"No, not Darnley. I cannot see one sound reason to promote him with her except it would rid my court of his simpering, fawning presence—and he'd mayhap take his crafty dam and sire with him."

"Then, of course," Kat added as they entered the corridor outside Mary Sidney's rooms, "your sister Mary's probably going to want to have her say in all these royal marriage doings."

Elizabeth jolted as if she'd taken a fist in the stomach. Her sister had been dead nigh on six years. Worse, if Mary Tudor weren't long deceased, Elizabeth would not be queen, so even Kat's reasoning had deserted her this time. Just when she hoped Kat was somewhat improved from the treatments Elizabeth's herbalist, Meg Milligrew, had brewed to help her, Kat's mind had slipped again.

"Do you ever feel her presence in this hall?" Kat asked as if naught were amiss.

"Mary Sidney's or my sister Mary's?"

"Queen Catherine Howard's, of course. They say her ghost walks here—or rather runs," she whispered. "More than one have seen her."

At least, the queen thought, Kat had that much right, for

she'd heard of the ghost from time to time. King Henry VIII's young fifth wife had been beheaded for adultery over twenty years ago. It was here Catherine had run from her bedchamber toward the Chapel Royal to beg her husband not to send her to the Tower, here where he had ordered her dragged away to imprisonment and death.

The queen's footsteps faltered when her companion bumped into her. Keeping Kat close was a double burden of late: by day she too oft lived in the past; by night, she suffered from frightful dreams. Elizabeth hated sickness, and she did not need the painful past hauled from its grave and paraded by. But she would care for Kat—as Kat had nursed and comforted her from before she could recall anything of her life.

Elizabeth glanced up and down the bright hall. Surely no ghosts lurked here now. On the outer edge of the building, several deep-set windows overlooking a kitchen court below threw light upon the old oak floor. Dust motes spun in the air amid the slant of sunbeams, for several casements were set ajar to let in fresh air. To their right were the doors of bedchambers that lined the white-washed hall which connected the state rooms to the chapel.

"I do not believe in ghosts, but for those in one's head, my Kat." Elizabeth whispered, too, until she realized it, and said more loudly, "My father once said ghosts are but unburied secrets and bad consciences, and surely he knew whereof he spoke on that. Let's see Mary now—our friend Mary Sidney—and talk only of happy times and things."

Elizabeth gestured for her yeoman guard Stackpole to wait down the hall, and knocked on the door herself. Elizabeth stiffened her backbone for that first sight of her friend, for it ever jolted her anew, not only that Mary was prisoner of a monstrous appearance but that she herself had escaped such a fate. Mary's young tiring woman opened the door, swept the queen a low curtsy, and stepped out, closing it behind her.

"No, do not curtsy to me," Elizabeth insisted and hugged her friend before she could bend a knee. As always, Mary wore a veil, a thin one this time. But with window light behind, the queen could glimpse her ravaged complexion. "What is the point of formalities here, as above all we are fast friends."

"Because you are ever, always my queen, too," Mary replied gently. "And it is so good to see your—your lovely face, Your Majesty."

"I have said you must call me Elizabeth," the queen insisted, squeezing Mary's pock-marked hands. "I am so glad you are here. I must tell you, I ordered full-faced masks for the masque this evening, so that you might attend and feel no fear of anyone staring. Every lady in the play will be dressed identically to you down to flaxen wigs, so no one will even know it's you. I shall order that we not unmask and let them all guess even who is their queen this night. And, of course, you may portray one of the five wise virgins in the play and not a foolish one."

"It is all so thoughtful of you, as are all the letters and gifts you've sent," Mary said, as she and Kat hugged, too. "But cannot it be enough that I am here at court? I must beg off moving among my former friends, even disguised. Everyone would be so curious as to which player is poor Mary Sidney. I cannot comply, and pray you will understand, my friend Elizabeth."

Mary sniffed once from behind the veil as she indicated where Elizabeth should sit. "It is bad enough to bear the pity of my children," she added quietly, "and my dear lord."

"A lord who is loyal and loves you yet, no matter what," Elizabeth insisted. It was as much a command as a question, for the queen would brook no disloyalty in her realm's marriages. She'd seen enough of that and the destruction it wrought.

"Of course, and Robin's been steadfast, too," Mary said as the three of them sat, Elizabeth and Mary on a padded bench under the single window and Kat on the coffer at the end of the curtained bed. "It was a joy to have our Robin visit Penshurst after his business journey, so I must thank you too for giving him leave to go from court for a time."

Robin was the nickname those close to Robert Dudley, Elizabeth included, called Mary's brother. As soon as the throne was hers, Elizabeth had named him to her highly visible post of Master of Horse and later Warden of Windsor Castle. She had secretly desired Robin from the days they were prisoners in the Tower, but when his wife Amy had died in mysterious circumstances, the queen had sent him away from court and tried to shield her heart from his power over her. She had long ago summoned him back, but tried desperately to keep him at arm's length. She loved him yet, and damn the man, he knew it.

"*Our* Robin?" the queen queried. "I hope you mean you and your kin, for he is not *my* Robin. But did he not return with you to court then?"

"Yes, and bid me beg you for a time and privy place to get—well, caught up on things a bit with you."

"Playing Cupid, Mary?" Kat put in, though Elizabeth thought the older woman looked as if she hadn't been listening, at least to them. She'd cocked her head and had been glaring at the door as if she heard something strange in the hall.

"I am merely relaying a message between two good friends,"

Mary declared as she passed Elizabeth a small silver plate with candied figs and suckets.

"Why did he not directly ask me to meet him?" Elizabeth demanded, frowning at her selection.

"He is going to be busy in the royal stables for several hours because your Araby mare is about to foal. But tonight after the masque . . ."

"Ah, good, for I've missed riding her," Elizabeth said, but her mind raced for a privy yet nearby place to meet him. She thought of the maze, for she was soon to meet her guests Templar Sutton and his wife there. She could get away after the masque, just for a few moments, of course. "Tell him the entrance to the maze then," the queen clipped out, "and if he stands me up for a horse, even my Araby, I'll have his head."

"Then he can haunt the maze," Kat said, her mouth full of a candied fig. "As for now, I warrant someone's listening at this keyhole."

"Stuff and nonsense," Elizabeth said. "My guard or Mary's maid is out there, that is all."

But to calm Kat's nerves, the queen got up and went to the door herself. She pulled it open and, seeing no one, stuck her head out. No guard, no tiring woman, no one in the whole corridor.

"Hell's teeth, I'll sack the lout for this!" the queen muttered and stepped out to look up and down the hall for her guard. Inside, she could hear Mary talking soothingly to Kat. Undecided whether to shout for the man or just step inside and bolt the door until he returned, Elizabeth hesitated when she heard someone.

Light, quick steps, probably a woman, Mary's servant, or

someone coming to explain that the guard had suddenly taken ill. A rustling skirt nearby, a panting breath, but no one in sight.

The air moved across the queen's flushed face as if someone had rushed past. Footfalls faded in the other direction, and the slightest aroma of gillyflowers wafted on the air, when the queen never wore that scent.

The hair on the back of Elizabeth's neck prickled; she broke out in an immediate sweat. Nothing—still nothing in the hall at all. Surely not Catherine Howard's ghost? And in broad daylight? Elizabeth pressed her back against door and stared in the direction the sounds and scent had gone. She jumped as the door behind her swept open.

"Lovey," Kat said, "are you quite all right? Who was it then?"

"Nothing to cause a stir." She shook her head to clear it. Obviously, the corridor was so strangely wrought with those deep-set windows that sounds echoed here from the kitchens and courtyard below. And scents no doubt blew in too, gillyflowers from Meg Milligrew's herb gardens. That was the logical explanation, and, she thought, like any lawyer worth his salt, she prided herself in her logic.

"It's nothing," she repeated, hoping to calm her pounding pulse.

Although her new baby had quieted at last, the crying seemed to echo in Mildred Cecil's very soul. Grateful when the wet nurse carried little Elizabeth to the nursery down the hall, Mildred closed the door to her bedchamber to mute further noise. At least little Robert was sleeping, but she could hear her eight-year-old Anne, squealing at some game of tag or bowls outside.

Mildred strode to the oriel window that overlooked the spacious gardens of their London house. She felt cooped up here, but her lord must keep close to the queen, ever at her beck and call. The court had moved upriver to Hampton Court, and he'd gone with her, leaving Mildred behind to oversee shifting her household to their northern home at Stamford ninety miles north of London, lest the plague increase here. Too bad it would take years to build a great house on the new land at Theobalds, for that would be much closer, even if it might never have her husband's heart as Stamford—and his son Thomas—did.

Always queen's business, the kingdom's care calling her lord, Mildred fretted, hitting her fist on the window frame. She hated herself for begrudging her husband's work for their realm and religion and their brilliant and bold Protestant queen. William Cecil thrived on it all, and his wife had been so proud of him, but lately it all dragged her down.

God help her, Mildred thought, her children, whom she loved like her own life, annoyed her, too, even her innocent babes, but especially her twenty-two-year-old stepson Thomas, whose voice she could hear now entwined with Anne's.

Peering out the window, she could not see Anne, whom they yet called Tannekin for her early childish pronunciation of her own name. "I'll tell my lady mother!" the girl screeched.

Doors banged. Footsteps sounded, coming closer, closer in the house.

"Ha, I've got you now, you ninnyhammer—you little tattale!" Thomas's voice boomed.

"Just you shut your trap! You pushed me in the rose bushes, and my gown's all snagged. I'm going to tell on you no matter what you say."

Anne burst into the room, but her first impassioned words blurred in Mildred's ears. The slender girl was red as a rose with sunhat askew, tendrils loose, and her skirts snagged indeed.

The handsome, tall Tom looked as if he would chase and harass her the more. But when he saw his stepmother, he halted and, crossing his arms nonchalantly, leaned in the doorway as if to flaunt his fine face and athletic form.

"I'd admonish you, Thomas," Mildred said, "to torment someone of your own size and sex, but I know that you do that too in your caperings and scrapes about town."

He shrugged. "She's the one who begged me to play with her. I can't help it she darted into the privet hedge. And don't bother to give me a dressing-down, as I'm sure Father will when his little Tannekin tells him I've been picking on her."

As charming a young man as Thomas could be, Mildred marveled that he could make himself so disagreeable. From the first, no love had been lost between them, for he oft placed on a pedestal his dead mother, who died when he was so young he could surely not recall her. Mildred sighed inwardly again, wanting to say something to soothe and forgive, but that's not what came out of her mouth.

"Your hard-working, disciplined, God-fearing father," she declared, "is driven to distraction by your wastrel ways, as am I. Here he was this past winter, trying to make a fine marriage match for you while he sent you to the Continent to study, and you—"

"And I spent his coin and chased other sorts of doxies besides this one, eh?" he said with a sharp laugh and wink at his stepsister.

"Mother," Tannekin cried, "I'm not a doxy, am I? What's a doxy?"

"Go downstairs and have Cook give you something cool to drink," Mildred ordered the girl, who obeyed, though she flounced from the room most unladylike.

"I'll give you good day and a view of my backside, too," Tom clipped out before she could scold him. "I don't need a pious lecture from you if I'm in for another drubbing from Father. Of your growing brood, we all know his precious little Tannekin is still the favorite, do we not?"

And he was gone. Mildred stood staring at the empty door, wanting to ward off his sly stab that Cecil preferred Anne to their heir Robert. Mildred had the strangest urge to run after the boy and choke him. She was too busy, that's all, so much to do here, so much to oversee. She wanted just to run away for good. How did her husband manage to keep his sanity with all his burdens of queen and country? He ought to be here more. The queen kept him away.

"Dearest, good news!" Her husband's voice from the hall so surprised her that she thought she had imagined it at first so she could vent her spleen on him. Home unannounced. In the middle of the day. And from Hampton Court upriver, not just nearby Whitehall?

"I could use some good news," she said, forcing a smile when he strode into the room and swirled his riding cape onto a chair.

"Since you are recovered from the birth," he told her, clasping his hands in his excitement, "the babe is thriving, and our household is heading for Stamford, Her Grace has bid me fetch you to court for a few days."

"That's a wonder, after how I behaved when she was here." She found herself resenting the queen's meddling instead of being grateful for her goodness, but she tried not to let on. Though Mildred was strictly Protestant with a Puritan bent, she usually enjoyed the queen's company. As two of the most learned ladies of the land, they delighted to speak Greek and Latin together. Yet, Mildred thought, to have all those people about, their eyes probing, their mouths moving as they talked and gossiped ... mayhap about her carrying on the day of the christening ...

"When shall we go then?" she asked, relieved at least to be escaping both London and rural Stamford and—God forgive her—her noisy, troublesome brood.

"Today, my love. I need to get back today."

"But—all the packing. The planning ..."

"Don't fuss. There will be no real frivolity at court, so the tenor of the times will suit you," he added, putting his arms around her. "And Templar Sutton's visiting, so the talk's all been very scholarly."

"And his wife, too?" she clipped out before she could stop herself.

"I thought you'd be glad to go with me." He tilted her back to study her face. "I had hopes it might lift your spirits."

Mildred wanted to scream at him that her spirits felt scraped raw, but she forced a stiff smile. "I shall pack my things while you look in on Robert and the babe. Oh, and your Tannekin's downstairs. And Thomas is in his usual choleric disposition."

"Instead of to Stamford, I'm sending him to join the Sidney boys at their Penshurst for a while, hoping their gentlemanly ways will rub off on him. I swear, I'll make him a man worthy of his heritage yet."

"Or one of us will die trying," Mildred whispered as she turned away to summon the servants.

Chapter the Second

"I HOPE NOT ONLY TO VIEW AND WALK YOUR MAZE, but to discern its pattern, Your Majesty," Templar Sutton said as he and his wife followed the queen into the maze the very day of their arrival at Hampton Court. "Ah, I heard it was of vintage hornbeam, but I see it's been patched with other shrubs, too," he observed, looking as delighted as a child.

"It is a bit of a hodge-podge and probably needs replanting and moving farther out into the gardens, too," she told her guests.

Behind the Suttons, Christopher Hatton and James Barstow, two young men of her court who had studied law under Templar at Gray's Inn, brought up the rest of their little party. Cecil was not here, for he had gone to fetch Mildred for a few days at court at the queen's express invitation.

"My father's advisor Cardinal Wolsey had this maze planted a good thirty years ago," Elizabeth explained. "They say that pompous priest used to chide lovers who tarried too long within. Since those are my state apartments," she said, turning to point, "I now have this view, though the hedges have grown so tall I can see naught but the entry and first fork in the path."

They all gazed briefly up at the sweep of windows that marked the royal rooms within the palace's rose brick facade. Set like a jewel in vast parklands, the moated palace was one of Elizabeth's favorites. Topped by a tangle of twisted chimney clusters, parapets, and flapping pennants, the sprawling Thameside edifice was built around a hundred nooks and crannies. It was a city in itself which could house nearly one thousand courtiers supported by hundreds of servants. Yet the orchards, gardens, gravel walks, and glinting river made life here seem rural, a mere half-day's barge journey from teeming London.

"I do not know," she admitted, "what other sorts of shrubs have been patched in here, but we enjoy this maze, Master Sutton, and I order it kept in good trim."

"Pardon Your Majesty," Jamie Barstow put in, pointing out the vagrant varieties of bushes, "but that one is yew and this one's privet."

"You may recall, Your Grace," Chris Hatton added, "that Jamie's father is my family's steward, who oversees our fields and forests. Jamie knows a little about a lot of things, whereas I know a lot about little."

Everyone laughed. The two young men, both twenty-four, had come to court at the same time, or rather, the queen had brought them. She had been quite taken by Chris Hatton's skilled dancing, deep voice, and striking appearance—and his well-turned legs—at a Yuletide masque she had attended at Gray's Inn. As her court was ever in need of engaging young men of good stock to escort her maids of honor and learn the intricacies of daily royal business, as well as for masqueing and dancing at night, she had summoned Hatton and gained Barstow in the bargain, too.

Fast friends, the two men had been educated together since grammar school in Northamptonshire. Sir Christopher Hatton, the second son of a fine old family, had entered Oxford and the Inns of Court as a gentleman-commoner, though he earned a degree at neither school. He was a lofty step up the social ladder from Jamie, who was a *pleb. fil.*, or commoner's son. Yet they were the most democratic and amiable of comrades, both obviously grateful to their queen for their promotions to court when others of their ilk never got so much as a booted toe in the door. They were so attentive that Elizabeth had found them also useful to make Robin fret and fume.

That the two young men were quite different from each other in appearance and demeanor made their firm friendship even the more remarkable in the queen's eyes. Chris looked to be a knight errant from an old romance: his thick, straight hair shone so black it looked nearly bluish in the sun, and roguish green eyes lit his countenance. Sleekly attired, classically handsome, he was of tall and manly form. Skilled at gentlemanly pursuits, he was a favorite with her maids and ladies as well as with his queen. Her Majesty had seen more than one of her women hang on Chris's every word and nearly tilt into him, as if they were metal filings drawn to a magnet.

Jamie Barstow, on the other hand, was not a flashing comet in the firmament of courtiers, but a bright-burning lantern.

Chestnut, wavy hair framed his hazel eyes and open, sun-browned countenance. Whereas Chris always made an entrance, Jamie's strength lay in the fact he seemed to be ever-present and properly prepared when needed. His riding and sporting skills were as fine as his friend's, but he had to work at dancing and courtly conversation. Stalwart of limb and steady of mind, Jamie emanated a warmth of character if not the heat of personality which flared from his friend.

"I shall follow your lead to see if you can discern the convoluted pathway here," Elizabeth told Templar, indicating he should step ahead of her at the first curve of hedge walls despite his somewhat doddering pace. The queen came next, then Bettina. The leaf-walled pathway occasionally came to a dead end, and one had to backtrack, the clever Templar included. Though the maze was currently getting the best of Templar's fine-honed mind, she intended to use his skills and knowledge to help Cecil advise her court lawyers.

For now, she tried to keep their conversation lighthearted. Yet the fact that Kat was ailing and the plague seemed to be spreading in her capital had kept her from allowing much frivolity lately. Even the masque she had commanded for tonight was from a sober Bible parable and not a raucous classical fable.

"I shall judge, Master Sutton," the queen declared, "whether your fine reputation as protector and teacher of England's common law has given you the talent to discern puzzles such as this, when one finds oneself in the midst of the maze instead of merely observing it from afar or advising others—or playing with a child's wooden toy."

Templar chuckled as he found himself again in a dead end and waited for the others to back out behind him. Elizabeth heard Bettina giggle. Though overmuch lightness in a woman oft annoyed the queen, she had seen that Bettina cheered her husband, and even, at times, seemed to counsel him circumspectly, as he evidently had trouble hearing. Taking her cue from that, the queen—whose ringing tones could make a bell seem mute—spoke loudly to him.

"One thing I'll tell you of maze mythology, Your Majesty," Templar told her as they began on another path, one she recognized as also wrong, though she'd not correct him yet. "In the pagan past they used to believe that evil spirits were unable to turn corners, hence, one was always safe within a maze."

"I shall remember that, Master Sutton."

"Though these corners seem as slanted as sharp, so that shouldn't help here," Jamie said, only to have Chris elbow him to silence.

"I thought you were going to tell Her Majesty the story of Fair Rosamund in her Bower, hiding from the queen," Bettina prompted her husband.

"Ah, yes, poor Rosamund," the queen said, piqued the woman dared think she did not know that tale. "When she discovered her royal husband's *affaire de coeur*, King Henry II's queen finally found her way into the maze His Majesty had made to shelter his mistress and forced the poor woman to drink poison."

"Bettina portrayed Fair Rosamund in a small tragedy we staged at the Inn, Your Majesty," Jamie piped up again.

"A woman on the stage?" Elizabeth inquired, though the idea rather pleased her. If females could be part of private masques, why not the more public stage?

"I bound up my breasts and everyone thought I was a lad," she explained.

"Well, perhaps not everyone," Chris teased and, this time, elbowed Jamie.

"She's quite skilled at playing parts," Templar put in.

"Though I admit my complexion is the olive hue of my mother and not that of a fair-faced woman like Rosamund," Bettina said with a fetching little shrug. "If I ever played in that masque again, I should take the part of the evil poisoner, Queen Eleanor of Aquitaine." Both hands flew to Bettina's mouth. "I mean, I am not worthy to play a queen, Your Majesty, but she was a French queen, and could, therefore, never shine as bright as you, pardon if I have spoken amiss."

"Not amiss, but it reminds me that a friend who was to be in our masque this evening is indisposed, and I believe you might do the part justice. It is no speaking role, and all ten women portraying the wise and foolish virgins will be costumed, wigged, and masked to look the same."

"Oh, the greatest honor," Bettina said, pressing her clasped hands to her breasts.

"Play-acting indeed to portray a virgin—after years of marriage to our mentor," Jamie put in with an impish grin.

The queen smartly smacked his arm with her folded fan. "One more comment about virgins, and I shall banish you where you can no longer make eyes at my Lady Rosie, for I have observed she has caught your eye. But I wager you a good gold crown—a coin, I mean, not a royal one," she added tartly, "that you'll not breech Rosie Radcliffe's well-defended bastions, Jamie Barstow!"

More laughter but from Templar, who might not have heard. He was already headed around the next turn, and on the wrong path again. But then the queen herself had been lost more times in here over the years than her pride would allow her to admit.

" *'Behold, the bridegroom cometh; go ye out to meet him!'* " echoed to the vast hammerbeam roof of the great hall at Hampton Court. The audience stirred as Chris Hatton, playing the bridegroom, strode toward the ten virgins waiting with their silver lamps.

The masque of the five wise and five foolish virgins seemed to please everyone, Cecil thought. As one of the few unmasked—those ornate, false countenances never suited him—he settled back to watch not only the parable performed but observe those watching it. The cast had commandeered the dining dais for a stage. In addition to the chamber's usual array of fine tapestries, Her Majesty had evidently ordered four more brought in from Greenwich Palace. Those illustrated the parable in which the Lord Jesus advised his followers to always be prepared for his return. A more intimate stage had been created by draping the Greenwich tapestries on poles around the dais.

" *'Then all those virgins arose, and trimmed their lamps,'* " the narrator's voice boomed out again.

In flowing white and silver robes and wearing full-length brocade masks, their tresses hidden by flaxen wigs, the women went through their paces. Five of them had planned for the arrival of the groom—women after his own heart, Cecil thought—and the five frivolous ones had used up all their oil and were left out of the wedding feast.

The queen, Cecil noted, was in her element, leading the wise virgins, of course, while the foolish five fumbled about, then cried and screamed when they realized their sad fate. Though all ten women were gowned, wigged, and masked alike, he could always pick out bold Bess Tudor, however much he heard whispering about him that some others could not recognize Her Majesty. Many of the maids were graceful and slender and of similar height, but he saw the way Elizabeth subtly steered the others through their parts. Her wily cousin Margaret must be in that mix, though damned if he was sure which one she was. He thought he could spot Rosie Radcliffe and Bettina, though.

Templar had told him that his wife had been pulled in at the last moment. She was acquitting herself well, and, no doubt, having the time of her life. It was that volatile Italian streak in her, Cecil thought, for she loved to be watched and wanted. He shifted in his chair so hard it creaked, and Mildred, through the slitted eyeholes of her mask, glanced askance at him. In the audience, Templar—the mask Bettina had insisted he wear kept slipping—looked proud enough of his little wife to burst, poor man.

Cecil wasn't surprised that the queen's latest favorite, Chris Hatton, was playing the bridegroom who symbolized Christ himself. Since Hatton was on display, Cecil assumed Jamie Barstow was behind the scenes somewhere. He'd heard Robert Dudley was back at court but didn't see him.

"'Afterward came also the other virgins, saying, "Lord, Lord, open to us."' But he answered and said, 'Verily I say unto you, I know you not. Watch therefore, for ye know neither the day not the hour . . .'"

Even the queen's closest servants were enjoying themselves, that was clear to see, since they weren't masked. Her Majesty's

so-called fool and principal player, Ned Topside, a clever, for-
merly itinerant actor, had obviously masterminded the staging,
which the queen kept subtly changing. Ned stood slightly to
the side as he read the narrative for the miming players, his fine
voice showing him as much to advantage as his face and form,
which were his real stock in trade. Like her father, Elizabeth
had always favored surrounding herself with fine-looking people.

Off to the side stood Kat Ashley, who seemed to be not
only delighting in the drama, but following it, too. With her
was Meg Milligrew, the queen's Strewing Herb Mistress of the
Privy Chamber, who also served as the royal herbalist. Though
the queen employed court doctors, she and Kat disliked their
bleedings and leeches. Lately, Elizabeth had relied more on
Meg's garden and apothecary tonics and elixirs to treat Kat's
dementia.

Cecil had noted the results were dubious, yet he had asked
Meg last month if she had anything in her bag of tricks for his
wife's strange state of mind. She'd given him a sweet-smelling
powdered mix to sprinkle in a glass of malmsey before Mildred
slept, but more than once, his wife had insisted he was trying
to drug her. Favoring the scent, she'd used the powder for fragrant potpourri instead.

But another reason the clever queen kept Meg Milligrew near
her person was that Meg greatly resembled her—or at least
could be made to. Their coloring, height, and weight, not to
mention some facial features, were much the same. Years ago
Her Majesty had ordered Ned Topside to tutor Meg in royal
deportment and speech. More than once, switches or substitu-
tions of herbalist for monarch had saved their necks. But, thank

God, Cecil mused, there had been no need for such of late, and he prayed it would remain thus.

Lastly, Mildred looked and acted pleased tonight, so that pleased Cecil most of all. Perhaps, he thought, the change of place or rest from the children's noise was the only tonic she needed. Hell's gates, who could understand the mind of a woman, especially ones as brilliant as those he loved most, his wife and his queen?

Her Majesty heaved a huge sigh when the masque ended. Usually performing in or watching such amusements put Elizabeth in her element. Yet her stomach had knotted like a noose, *not* like these damned silk and gauze garters which kept loosening her hose. She needed to slip out to meet Robin as she had promised, but she didn't want to let on, even—especially—to those close to her.

Though Cecil and Robin worked together well enough these days, tension between them always lurked just beneath the surface. Kat had heard her promise Mary that she would meet Robin, but she'd probably forgotten already. And she hardly needed her servants whispering that Robin was back in her arms let alone in her good graces. Disguised though Elizabeth was, people knew her when they heard her voice, and it might take some ado to sneak out.

Poking her head behind an arras, with a flick of her wrist, she summoned her hovering guard Stephen Jenks and edged toward the fringe of the crowd. Jenks had served her well, even in the years she had lived in dangerous exile from court life.

Though his wit was for horses, he was skilled with a sword and was ever loyal. However many gentleman pensioners and yeomen guards she had about her person when she ventured out, Jenks was her best buffer against all physical danger. He was nominally part of Robin's staff to select and train the three-hundred-some horses from her royal stables, but Jenks was at her beck and call whenever he was needed. And he was needed now to ascertain that Robin's reason for not attending the masque was the truth.

Jenks rushed to her side. She'd told her people that, unless she unmasked, they were not to show obeisance or address her by name or title this evening, and she was heartened to see Jenks remembered. He stopped so swiftly that his sword clanked in its scabbard and the fringe of hair over his earnest blue eyes bobbed.

"Do you know if my Araby mare has foaled yet?" she asked. "And if she's being tended properly and by whom?"

"Didn't Lord Dudley tell you then? The new foal's a white stallion, a hellion to break someday, he said, as he oversaw the foaling. Probably means to surprise you himself, though don't see hide nor hair of him here tonight, masks or no."

Then Robin had told her true, she thought, much relieved. He might be adept at twisting or turning the facts, but not Jenks. Perhaps Robin even planned to take her to the stables to see the new foal by torchlight. That thought rather pleased her.

"That is all for now," she told Jenks. "Except, send Meg to me and be sure Lady Ashley doesn't wander off."

He disappeared behind the scenery while the queen surveyed the room. The lawyers—Templar, Chris, Jamie, and Cecil— huddled together over some issue, though everyone but Cecil was still masked. She surmised that Mildred and Bettina were in the crowd, but she wasn't sure. The queen had commanded that the women remain masked and continue to mime their parts, supposedly to drive home the parable's point of being prepared for disaster.

Actually, Elizabeth knew it would be easier for her not to be missed if all stayed costumed and covered. If she dismissed everyone and headed for her rooms, she'd have her ladies in her wake and that would never do. If only her servants, who had been with her through thick and thin, knew who she was for certain, that suited her right now.

"You know what, Your Gr—milady?" Meg whispered, still cradling the basket of fragrant strewing herbs with which she'd decorated the dais earlier. "I actually approached Lady Rosie by mistake just now, since I thought that's who Jenks had pointed out was you."

"I intend to go alone to see Mary Sidney," Elizabeth said without ado, "to show her the costume. But I don't want everyone to know I'm gone or where."

It galled her to lie to her faithful servant, especially since the queen of England was slinking off like some milkmaid to see a man when she should simply have commanded Robin to attend her. It was sheer tomfoolery, yet the fact no one could gainsay her even if they knew excited her—as did meeting him at night in the maze.

"Then I'd best keep a sharp eye on Kat," Meg murmured.

"I won't be long, but either you or Lady Rosie need to be with her. And don't try that new herbal cure on her until I get back—or if she's weary and goes to bed, we'll test it another night."

"The betony," Meg said with a nod. "I'm praying it will halt her nocturnal visions—her plain, old nightmares."

"I meant to ask, have you planted gillyflowers in the kitchen herb gardens?"

"Did you tell me to put some there, and I forgot?"

"I simply said, *did* you plant them there?"

"Nary a one there 'cause the brewers were filching them to flavor their beer," she whispered as if they were discussing some capital crime. "But I need them for strewing herbs and potpourri. This year, all the gillyflowers are in the riverside gardens. I planted fewer than usual since their perfumes are a whit oldfashioned. But next year I can put them in the kitchen gardens, if you wish."

"Never mind. Be off with you then."

Elizabeth headed for the door, moving into the shadows. Looking back over her shoulder twice, as if she were some stealthy cutpurse, she went out into the hall nearest the maze. A guard stood just inside the door. She nodded silently to him. He could think she was any lady stepping out for a breath of air or a tryst. When he opened the door for her, she darted into the darkness, feeling wildly, if momentarily, free.

"Next time, Robin, you shall come to me," she muttered to herself in rhythm with her strides on, then off, the gravel path. "Never again," she rehearsed her opening words, trying several voices—annoyance, teasing, then raw command. "Never again!"

She was pleased that, once she was outside, the blowing night did not seem as black as it had at first. A full moon enhanced the wan light from palace windows. She used the moonshade of a huge oak to lift her white and silver robes to tie her damned garters tighter. No good having her stockings trip her up.

Remaining masked lest someone see her, she took a moment to survey the walkways and gardens in their eerie light. This, indeed, would have been a better setting for poor Catherine Howard's ghost. The scene, usually so familiar, seemed an alien landscape now. Shivering, she hugged herself and moved toward the maze.

She wished she'd brought Jenks or Meg, for she could trust them to keep their mouths shut about a tryst with Robin. And yet she'd wanted to come alone. This was the place where Kat had told her that her own parents used to meet by moonlight, before everything went so bad between them.

When she saw Robin was not yet here, she whispered, "I will kill him!" In her topsy-turvy relationship with the man, *she* was the one with the power, yet he seemed in control. Tonight, he'd best not keep her waiting, especially when he was the one who had arranged this, though she had named the place.

Again she felt her garters slip and tried to pull them up by hoisting the layers of petticoats she wore. Silk to hold up silk was foolhardy, and she'd tell whoever made them that they would never sew such for her again.

When she heard the hedge rustle, she loosed her huge hems. Her head jerked around. Her mask went askew, and she bent to readjust it to see out the eyeholes, leaning forward as if she would spring to a run. Yet she stood her ground in the gaping maw of the maze. If the blackguard was playing games as usual, if he thought to jump out and frighten her, she would show him she was not afraid.

She peeked into the maze, then shuffled in without making a turn. Though she'd sensed someone near, just as in the palace corridor this morning, she saw nothing. Surely, in the breeze, she only fancied she heard someone breathing. Robin used to say she made him breathe heavily, yet this was shallow, almost silent.

"Damn the man!" she muttered.

As she turned to leave, someone pressed against the back of her skirts. Thinking Robin would dare to embrace her from behind, she gasped in anticipation through the slitted mouth of the mask.

She saw—or felt—two dark hands fly before her face. Holding something? A necklace, a gift from him? Something around her throat but so tight—too tight.

Elizabeth gagged and gulped for breath. She tried to elbow the person, but hit only empty air . . . breathed black, empty air. Her attacker yanked her into the maze and tripped her. She was shoved facedown in the grass in the first dead end, a knee pressed in her back. Not Robin, not like this.

Her mask bumped away, her wig snagged in the hedges. She sucked for air but only tasted grass. Nothing in her throat, her bursting lungs. She tried to kick, but her skirts trapped her legs. Tried to talk, to order him—someone—to stop.

She clawed at her throat to get her fingers between her neck and the ligature which cut her, suffocated her, making all the lights go out and choking—her life—away.

Chapter the Third

 A WOMAN'S VOICE BROUGHT HER BACK FROM OBLIVION.

"Did you fall? Are you hurt? Oh, it can't be you!"

Not Kat or Rosie. Was it that ghost again, talking this time? Would she just pass by? Elizabeth sucked fresh, cool air into her mouth, her throat, her lungs.

Her eyes flew open. She was dizzy, and the moon above the woman's head seemed to be two moons snagged in the tops of hedge walls. Stars dipped and doubled and danced.

It took her a moment to realize who and where she was and even longer to know who knelt over her. Bettina Sutton, still costumed and bewigged, her mask hanging from its ribbons around her neck.

Then everything came flooding back.

Weakly, Elizabeth reached for Bettina's wrist. "Sh!" she managed, then got a gasping, coughing fit.

"I—I can't believe it's you, Your Majesty," Bettina cried when the queen quieted. "What happened? Look, two garters knotted around your neck, and it's all scratched! Should I fetch your guards and doctors?"

Elizabeth managed to shake her head. It hurt. She hurt all over. Bettina helped her to sit up.

"I want to stand," Elizabeth rasped, but when she did, her legs went wobbly, and she steadied herself by leaning on the shorter woman. "Walk me away from here—out there."

Sheer determination took Elizabeth to the big oak where she leaned panting against its solid trunk. "Why—are you—out here?" she managed. She could tell Bettina dared not ask her the same.

"It's all been so wonderful, our visit here, and Templar was tired," the woman stammered, obviously nervous about touching the queen's person but about loosing her, too. She held her arms out, as if she'd catch her if she fell. "I just wanted to soak it all in before I slept, and of course, I knew this area from your taking us around. Oh, Your Majesty, what happened?"

"Did you see anyone else afoot?" the queen countered. "Someone running, even someone distant when you came upon me?"

"No one, I swear it."

"Then what happened to me is that I was walking alone and tripped. But I don't want anyone to know I was—clumsy. I shall reward you on the morrow for lending me assistance and telling no one of this."

Even in the darkness under the big tree, Elizabeth noted well how the woman's eyes flew again to her throat, then to her face. Bettina nodded shakily. "Even one as poised and graceful as yourself, Your Majesty, who knows the turns of that dark maze, could trip. Yes, I understand. I must learn to be more wary myself walking out alone."

"You are certain you saw no one else, even at a distance?"

"Guards on the palace doors, of course. Forms in the windows. But no one out here—but you."

That might mean her attacker had fled into the maze instead of out, the queen reasoned. And the entry was the only exit. "Then go to the guard on the door and say the queen has need of Stephen Jenks, Meg Milligrew, and Ned Topside here at once. The men are to bring torches. Then return to me until they arrive," she ordered and weakly gestured her away.

"Jenks and Meg and Ned," Elizabeth heard Bettina whisper to herself in rote as she hurried away. "Jenks, Meg, and Ned."

From this distance, the queen watched the entry to the maze to be certain no one emerged while Bettina did as she was bid. The world slowly stopped spinning, but the queen's neck began to sting. Tenderly, she fingered the two wide silk and gauze garters still around her throat.

They felt like the ones all the women wore for the masque, the slippery ones she wore even now. She'd not disturb them further. Any knots or snagged hairs were all necessary proofs she and her people must explore after they searched each turn of the maze for who could be hiding there. Strange, though, that she fancied she smelled the same faint gillyflower aroma on the garters as she'd noted in the corridor outside Mary Sidney's room. Had she smelled that in the maze when she was attacked too? Elizabeth of England shuddered once and began to shake.

———

"Does this marigold cream soothe the sting, Your Grace?" Meg asked as she laved the ligature and scratch marks on the queen's neck in the royal bedchamber later. "You've got two welts coming, too, I must put beebalm on."

"Just give me another swig of that horehound tonic, and find me a neck ruff to wear. An older, high, soft one. No starchwort in it."

"That will start a new craze."

"I'm the one who's crazed," Elizabeth said, jumping up again to look out the oriel window with its casement set ajar. The torches Jenks and Ned held aloft—she'd seen drawn swords in their other hands when they began—moved methodically through the paths of the maze. But they must be nearly at the goal and had evidently discovered no intruder yet.

Despite her impatience, Elizabeth was grateful for some time to recover her breath and her wits. Rosie was sleeping in Kat's chamber, and her other ladies had been sent to their beds. She had ordered the guards doubled on the privy entrance to these rooms, and her yeomen, as ever, guarded the halls. Yet the brutal attack on her person had damaged her composure and courage.

"What keeps Lord Dudley when I sent for him posthaste?" the queen demanded, more of herself than Meg. "He should think he's died and gone to heaven being summoned to my bedchamber this time of night."

She had fretted at first that someone might have struck Robin down, too, but she knew better. Like Jenks, the man could handle himself with a sword or fists, let alone that glib, honeyed tongue of his. She did not believe for one moment he was the one who had hurt her, for he had all to gain through her and naught without her. Indeed, the man's rampant ambition made him want to wed her and rise high, so how dare he not keep their tryst and come early.

" 'S blood, he has a lot to answer for," the queen ranted on when Meg said not one word about Robin, whom she used to adore but now couldn't abide. "I vow, trouble follows that man everywhere!"

"Then it is not good he follows you everywhere," Meg blurted. She clapped a hand to her forehead. "You mean Lord Robert was to meet you out there at the maze? Alone? But—"

"I swear, bottom to top, this court and kingdom would go to hell in a handbasket without me," Elizabeth muttered, leaning again into the deep-set window to watch her men. "My guard Stackpole claims a linkboy he didn't know brought him a note from me *not* to guard the hall outside Mary Sidney's room earlier today, where I had just told him to stand watch." The queen began to pace, flinging gestures. "He can't find the note, of course, but says it was wretchedly scribbled, as if *that* would be my hand. Then Robin deceives or deserts his queen."

"I thought he's supposed to be in the stables, Your Grace. You just sent your guard to fetch him there."

"And where is Cecil," she demanded, ignoring Meg, "for he's been sent for too, though I don't favor facing him at first with my throat looking like this, so hie yourself over here with that ruff!"

"You need Kat or Rosie for this," Meg protested as she bent to look through the coffer containing gloves and hats.

"Kat's not to know, as I don't need her more upset. We can't have someone out of control privy to this. Now give me that ruff!" she cried and snatched it from Meg's hands the moment she turned one up.

Bending her knees to dart a look in the mirror, Elizabeth straightened the unironed ruff. She had removed her soiled and grass-stained costume and quickly donned a dark blue gown. Her own hair still looked a mess from the wig and the rough handling. But, for now, this would have to do.

When a crisp knock resounded on the door, she nodded for Meg to open it. Robin filled its frame and the room with his very presence. She locked her knees and stared him down.

"Your Grace," Robin began, looking both flushed and out of breath as he hurried in, "I was beside myself when you didn't come."

"I?" she countered icily as he went down on one knee with his head bowed. "It is *you* who did not arrive as *you* arranged."

His head snapped up. "I was early and never left and in the very place you commanded," he insisted.

"I cannot believe your sister was confused when she told you."

"She said the maze, but then this," he insisted and produced a folded piece of paper from the neck of his doublet.

The queen snatched it and read: *Robin, I shall come to the stables instead. To see the foal but more to see you.*

It was someone who knew about the foal and their plans, she thought, panicked. Someone who knew far too much.

"This isn't signed, Robin."

He rose, his handsome face puzzled and wary. "I didn't expect it would be in case someone else came across it, my queen."

"Someone else came across it, indeed," she clipped out, sinking back in her chair and nervously fingering her ruff to be sure it was in place. "That's because someone else sent it. It's not my writing."

"Do you think after all your letters I yet treasure I do not know that? But I believed it could have been dashed off in the heat of the moment or even written by Kat or your herb girl here. Or that you disguised your hand, my clever queen. But— you mean you were at the maze?"

"Yes, your clever queen was at the maze," she muttered, glaring down at the note, though it hurt her neck to so much as flex it like this. "My lord, I shall summon you in the morning, but leave me now and this note, too."

"You know I would never keep you waiting. You know I adore and—"

He halted in mid-plea, evidently when he glimpsed her expression. Robin had never been a member of her secret Privy Plot Council. Though she had longed to trust him fully, she feared she never could. Now, at least his exit was both smooth and swift.

"Meg," she ordered when the guard outside closed the door behind him, "send someone to find what's keeping Secretary Cecil and go fetch the men from the maze posthaste. 'S blood, they must be done by now. But first, tell me what scent you think is on this forged note," she commanded and extended it arm's-length to Meg.

Meg sniffed once, again, then nodded. "Now that's a coincidence. Here you asked me about gillyflowers earlier today, and that's it for sure."

Jenks and Ned had thrust their torches into each corner, node, and turn of the old maze. After they met at the goal with its stone bench and sundial, they began to work their way back out by different paths. So as not to call even more attention to themselves, they had doused their torches. Ned, who loved to tell tales and play parts, had already told Jenks that, if courtiers saw them from the windows, their story would be that they were looking for a jeweled pin the queen had dropped earlier in the day.

That riled Jenks. Ned was always trying to take over, always talking his way in and out of things, when Jenks wasn't so good with words. And Jenks knew they were headed out empty-handed. Whoever had attacked Her Grace had had plenty of time to hightail it.

Jenks was nearly back to the entrance, where they had found the queen's mask and wig, when he heard someone shuffling into the maze just across the last hedge wall. The culprit returning to the scene of the crime? Coming to remove clues, or to scuff out the footprints they would search for at dawn's first light? It wasn't Ned, who was a ways behind him. Edward Thompson, alias Ned Topside, the flap-mouthed wagtail, might be sure-footed on a stage, but protecting the queen was Jenks's bailiwick.

His sword at the ready, his muscles tensed, knees bent, Jenks waited until the form cleared the entrance, then lunged. He hauled the person—a shapely woman, who squealed—into his arms and—

"Meg?"

"Jenks! Devil take it, you scared the daylights out of me. I thought I would be strangled, too. Loose me this instant!"

He did, reluctantly, then tried to take advantage of the situation as he'd seen Lord Robert do more than once with Her Grace.

"Sorry, Meg. You know I long to protect you. You should've called out."

"And drawn a murderer to me if he's still out here? You'd best watch grabbing women or Her Grace will toss you in the Tower."

"She would not. She trusts me. But are you all right then?"

He sheathed his sword and grasped her shoulders with both hands, then moved one hand to lift her chin, also as he'd seen Lord Robert do. "I wouldn't ever scare or hurt you apurpose," he whispered. His mouth was close to hers, but he felt his tongue and lips swollen with the words he wanted to say. She smelled wonderful as ever, of summer gardens and the sweet hay they fed the horses. "Besides protecting Her Grace," he whispered, "I always want you to be safe, too, Meg."

Her eyes widened. When she lifted her chin even more as if to see him better in the moonlight, he leaned down to kiss her. He had yearned to for as long as he'd known her, and not just because he adored the queen and Meg resembled her so. And now that Meg was widowed...

It galled him sore to hear Ned coming. Meg stepped back from Jenks as if she'd been burned.

"Ho, now, you two," Meg said, turning toward Ned. "She sent me to fetch you both straightaway and said to rope off the maze before you leave. Then hie yourselves to a privy plot meeting. Ned, are you all right then?"

"Of course, I am," the freebooter told her and dared to smack her bum right through her skirts as he passed. Jenks could have brained him for that. And for the fact that however rough or rude Ned Topside treated Meg, her eyes still followed him. A fig on it, Jenks would give anything to let her see Ned Topside for the skirt-chasing bed-swerver he really was. Though caring for the queen would always be his first, best cause, he'd have to move fast to make sure Meg was his at any cost.

"I regret keeping you up so late or turning you out of your beds," Elizabeth began as she opened the meeting in the with-drawing room of her state apartments.

It had been a long time since she and her loyal band of Privy Plot Council members had been forced to solve a crime. And never had Elizabeth of England ordered an investigation begun because of a direct attack—an attempted murder—by hostile hands laid upon her royal person. She had advised Cecil, Ned, and Jenks of the crisis, and shown them her neck abrasions. Cecil looked as if he had something to say already, but she gave him no opening.

"Our numbers are woefully short without Kat and my cousin, Baron Hunsdon, present but, as you know, he is keeping a watch on our Scottish border this summer. I miss the services and dear presence of my artist, Gil Sharpe, but pray he will profit himself and our court later by his time studying his craft in Italy. If need be, as our investigation progresses, I may bring in others I can trust.

"But, I admit," she plunged on, gripping her hands on the table, "the fewer our numbers, the better for secrecy now. I do not want this attack noised about. And who knows," she added, her voice breaking, "what Kat would blurt out if she were privy to this now, so this group must needs probe this diabolical deed."

At last she took a breath and glanced around the table. Cecil had looked grim since she'd shown the marks on her neck. She also had a purplish bruise coming on her forehead—fortunately one her hair could hide—and scratches on her right cheek from being thrust into the maze hedges, not to mention grass stains she'd displayed on her mask and the gown. She'd have to exchange those with another identical masque costume by tomorrow or Kat would know for certain that something dire had befallen her mistress. Her beloved First Lady of the Bedchamber still fussed with her gowns, though Rosie Radcliffe now bore the burden of Kat's duties as Mistress of the Robes and kept an eye on her jewel cases, too.

Ned and Jenks leaned forward avidly. Meg looked flushed with excitement. Yet everyone seemed to hold back, waiting for whatever William Cecil would say.

"First of all," he began, "forgive me, Your Grace, but I cannot fathom you walked out alone."

"I admit it was to see Lord Robert Dudley privily after his time away. Just a walk in the moonlight."

"Which went sore awry."

"I'll not have chiding or lectures, Cecil. You are not my parent, nor some prelate or preacher."

"But I am ever your loyal servant and, you have said, your friend. Be that as it may, Meg mentioned," Cecil continued, "that Lord Dudley had a note changing the assignation—"

"Merely a meeting," the queen interrupted.

"A meeting," Cecil amended. "And you have that note?"

She drew it from her lap and handed it to him across the narrow table.

"Perhaps from a woman with that heavy scent on it," Meg put in, wrinkling her nose and fanning her face even from where she sat. "Gillyflowers. Your Grace, is that why you asked me earlier today about gillyflowers—no, you didn't have the note then."

"Hell's teeth, what about gillyflowers?" Cecil asked, sniffing at the scrap of folded parchment, then sneezing into his sleeve.

She was not, Elizabeth thought, going to tell them the foolishness about Catherine Howard's ghost and prayed that had not been some sort of harbinger of doom. The scent drifting up from the kitchen herb gardens was probably not gillyflowers at all, since Meg said none were there.

"Well," Meg said, "no one wears that scent much anymore, though I've been using that kind of dried petals in some of Kat's tonics with valerian and chamomile. It lends a spicy taste, and she always liked the smell of them."

"Leave poor Kat out of this," Elizabeth ordered.

"Probably not a woman who overpowered you anyway," Jenks put in, hunching over the table. "Not to take you down and choke you like that. However slender your form, Your Grace, you are strong."

"Jenks," Ned said, his voice condescending, "the would-be murder weapon was two gauzy garter ribbons, the ones *women* wore tonight. It could well have been a woman, a strong one who had the advantage of surprise over Her Grace."

Meg spun to face him. "What do you know about the garters Her Grace's ladies were wearing?"

"Your Majesty," Ned protested, gesturing grandly, "I oversaw the entire masque and knew what the women wore, that's all, so . . ."

"Enough!" Elizabeth cried, smacking a fist on the table. "It could have been a man or a strong or zealous woman for all I know. Someone tall enough, however, to be able to lift these garters over my head. And tie this strange knot in them."

"A common slip knot, used by sailors, farmers, even some falconers," Jenks said. "We use them in the stables, when colts need tight control, even before we start with bits and harnesses. The more the colt tugs, the tighter the rope or strap gets, but it's just as easy to loose, too. Let me show you."

"No, not with these, as I mean to examine them closely in better light tomorrow," Elizabeth said.

"What about Lord Robert?" Meg blurted. "He knew where you'd be, Your Grace, and must know those knots."

"Impossible," Jenks argued, though he didn't raise his voice as he usually did when he defended his master. "I don't care if some people still wrongly think Lord Dudley had his wife killed. I heard tell he was pacing back and forth in the stables, though they said he did leave after the foal was born to clean up and change his clothes."

"It wasn't Robert Dudley," Elizabeth protested. "He has everything to lose if I lose my life. At any rate, whether my attacker—and perhaps, potential murderer—was man or woman, I was, as Ned correctly says, at a great disadvantage to be so taken by surprise."

"Perhaps your attacker was, too," Cecil said, leaning across the table to return the note to her. "Almost everyone was masked, including you, Your Grace. Perhaps we have not an attempt at a royal assassination but a case of mistaken identity.

Your attacker erroneously believed he or she was strangling someone else. Even though it must have been dark in the maze, when your wig came off to reveal your red hair or your mask slipped, he or she ran, appalled."

"If you ask me who I'd put at the top of the list," Meg muttered, still looking upset from her dressing-down over her Robert Dudley theory, "it's Margaret Stewart, the Countess of Lennox. I see her giving you snide looks all the time, Your Grace."

Elizabeth and Cecil exchanged lightning glances. She could read that he'd been thinking the same. In these privy plot sessions, Elizabeth had always given her people leave to speak freely, and Meg had boldly done so. Margaret covertly championed Mary, Queen of Scots. Had Meg hit the nail precisely on its Papist plot head?

"And we all know," Ned said, "that her husband, Matthew Stewart, is tall and—as the wily Scots say—a braw man."

"He's not at court right now," Cecil said before the queen could reply. "But their lanky, nimble-footed son's been lurking about and perhaps would only be too happy to do the deed for his mother. Margaret Stewart seems to command him with an iron hand, despite the fact he's nearly twenty. Would that I could control my eldest that way," he added, under his breath.

"I know the Stewarts have sent privy correspondence to Mary of Scots," Elizabeth admitted, "even probably plotted against me over the years, so perhaps they are becoming desperate. Margaret was highly insulted I named her as one of the five foolish virgins, and her son was masked in the audience."

"Then too," Meg put in, "the countess is old enough to

favor gillyflower scent yet, out of fashion though it is. I never get close enough to her to know what potpourri she carries in that gold filigreed pomander of hers."

"Hm," Ned interrupted, narrowing his green eyes, "the pomander studded with bloody-hued garnets which she swings on its chain as if it were an orb of the whole world."

Elizabeth glared at him for his usual overblown bombast, but perhaps they had all leaped far afield. Surely, the Stewarts would not risk actually laying hands on their queen—or at least would have finished the job had they set out to do it. Yet in this search for a serpent in her court, they must look under every stone.

"Meg, you must discover what scent the countess favors," Elizabeth commanded, "and that of other women who were at court tonight. Try offering them some new fragrance or potpourri you've concocted, and ask them what they've used before."

"I could try to ingratiate myself with the countess—spy on her, Your Grace," Ned suggested.

"Indirectly mayhap, for she would never trust you outright. And you must feign to plan another amusement where each person who will take part must give you in their own handwriting what sort of costume they would like to wear."

"Why feign it? I could indeed create something for a large cast of actors—and suspects."

"No, spend your time and effort on this," she ordered, thrusting the small paper at him. "Then I shall examine those notes to compare handwriting. And be certain they include some of the key words here for comparison.

"Jenks, see if you can turn up the note my yeoman guard

Stackpole said he had, or at least ask him if he recalled if it had a scent. Also, get a description of the strange linkboy who fetched the note to him and track him, if you can."

Jenks nodded as Ned perused the note. "I'll have Lady Rosie ask for all the women's garments to be returned forthwith, their garters included," Elizabeth continued. "She's been helping Kat oversee the wardrobe, so perhaps she can account for or trace such unique garments."

They gazed silently at the silvered ribbons wrapped with gauzy tissue, carefully knotted. Cecil drummed his fingertips on the table. He'd been frowning throughout, but now looked as if his countenance could splinter.

"My lord, are you quite well?" she asked.

"Hardly, Your Grace. I fear, at the least, we have before us an attempted murder on a mistaken noble victim on royal property. And, at the most, high treason against your most precious person. Could someone besides Robert Dudley have known where you would be and lain in wait there?"

"Only Mary Sidney and, for obvious reasons, I trust her with my life," she said, gripping her hands on the table. "But when I told her where and when I would meet Lord Robert, Kat thought she heard someone listening at Mary's keyhole. I looked out and—she was mistaken."

"Then your attacker could be some random wretch," Cecil said, "who merely saw you leave tonight and went out the same or a different door behind you. We can delve into that."

"I first stopped under the big oak. I saw no one enter the maze, but I wasn't always looking."

"We'll have a devil of a time determining a possible culprit, since nearly everyone in the audience was thoroughly disguised at your express command. And since you want this kept quiet."

"Not so much because I don't want gossip about me and Lord Robert again, but more to avoid inciting panic—nor will I give any satisfaction to my enemy who might be behind the attack."

"Or," Jenks put in, "your attacker could have been some random oaf who walked in from the road or river, then just spotted a comely woman alone."

"In short," Elizabeth said, "we may never know. But we are going to try desperately to."

"Thank God, Bettina Sutton stumbled on you," Cecil said, rubbing his eyes with thumb and index finger. "You must promise not to go off alone ever again."

She was going to tell him that only she would decide what she did, that no one could frighten the Queen of England, no implied threat, terror tactic, or direct attack. But she knew he was right. The times had suddenly changed, for her, for all of them who were the crown or served the crown. And this was no time for a display of Tudor temper, no matter how effective a tool it could be at times.

"You must return to your wife, my lord," she told Cecil as she rose. Everyone else stood, scraping back their chairs. The queen stepped away with Cecil. "How did Mildred fare in the short time she's been here?"

"I am certain she enjoyed the evening, Your Grace. Yet her countenance hidden behind that mask made me so uneasy," he admitted, "since I could not watch her expressions to read her moods as I have been wont to do, and even that desperate form of detection has not served me well..."

His voice trailed off again. Poor Cecil, she thought.

"This meeting is adjourned," Elizabeth said, when the others still tarried. "Dear friends, I know I have enemies, some of them, as ever, my own courtiers and kin. But we must pursue and capture the murderer from the maze."

Chapter the Fourth

"HOW IS KAT THIS MORNING, ROSIE?" ELIZABETH ASKED as the pretty young brunette bustled into the queen's bedchamber without the older woman.

Picking at her breakfast of ale, manchet bread, and stewed carp, the queen was still in her nightrail and barefooted, for it was warm in the room. She did not wear her robe but had draped it about her neck to hide the bruises there. She'd pulled her hair down to cover her forehead bruise, and covered the scratches on her cheek with Meg's concoction of alabaster face cream. Rosie evidently noticed nothing strange and proceeded to open the windows to let the July breeze chase the sunlight in.

"You're going to be upset," Rosie said, so dismayed that as she walked back toward the table she wrung her hands, "so I might just as well tell you straightaway."

The queen's goblet clanked against her breakfast plate. Rosie was never an alarmist. "Have you finally accepted Jamie Barstow's attentions?"

"He's very kind, honorable, too, Your Grace, but it has naught to do with Jamie."

Elizabeth's insides lurched. "Kat's not failing?"

Rosie shook her head. "*I* failed you. Last night she drank that new tonic of Meg's before I could stop her. I coaxed her into bed, though she kept insisting you needed her. When I went to use the garderobe, she slipped out. I finally found her, though."

"Slipped out where? Is she all right?"

"Yes, but she had wandered around who knows where and ended up in the corridor outside Mary Sidney's chamber where she was looking in each keyhole. Still, I think the tonic did her good as she finally slept without being haunted by her usual nightmares."

Rising, the queen held out her hands to Rosie who rushed to hold them. "Do not take this amiss, dear friend," Elizabeth told her, "but I see I must not put the burden of Kat's care so much on you. Because you are so scrupulous and trustworthy, I fear I expect too much at times, and it is not fair to you."

"I want to help. You know I do."

"In the few years you have been among my ladies you have helped a great deal. The others smirk and gossip and giggle, but not you. I trust you with my jewels, my wardrobe—and with my dear Kat, but I shall have others, especially Mistress Milligrew, help you more. And having said all that," she added, loosing Rosie's hands with a deep sigh, "I do have one more favor I would ask of you."

"To put off Jamie, Your Grace?"

"No, if he is behaving as you say, not Jamie. That is—well, I mean this not as it sounds, but, for now, that is your affair."

"Name anything I can do for you, Your Grace."

Their eyes met and held. It bucked Elizabeth up to have an attendant and friend who helped fill the void left by Mary Sidney's absence and Kat's decline. Though the queen had never said such aloud, she admired Rosie's no-nonsense attitude toward men. The maids of honor, her unwed ladies, were always being swept away by the gentlemen of her court, who had seduction at worst, marriage at best in mind.

Rosie's admiration of Jamie Barstow notwithstanding, the maid alone seemed to see masculine flatteries for what they were and steered the steady course of spinsterhood. Even when among the queen's married attendants, her ladies of the bedchamber, Mary Radcliffe, dubbed Rosie, was a touchstone reminding the queen of her necessary virginity, however much Elizabeth loved being cosseted and courted. Soon, she should invite Rosie to become a member of her Privy Plot Council. This task would be a sort of test.

"The favor is simply that I ask you," Elizabeth said, gathering her robe closer about her neck, "to collect personally the gowns and masks from the ten ladies who played the parts last night, even their shoes, stockings, and especially those distinctive garters, and clearly note which things come from which woman."

The queen fully intended to see who came up short garters, but she also meant to peruse the hem of each gown and every slipper for soil or grass stains. Surely, discerning her attacker would be easily accomplished.

"The garters? Those slippery things? But Kat made so many of them and even handed the extra ones out at random, to men and women, too. It did keep her happily busy half a day, and we'll probably see them pinned for a jest on men's sleeves or as tippets on hats or . . . Whatever is it, Your Grace? What have I said?"

Deflated and furious, the queen almost couldn't speak. So much for easily finding her strangler.

"It's a disgrace that Templar and Bettina Sutton were allotted those small chambers on the ground floor beyond the kitchen wing!" Elizabeth groused to Cecil as they walked toward her withdrawing room mid-morning. Cecil was toting a pile of bills, grants, and dispatches she'd just signed.

"Your Grace, you know your palaces are cheek-by-jowl when you are in residence, not to mention that the threat of growing plague in London makes the salubrious air here an attraction to your courtiers—as much as your presence is, of course."

"I want the Suttons moved. Templar is your mentor and friend, and I may owe Bettina my very life. See that some better chambers are opened by sending someone to their country seat. 'S blood, my courtiers long for their own homes in these warm summer months when the roads are good, do they not?"

"They do indeed, Your Grace," he said in such a heart-wrenching tone she stopped walking and turned to face him.

"You too, my Cecil?"

He shrugged slightly and frowned down at his armful of papers. "I visited Stamford in the spring, but it is my new land

and building project at Theobalds I long for. But never," he added, nodding to enunciate each word, "at the price of leaving my queen when she has need of me. And with this nearly fatal attack upon your royal person, we must be steadfast and vigilant."

Touched, she placed a hand on his arm. "Indeed, Sir William, Principal Secretary Cecil, Master of the Court of Wards, Chancellor of Cambridge College—and many more honors yet to come—your queen ever has need of you, and especially now. But when I soon visit Cambridge as we've planned and stay at my old home of Hatfield en route, Theobalds is but a scant few miles' ride. And so, I shall go to see your land and building project there."

She was amazed that tears glazed his eyes. "It's not worthy of your presence yet," he insisted, "though I intend to make it so someday when the Cecils can house the queen's majesty and your court for a fine visit. So far, despite the spacious grounds, it has but an old moated manor house I've scarce spent a night in—and, they say, it is haunted."

"Haunted?" she repeated, as her mind flashed to her strange experience in the chapel corridor yesterday.

"And a further curiosity I hope to take Templar to see," Cecil went on, "though I warrant you would fancy it, too, Your Grace. A water maze."

"Indeed? I've never seen such. Flooded by a stream or moat?"

"A sturdy stream feeds both maze and moat. The hedges are planted in barrels with stone ballast, and one must row oneself through the shrubs. Templar will love it."

"Speaking of Templar, I had asked Bettina not to tell anyone what happened last night, but I never intended for a wife to keep such from her husband, so I must correct that, if she hasn't told him already."

"How could a woman keep that in? To rescue and revive her queen?"

"Perhaps if we put Templar's and your fine minds together—with mine, too—we shall discover not only someone we suspect but someone we can question and imprison. When we restage the crime tonight, I intend to take Templar and Bettina with us."

With Cecil in her wake, the queen swept into the room where the Suttons awaited. As he bowed and she curtsied, Elizabeth found herself assessing them as she had everyone so far this morning by their height and musculature. Her attacker had been tall enough to easily reach those garters over her head and strong enough to throw her down. Templar was tall enough, but his body seemed almost frail, however firm and resonant his voice. Bettina was not only petite but had breasts like a shelf—though they were bound up last night to get her in that dress. Yet, she surely would have felt Bettina pressed up against her back. No, her attacker had either been a muscular man or a tall, spare woman of some strength.

Elizabeth welcomed them and indicated they should sit across the small, round table from Cecil and her. The Suttons' eyes grew wide as Cecil put down his papers to pour wine and the queen herself passed the plate of sweetmeats.

"This privy audience is a great, great honor, Your Majesty," Templar said.

"Master Sutton, I believe you retired to bed directly after the masque last night," Elizabeth began.

"As ever, I lull myself to sleep by concocting legal conundrums for my students to debate. After dinner each night at Gray's Inn, I write out a legal problem and place it before the salt, so that two of the inner benchers may argue it, and I retire to bed immediately after hearing their *pros* and *contras*. But I wish to extend an invitation to you to visit our law school at the inn, Your Majesty. You have graced us with your presence on holidays, but you would honor us even more if you would come to see the daily making of an English lawyer."

"I believe I have your curriculum and encouragement to thank for the fine men and advisors I have around me—my lord Cecil, especially, of course. Indeed, the Inns of Court are a finishing school, our third great, if unnamed, university. Certain of my long-time courtiers, members of Parliament, and lately, Chris Hatton and Jamie Barstow, are the fine products of your tutoring."

"Ah yes, those two young bloods," Templar said with what Elizabeth construed to be a rueful shake of his silver head while Bettina fidgeted, crossing her legs and rearranging her skirts yet again.

"Perhaps," the queen said, "you will also favor me with assessments of each man's strengths and weaknesses—and huggermugger stories of their student days with you." To her amazement, now her serious, serene Cecil looked like the lad caught with his hand in the plum pudding. "On occasion I need something to hold over all their heads," she added with a forced laugh.

"It would be my greatest pleasure to tell you tales out of school, Your Majesty," Templar said with a solemn nod. "But I must add, despite some youthful indiscretions and tomfooleries, you have chosen your chief secretary well. He is my ideal of the perfect lawyer: detached yet dramatic, persuasive yet practical, and cautious yet challenging. And I assure you, there is no profession where an ignoramus or impostor is more easily detected and exposed than in the pursuit of a calling to the law."

Elizabeth sensed she was hearing one of Templar's lectures. "Then let me lay out a problem, a conundrum, as you say, Master Sutton." He sat intently, as she explained what had happened last night and how Bettina had been her salvation. It touched her to see Templar reach out to grasp his wife's hand in pride of what she had done. And it moved the queen deeply to sense these two such different people had evidently built a strong marriage, when she had known so many fragile or fragmented ones.

"I can tell that Bettina did not inform you of this before," Elizabeth told Templar. "I especially admire anyone who can hold his or her tongue on such a thing and will reward it—judiciously."

"Ah, Your Majesty," Templar replied, "your wit is a match for any lawyer I have seen called to the bar. Now, since Bettina and I—and obviously Cecil—know of this terrible and treasonous attack on your person, what can we do to help ferret out and bring the perpetrator to queen's justice?"

"Come, Kat," the queen commanded that afternoon as she sat with her ladies in her withdrawing room. "We shall take a walk outside to the Thameside gardens. Ladies . . ."

Like colored flowers turning to the sun, her maids of honor and ladies of the bedchamber popped up from their seats, where they had been bent over embroidery, reading, or whispering. Elizabeth had included Bettina in their company today and motioned for her to attend also. She'd have asked Mildred along, too, but Cecil said that she'd gotten pounding head pains during the masque, and had since been keeping to her bed.

The queen had hoped to send Meg to her with a tonic, but her herbalist was still off somewhere. Perhaps she was concocting a new potpourri to offer her women so she could question them about their scents. As far as the queen knew, she hadn't smelled gillyflowers on a single one of them, for lighter rosewater fragrances, like she herself wore, were now in style.

"A walk," Kat said, getting up stiffly while the other waited for her to catch up. "I'd like that."

The queen set a slower pace than usual, for the day was warm and humid. It amused her that several of her maids had already copied the wearing of the soft ruff she wore, but it galled her sore that some had taken, as Rosie had predicted, to gaily wearing Kat's overmade ribbon and gauze garters on sleeves or at belts.

When they passed the maze, Elizabeth noted well that Jenks and Ned had roped it off. The queen had told Ned to put out the word that it needed to be clipped and raked. Actually, she did not want it disturbed until they had an opportunity tonight—when the moonlight was exactly right—to return to the maze and mime her attack. Bettina met her gaze and nodded. With Jenks and Ned along for guards, the Suttons were pledged to accompany Elizabeth and Cecil to re-enact and reason it all out together.

Everyone chattered about the most frivolous things, the queen realized. How an attempt on one's life could change one's outlook, making daily duties seem so trivial. Besides, she was grieved by the plague marauding through her capital city, even encroaching on the southeastern shires. If it came closer, she'd be off early to old Hatfield House, buried deeper in the country-side.

"Gracious," Kat said and tugged at Elizabeth's sleeve as if she were a child, "there's that lad of yours, looking as if he's up to no good when he should be saddling your father's horse."

Heads turned toward Kat and the queen. The chatter stopped, then when Elizabeth did not react, began again. However confused Kat had been, she'd not forgotten names before.

"That's Jenks, Kat, and I will have a word with him. Wait here with everyone."

She traipsed off the gravel path to see what he had to say. He bent in a bow, smoothly sliding his swordpoint out of his way so it wouldn't skewer the ground. She realized she had not felt a man's sword belt or hilt against her last night from behind either, and most courtiers wore them when dressed—well, to the hilt.

"Pardon, Your Grace, but didn't think you'd mind if I followed you out here. Lord Dudley says he'll escort you to the stables when you're ready."

"Tell him an hour, and if he's late, I will marry him to one of the scullery maids. Say on."

"Your guard Stackpole swears up and down he can't find the note," he said, speaking fast and low, though no one could overhear. "Can't read anyway, it turns out, but the Countess of Pembroke's tiring girl been taught to sound things out and she read it for him. Stackpole doesn't know a thing about scents but the girl says it smelt fine. As for that linkboy, can't find hide nor hair of him—raven-haired, he was, with a red welt on his chin."

"Was he a boy indeed? Short or not?"

"Tall, Stackpole said, and the tiring girl saw him, too. A lad of middling weight with big shoulders."

" 'S blood, next we'll learn he was dragging two silver garters about," Elizabeth muttered.

"And something else, too, Your Grace, something personal."

"About my person?"

"I guess I never say things right. About me."

"Say on."

"I know it's not a good time, but when e'er I see you, it's with all sorts of folks about, and I need your permission."

"My permission for what?"

"You are ever the first lady—queen, I mean—in my life. But I was hoping if I courted a—a woman, you'd give me your say-so."

She had seldom been more astounded. Quiet, dutiful, straight-arrow Jenks? In love? Ned needed a good watch at all times, and she nearly wore herself out guarding her women from flirtations and dangerous tangles of the heart and body, but she had not fathomed Jenks. And then she knew who he meant, and her heart went out to him. Meg had ever been hopelessly, but foolishly, enamored of Ned Topside.

"And will you name the one you love?" she asked.

" 'Tis Meg Milligrew, Your Grace. I mean, now that she's widowed and all. Since we both serve you, we would never leave. Like Kat Ashley and her husband years ago, 'fore he died."

"Jenks, you have my permission to approach and court Meg, if you are certain about your intentions *and hers*."

"Hers—well, I'm clod-foot at women's feelings, 'cause horses are so much easier to read."

The queen fought back a grin. "Let me know how things proceed, Jenks. Perhaps Meg will, too," she added and shot him an encouraging smile as she returned to her waiting retinue.

The entire world was falling in love if they weren't already in that hopeless state, she thought, entirely frustrated, though she made conversation and responded to her ladies' chatter. Cecil was fretting for his Mildred; Bettina and Templar, though apparently mismatched, seemed to be quite suited. Jamie Barstow had evidently found the chink in Rosie's armor. The queen herself was attracted to both Robin and Chris Hatton, however much younger Chris was.

And then there were the politics of love. Cecil, her counselors, and her Parliament had more than once requested that she wed, though she had managed to put them off yet again. Hell's teeth, Mary, Queen of Scots was looking for a second husband already, and Elizabeth must play a part in that to be certain she wed someone who could be trusted. Someone ambitious but malleable to the will of the Protestant, English queen even when he bedded with the Catholic, Scottish one.

She strode the rest of the way to the gardens, hardly hearing the chatter and giggles about her. But the moment they reached the flowers, she decided to toss out her bait. "Look at these pretty gillyflowers, everyone. I can smell them from here."

"A spicy smell, rather too strong," Anne Carey put in, wrinkling her pert nose.

"I like it myself, and so does our queen, even tucking gillyflowers in her bodice or her hair," Kat declared, stooping to behead a flower and thrust it at Elizabeth. For once she was about to correct Kat when the old woman continued, "Queen Catherine Howard may be too young for your father, lovey, but he's so enamored of her, that, just like other old husbands with flibbety-gibbety wives, he'd do anything to please her."

"You must take your sister riding while she's here, as she won't come out of her chamber for me," Elizabeth told Robin as they walked toward the vast brick and wood stable block.

"Mary does ride out, sometimes even alone like last night. I would have gone with her, but I couldn't leave the foaling and she wouldn't hear of a guard going along."

"At night? Last night? And alone?"

"Don't fret," Robin soothed. "She said she's likely to go mad cooped up. You know she's always glad to see you, but just can't abide anyone else around. Enter my realm, my queen," he smoothly shifted the subject, and swept Elizabeth a bow as they stepped into the long corridor of slatted wooden stalls.

Despite her delicate nose, Elizabeth had always loved the smell of the stables, well-tended ones, at least. Once one adapted to the undercurrent of animal smells, the nostalgic ones were discernible: straw, leather, soap, and polish—men. And sounds like the creak of saddles, the snorts and stomping of the big beasts. It all reminded her of the few happy times she'd shared with her father. She had become an excellent horsewoman to please him above all else.

"What do you think of our new arrival?" Robin asked her and pressed her hand on his arm close to his solid ribs as he swung open a stall door with the other.

The white mare Fortune, the queen's favorite mount before

the animal's belly swelled, stepped forward to nuzzle the gloved royal hand and crunch down the offered apple. Robin smacked Fortune's flank and she sidestepped to reveal her gangly foal, who went noisily back to suckling. For one rapt moment, the queen and her Master of the Horse just grinned and stared at the new stallion.

"What shall you name him then?" Robin asked.

"Destiny, I believe."

"Ah, Fortune and Destiny, names after my own heart, but it is truly you who are after my own heart—or I wish you were," he teased, his voice rough with the sudden passion that could flare from him without warning.

Though her stomach cartwheeled, she decided to ignore that. "You do a fine job with all of this, Robin." She gazed around the vast stable block with grooms busy at their tasks. "And I hear your implication about your fortune and destiny, which I am certain will be on the rise."

"Meaning someday you will not rip to shreds my patent for the peerage as you did before everyone when you were—were angry? Someday you will actually give me the earldom you have promised?"

"Yes, Robert Dudley, yes! I had to be certain I could trust your loyalty to me, even if I asked you to wait—to sacrifice or take on some task that seems dangerous or difficult."

"Such as what now?" he demanded. He closed the stall door and leaned against it with his arms crossed and his brow furrowed.

"We read each other well yet, do we not? The earldom of Leicester will yet be yours, for I would raise you high."

"My queen!" he cried and went down on one knee in the straw, head bent.

"Do not thank me overmuch. And put from your mind that we shall wed, my lord. That is not why I will create you earl when we return to London this autumn, though I do have a queen in mind for you."

His expression looked both ravaged and raptured when he raised his face. As ever, she could see his mind working to catch up to hers. "You don't mean to offer me to Mary of Scots?" he cried, exploding to his feet. "Hell's gates, I know you've wanted to push her toward someone you can trust, but she'd never have me."

"She will if I find a way to convince her, coerce her."

"Not with your Master of the Horse whom she will see as your cast-off, former favorite."

"I must find a way, my lord. The last thing I need is the Stewarts dangling Lord Darnley before her with his Tudor ties and noble Scottish blood. I cannot abide or allow an alliance between my cousin Margaret and Mary of Scots, damn them, connivers both."

"But—you cannot ask that of me, not when I will always love you, and I know you would never command me to—"

"Shh," she said and pressed her gloved fingers to his lips. "We will discuss it privily later. Besides, when has love ever had a thing to do with royalty and realms?"

Fighting tears, she turned slowly, sadly away, and he hurried to keep up. They walked from the stables into the blazing afternoon sun. He'd fallen silent, and she ached to think that she had broached the subject with him—or that she would ever actually send him away, and to the woman she feared and detested more than any other.

For, despite their problems, Elizabeth had always felt better with Robin around. And to think that Cecil had said once Robert Dudley was just waiting for a chance to rattle her so that she would realize she loved and needed him—even as a husband, a king.

She nearly lurched to a stop, and, thinking she had stumbled, Robin's hand shot out to steady her elbow. Surely, she thought, Robin could not have been the one who laid hands on her in the maze. No, as she had reasoned out before, his future hung on her good will. Besides, the foaling gave him an alibi. Unless after that, while he was supposedly changing his clothes, as Jenks had mentioned, he'd waited in the hedges for her. Thinking just to shake her up, he'd not known his own strength. He'd meant to rescue her himself before Bettina came charging in ...

She pulled free of his touch. Her attacker had been at least partly victorious if he could make her believe even her closest friends could be guilty. She shoved down another stab of panic when she recalled Mary Sidney had been abroad last night. Of course, her dear friend wanted only the best for her brother, so did that entail forcing her into Robin's arms? Or worse?

No, the queen told herself, Mary had no motive for harming her sovereign and friend. Surely, surely she could not blame Elizabeth for the fact that she had caught the pox from nursing her queen. Friendship overcame such trials and tragedies, didn't it?

"Devil take it," Robin muttered, startling her again, "but would you look at that!"

"What's wrong with that horse?" she asked, following his

gaze. Around the far side of the stable block, a groom led a limping roan with what appeared to be long cuts across its throat and neck.

"I've warned him, but I've a good nerve to beat that spoiled, sadistic bastard Darnley to a pulp for whipping every horse he rides," Robin muttered, as he smacked a fist into a wooden gate then kicked it open. His sudden shift to violence upset the queen as much as the sight of the poor horse. "He whips his hunt dogs, too," Robin raved on. "The little priss is not quite twenty, so he'll only get worse. He looks like such a handsome, graceful lad, then acts like a brute in private."

"Then I must admit I hardly know him—and he sounds like his mother's boy indeed," Elizabeth said and tucked that new bit of knowledge away for dealing later with the Stewarts and her Scottish problem. For first, in the moonlit maze tonight, she had her own to solve.

Chapter the Fifth

"IS YOUR HEAD PAIN BETTER, MY DEAR?" CECIL ASKED his wife, as he hurried into their small suite. It consisted of a bedchamber and outer room, the latter which, when Mildred was not here with him, was filled with his own scriveners and secretaries. The household maid they'd brought from London peeked her head out of the bedchamber, saw it was him, and closed the door to give them privacy. Mildred turned slowly toward him from where she'd evidently been staring out the casement window.

"Like you, my head pain comes and goes," she said, standing her ground. "I didn't want any of that elixir, even if it is from the queen's herbalist. It makes me sleepy, and I don't want to sleep. There is much too much to do around here."

He assumed she was being shrewdly flippant, for he'd not spent much time with her since they'd arrived. He'd been late to bed, risen early. He'd left for the Privy Plot Council meeting last night and would be back out in the maze after dark tonight, none of which Mildred could know about.

"This evening, let's go over our plans for building Theobalds," he proposed with a smile, as he dropped his leather satchel on the table and gave her a quick hug. "It will have to be before dark as I have a meeting later."

"You're the one who loves poring over the minutiae of measurements on those diagrams, Will," she protested as she weakly returned the hug. Mildred was a hardy, vigorous woman, so her apparent feebleness dismayed him. He needed some better tonic for her and soon. "When they become reality," she went on, "I shall advise you on furnishings and ornaments on little Robert's behalf."

"Since the house is to be his inheritance, I thought you'd be pleased to contribute even in the planning stages."

"If you put one tenth of the funds and time into Theobalds as you have into expanding and refurbishing your family's ancestral Stamford home for your Tom, I'll be eternally pleased."

"The queen may visit Theobalds soon, and I'd like to have Templar come see that water maze, too," he said, bending over the table to roll open a parchment diagram of the ground floor. "They'll be excited to see it early."

"Ah," she said, remaining at the window while he poured himself a glass of ale, "Bettina will be excited to see it, too, I suppose."

"I'm not certain, but the Suttons seem to be inseparable."

Glancing up, he could tell she almost said "lucky them," or something of the sort. His hopes fell that being here at court would buck her up. Mildred's mental malady baffled him. She had once been so calm and confident, so sure of him and proud of his achievements. But since Robert had been born lame with a bent backbone, icicles could have hung from her, though that was better than her occasional fiery outbursts.

Surely, he agonized, as much as she knew he admired Elizabeth Tudor, it couldn't be jealousy for the time he spent with his royal mistress. She wasn't *that* sort of mistress, and he'd never been untrue *that* way in all their years of marriage.

"Her Majesty only mentioned she'd drop by because she'd be nearby," he rushed on, letting the parchment recoil itself. "She'll be staying at Hatfield en route to a visit to Cambridge."

"Cambridge? Your old stomping grounds, as they say. After all, she did name you Chancellor of Cambridge when you didn't even finish a degree there, but of course, Her Majesty must know that and why. Your only grand mistake, you once said and yet you risked all for it, your family's wrath, all your plans, all your dreams."

He smacked his goblet down. He did not need to be reminded of those days when passion and not prudence ruled his life.

"After all," she went on, "I rather think—"

A rap resounded on the hall door. Mildred nearly leaped to answer it as if she welcomed the excuse to say no more. It was Jason Nye, one of his most trustworthy assistants.

"Lady Cecil, milord." He greeted them with a nod. "You said, milord, to tell you if Matthew Stewart came back to court, and he just rode in. Don't even think his countess or son knows he's back yet."

"I'll be right there," Cecil said and rushed to seize the correct leather satchel from his array of them in his brass-bound coffer.

"My dear, let's dine here and go over the plans. . . ." he began as he spun around to bid farewell to Mildred.

She was not in the room.

"Her ladyship went out in a hurry," Jason said, standing wide-eyed in the open door and gesturing into the hallway.

"So I see. She needs a breath of air, I believe."

"Aye, that's it. Saw her walking in this very corridor late last night, too."

"No," Cecil corrected him as they dashed out and Jason closed the door behind them, "Lady Cecil was not herself last night and kept to her bed."

"Must have been someone else, milord," he amended, but it was Cecil's own words which echoed in his head. Mildred was not herself, so who was she of late? He obviously needed more than a single servant girl to watch her. Thank God he had her away from the children for a while. He was actually starting to fear that in her strange moods, she might do damage to herself—or to someone else.

"We're going where, Your Grace?" Rosie asked. "The kitchens?"

"The flower garden was one thing," Anne Carey put in as the two of them stretched their strides to keep up with their royal mistress, "but the kitchens? The hearths will make this hot day absolutely stifling in there. Your Majesty, are you certain you meant the kitchens?"

"You two sound like that parrot my brother once had," Elizabeth teased them. "I believe I am queen here, and will visit my kitchens if I so desire, when I so desire."

"I've seen them, vast and smoky," Anne said, still sounding

miffed, as two yeomen guards fell in behind the three women. "Hold your skirts close, or you'll get grease-speckled, Your Grace. But it will give the staff something to talk about besides what such-and-such dish was fit for you, or what lord just dumped what for his dogs."

The queen ignored their prating. She was not paying a surprise visit to the kitchen block on a whim. Nor was Stackpole one of the guards with her for no reason. The scent of gillyflowers in the so-called haunted gallery outside Mary Sidney's rooms had—damn, had haunted her. Despite the fact Meg Milligrew had claimed there were no such flowers in the kitchen herbal beds, she must be mistaken. That spicy scent was distinctive and she was intent on tracking it.

Like the entire sprawling palace of Hampton Court, the kitchen block was a veritable warren of chambers. Commonly called Cooks Court, it encompassed numerous passageways and backstairs connecting pallet chambers, irregular cobbled courtyards, and work rooms. These included a bakehouse, brewhouse, dove house, pastry house, flesh storage, confectionery, boiling house, garnish room, larders, the wine cellar with its three hundred barrels, and an ale storage. The great kitchen block, which produced the prodigious meals for up to one thousand courtiers twice a day, was staffed by eighty servants with a system of rank all their own, from chief cook to scullery maids and slop boys.

But now, as the queen entered unannounced, multiple hubbubs slowly ceased as heads turned and workers elbowed others to silence.

"I came to tell you how much your hard work is appreciated," Elizabeth declared in ringing tones. She noted well the mingled aromas that assailed her, but none seemed the scent she was seeking. Still talking, greeting folk who beamed or looked as if they'd cry in pride at this arm's-length glimpse of her, she led her small party through the garnish room, where a roast peacock was having its feathers arranged and a crown-shaped marzipan was being colored and decorated. Soon, Roger Stout, the garrulous chief cook, appeared and trailed along, over-answering each question as fast as she asked it.

The intensity of mingled smells amazingly increased as they stepped out into a court which boasted not one but two herb gardens stuffed with the green and flowering savories Meg helped to oversee. The queen sniffed. Yes, the scent was here, but faint. Trailing gawkers and her original entourage, Elizabeth perused the beds of herbs, recognizing most, but, as Meg had said, she saw no pale rose-hued gillyflowers with pinked edges here. She turned to Roger Stout again.

"I would have sworn I smelled gillyflowers strongly in the upstairs gallery where I was walking yesterday," she told him, pointing. "There, just to the east."

His face, like a plump apple, permanently bronzed from peering into pots and at spitted, rotating joints, broke into a relieved smile. "Yesterday? Aye, Your Majesty, we were crushing cloves, pounding them to powder, right here. As for gillyflower petals, we had none, though they ever lend a faint clove spice smell, aye, and taste to everything. Not that you were mistaken, Your Majesty, but perhaps you just thought it was gillyflowers and here it was our precious cloves, though they're much stronger—more expensive, too. Aye, we take a care not to drop a one, we do, and not to give too many out when servants come abegging or bartering for cloves for their lords and ladies."

"Cloves, was it? My courtiers want cloves to spice their own foods when they eat *gratis* at my table?"

"Not so much that, but chewed whole, for sweetening the breath, Your Majesty, like lovers wont to do, eh?" the man finally managed a short answer.

She favored Master Stout with a nod, then turned to her guard Stackpole and said low, "Is this clove smell what was on the note, do you think?"

"Not sure, Your Grace," he boomed out. "All I know is that note smelt good."

So far, the queen thought, her wretched attempts to tie proofs to her strangler had made her path wider, not narrower. Many of her court could write notes and hire some apprentice from town or even an itinerant ruffian to deliver them. Many flaunted those silver garters, and could have cloves, chewed or stored, about their persons, let alone gillyflowers. Elizabeth made her way out of one of the numerous exits from Cooks Court, but she considered her foray into it a dead end.

As she walked around to the riverside lawns, hoping to calm herself, she glared at the roped-off maze, then decided to walk its outer circumference. She was perspiring and knew Rosie and Anne were shooting each other arrow-tipped looks, evidently wondering if their queen had taken leave of her senses. Stackpole, toting his ceremonial pike and sword, huffed along as if he was exhausted or chagrined. Only the other guard, Geoffrey Clifford, kept up well.

Indeed, she was angry with herself as she still had no notion what she was looking for. A break in the outer hedges perhaps, which was not discernible from within but which someone inside the maze could have broken out to escape?

"That pin you lost in the maze yesterday," Rosie piped up. "Do you think you lost it outside the hedges instead of in? And I didn't notice one missing from your jewel boxes."

"If it's lost, how do I know where it is?" She spun to face the two of them. The sheen of sun and exertions gilded their pretty faces, and they both plied their fans so fast they even sent a breeze her way. In her inner tumult, she'd quite forgotten her own fan, which dangled at her wrist.

Elizabeth decided it best to lessen the number of observers. She was tempted to keep Rosie with her, for she hoped to include her in her Privy Plot Council. But she supposed it would build morale among her people if she told them first—at least Cecil. If she sent one lady back, she'd be hard pressed to explain keeping the other with her.

"Stackpole, accompany Lady Anne and Lady Rosie back to the palace. Clifford, come with me." Indeed, she was not keeping Stackpole with her, when he seemed so dense. Clifford she had known and trusted for years.

Despite their protests and fussing, the two women headed back toward the palace with their plodding guard, while the queen, trailing Clifford, walked on. Near the back of the maze's exterior, closer to the goal within, trees shaded the area. She saw no breaks in the venerable hedges here at least. Standing on tiptoe, she scanned the trees and their foliage. Could someone have climbed in or out of the maze via a big tree limb? But none seemed to hang far or low enough. She supposed someone could have used a ladder, but damned if she was going to look for ladder marks around this huge stretch of hedge. She'd send Jenks and Ned out to do it.

"Seeing I'm taller, Your Grace, what is it you're looking for, if I may ask. Not some pin you lost, for certain."

"I was pondering whether I should have the maze replanted here or moved. Go along this back length, and see if you can spot any breaks big enough to see through or get through, as that would quite ruin the whole effect."

As he instantly obeyed, she realized Clifford might also be a good man to swell the ranks of the Privy Plot Council. Of course, there was always Chris or Jamie, both young but always ready and able to assist her.

She watched Clifford move slowly away to scrutinize the hedges. Deflated she was still getting nowhere, she paced the opposite direction, around the farthest back corner of the maze where the tree trunks were the thickest.

A bright blur of color near the distant, shady grape arbors snagged her gaze—the peacock blue of a man's doublet beyond the low brick wall. A tall, slender man had a lady pressed against a tree in wildest, passionate abandon. If the queen had not been too warm already, she would have blushed, for even from here, she could tell the blond man—who was that?—ground his loins against the lady's thighs and belly.

No, she was sore mistaken. They were both men. Sodomites? It was a crime which, if proven in court, was punishable by death, so it was almost never prosecuted. At least they both looked quite young, for it would be a pity if they had wives. She would send Clifford over at once to learn their names and see they were banished from her court.

She narrowed her eyes, shaded them with her open fan, and realized where she'd seen that peacock blue doublet before—and the blond man in it. One whom she'd heard only today was selfish, sadistic, and—now this. It was Henry Stewart, Lord Darnley, her cousin Margaret's son and heir.

Since the queen was evidently out somewhere—and courtiers hardly hung about when she wasn't here—Cecil used her empty presence chamber to meet with Matthew Stewart, Earl of Lennox. He'd managed to waylay him even before the man could huddle with his wife and son.

Cecil, who had spent time in dealing and treaty-making with the wily Scots, had a certain grudging admiration for their stiff-necked independence, but the sandy-haired, strapping Lennox had always vexed him. Cecil knew the man could put on or off the burr and broad accent of his speech, but with Cecil, he always flaunted it.

"Och, and wha' a great honor the queen's own secret'ry hies himself to me the moment I arrive for a braw greetin'!" Lennox declared, though he looked like he had one of those Scottish thistles up the tartan trunks he always wore.

"I knew you would be most anxious to hear Her Majesty's reply to your continued petitions and pleas about—"

"They be my lawful and rightful requests, mon, if you mean tha' I should be allowed to go home to Scotland to petition—not plead—for my bonny ancestral lands to be returned to me. You ken wantin' land and house for your heir, dinna you?"

"I do. However, since the queen does not wish for you—and your heir, Lord Darnley—to have to bend the knee in supplication to the Scottish queen, she has refused—"

"Ah, my Lord Lennox, back from visiting his friends," the queen's voice rang out behind Cecil as she swept into the room with but one yeoman guard, who bowed his way out and closed the door behind himself. To Cecil's surprise, Elizabeth extended her hand to Lennox, who smoothly kissed it as he rose from his bow. Not only her sudden arrival had shocked Cecil but——he could see the wariness in Lennox's eyes, too——her demeanor toward the man had changed. Though the queen kept the earl, his countess, and their fawning whelp about the court to keep an eye on them, she could neither trust nor stomach the lot of them.

"My lord Cecil," Her Grace said, "has this travel-worn man come straightaway to ask again that he and Lord Darnley be allowed to visit Scotland to see about the return of their heritage and holdings?"

"I summoned him because you——"

"And have you explained my answer to him?"

"I was about to, Your Grace, when you so fortuitously joined us."

Cecil expected her to take her leave, for they had decided he would buffer her from the Stewarts by being the one to refuse them permission to return to Scotland, while the queen simply insisted she could not bear to part with her kin. Under no circumstances were they to go, especially Lord Darnley, whom his parents had tried to dangle before Mary, Queen of Scots in France when she was first widowed.

"Then I shall explain to the earl," she said with an almost beatific smile. Cecil noted she was windblown and perspiring; her usually pale complexion looked heated, and the corners of her mouth were tight. He stood awed anew at Elizabeth Tudor; she had no need for Ned Topside about her court to play parts or create a fiction. She was in her element now, though it frightened him that he did not know what in hell she was going to say or do next.

"Since you've been away, my lord Lennox, Secretary Cecil and I have been discussing his new lands at Theobalds, the house he intends to build there for his second son, since his heir will have his family lands at Stamford. Isn't that right, my lord?"

"Indeed, Your Majesty," Cecil put in and shut his mouth again.

Lennox looked as rapt as Cecil felt. It was obvious the canny Scot had not the slightest clue what was coming next either.

"I shall leave it up to you to tell your wife and son the happy news," the queen declared to Lennox. "After having considered your request again, I am giving you and Lord Darnley leave to go to Scotland to ask Queen Mary and the Scots lords for your lands back. Surely, they will not begrudge the family of my dear cousin Margaret their ancestral lands!"

Cecil thought Lennox's stiff jaw might hit the floor. His eyes darted to Cecil, evidently for confirmation of this sudden shift in the royal wind.

"One favor only, I would ask—no, two," Elizabeth added.

"Anythin', Your Gracious Majesty, och, anythin'," Lennox said, though Cecil sensed he was flinching for a blow.

"First, you must promote Robert Dudley as a possible candidate for Queen Mary's husband," she clipped out. Hell's gates, Cecil had known that was brewing. But she was much mistaken if she thought Lennox and Darnley were the proper messengers—or that Mary of Scots would ever countenance Dudley. "And secondly," the queen said, "you must leave your countess behind with me for company, as I don't know what I would ever do without her."

Even after Lennox thanked the queen profusely and bowed himself from her presence, Cecil was so in shock he hardly heard the queen's question.

"I said, well, my lord?"

"I meant to tell him the utter opposite, which you yourself commanded only yesterday, Your Grace."

"One of the things I value most about you, Cecil, is you never gainsay me in front of others, but only scold me in private later. You think I've taken leave of my senses, like poor Kat, don't you?" she demanded, tapping her closed fan on his arm.

"Never. Not you. Yet I cannot fathom you think Queen Mary would take Robert Dudley, and especially not if Darnley's paraded before her. She'd balk like a fractious filly at Dudley and dash right into Darnley's puny arms. You said you wanted someone loyal to you for her or one who would bring her down."

"Exactly," she said. "If you'd discovered such proofs as I have stumbled on today, you would grasp my reasoning. And by such hooks or crooks, I shall somehow trap my would-be strangler, too."

"Met by moonlight in the maze," Ned Topside declared in his velvety voice. "I believe I shall use it as the opening of the play I am writing for the courtiers."

"Leave off, Ned," Elizabeth ordered, though Meg Milligrew looked thoroughly enchanted. "As soon as the Suttons arrive, we have work to do. And I told you, we do not need a play with a huge cast but only the suggestions of one so you can collect all their handwriting."

"I've been doing that, Your Grace, and have nineteen samples already, none of which seems to match the note we have as evidence."

Elizabeth frowned. She had clearly commanded that she and Cecil would assess the handwriting, but what was important now was getting through this re-enactment of her attack.

"'S blood, I think the moon's in the same spot, so we shall start without the Suttons," she announced. "Much happened before Bettina came on the scene, though I'd covet Templar's helping us to reason it all out."

"I saw him today, busy as a bee, talking to some courtiers," Meg put in from her position between Ned and Jenks. "Overheard him telling Sir Chris Hatton he should be ashamed of himself for not studying harder, not using the brains God gave him to go with his external trappings, as he put it. That's a good one—external trappings."

"I shall ask both of them about that, but let's begin," Elizabeth commanded. "I wasn't going to mention this for modesty's sake with you three men here, but we can hold nothing back in turning up our villain. I first paused under that oak out there and then again right here because those garters kept slipping. So, I bent over like this," she said, and mimed fussing with them.

"And bent your knees and your back to do so," Cecil observed.

What he implied hit Elizabeth with stunning force. She'd been insisting on a person tall enough to reach garters held taut between two hands over her head. "Good point," she admitted, though she could see Ned, Jenks, and Meg didn't follow. "The trouble is, it only broadens the range of possible attackers again.

And besides, stooping or bending to care for the garters, I also bent to adjust my mask, then leaned like this to begin to run back outside the maze."

"Then it is possible," Cecil said, "that your attacker was shorter than we surmised or that mistaken identity was indeed a factor."

"In other words," Ned put in, "the strangler could have been after someone else who was shorter than Her Majesty."

"And," Meg added, "in that flowing costume, one with bigger breasts."

"So, the intended victim could have been Bettina," the queen concluded. "Someone saw her go outside and followed her. Dear God in Heaven, where is she now, for we must question her about possible enemies. Even if Templar walks slowly, Bettina knows she is needed here and now!"

"What if someone was after her before and got her now?" Meg whispered.

"Sh!" Elizabeth ordered as she, with all of them, turned toward the distant sound of flying footsteps on the gravel walk, then softer on the grass. The queen recalled her waking nightmare in the haunted corridor, for she was suddenly certain this could bode only evil, too.

INSTINCTIVELY, JENKS AND NED DREW SWORDS AND stepped in front of the queen. Cecil moved to buffer her, too, while Jenks pulled Meg behind him.

"Speak of the devil," Ned said in a stage whisper, "it's Mistress Sutton. Did she think she was supposed to come swooping in to save you as she did last night?"

Elizabeth stepped from the maze as Bettina came closer, running, panting. She held her skirts off the dew-wet grass, and her breasts bounced.

"Oh, I'm so sorry I'm—we're late—Your Majesty, but I can't find Templar anywhere." She skidded to a stop; her curtsy went so far off balance she almost fell. Ned reached out to steady her.

"My herb woman saw him this afternoon," the queen tried to assure her. "Have you seen him since?"

"At supper in our new chamber," she said breathlessly. "We changed rooms today, thanks be to you and William Cecil, and I thought Templar was still somewhere between the two locations, but he never would have been late to help Your Majesty. He said he'd meet me, and we'd come out here together. I—I believe he was doing a great deal of thinking about your plight. But with what happened to you last night, Your Majesty, I fear for him. Perhaps he came out on his own to look around or wanted to see the maze again . . ."

She began gasping. Tears matted her lashes, that much the queen could see in moonlight, though her face was mostly in shadow.

"We shall find him," the queen promised. "If he was walking out here in the dark, perhaps he fell. I hope he didn't ignore the rope to come into the maze. Ned, fetch my yeomen guard with torches. Those will be brighter than lanterns. And do not send out a general hue and cry yet. No need to embarrass Master Sutton with much ado when we find him. Jenks and Ned, bring us torches here too, and we shall search inside the maze while the others look outside."

"I'm so grateful," Bettina cried, wringing her hands. "He loved—he loves this maze."

As word of the search spread, some courtiers appeared among the queen's guards. Even Kat showed up, trailing after Rosie. Elizabeth nearly ordered the two women back inside, but let them stay. With torches, Ned and Jenks were ready to lead the way into the maze. Templar's fascination with it and the idea he might try to visit the spot where she'd been attacked made the queen believe it was worth inspecting. Besides, he was hard of hearing, so if he had come inside on his own before dark, then fallen, he might not hear the searchers to call out for help.

"Jenks, Ned, lead on while the yeomen search the grounds. Meg, you and Rosie stay here at the entrance with Kat to be certain others don't enter. We don't need a crowd in here, too. My lord Cecil, best you return to your wife and assure her so she does not become agitated or alarmed if she sees or hears this hubbub."

"I am ever grateful for your concern and care for her, Your Grace. I'll look in on her and be back out directly, for we must find him. His mind may be steady, but his feet are not. Keep a stout heart, Mistress Sutton," he added and was gone at a half run.

As they entered the maze with flickering torchlight, the hedge walls seemed to swallow Jenks, Ned, the queen, and then Bettina. Sharp shadows leaped from each turn. Shifting shapes were starkly illumined, then devoured by blackness. The little entourage went on, methodically inspecting each turn and dead end as the queen commanded. Suddenly from somewhere behind, Meg's voice jolted them.

"Your Grace! Wait, please!"

Meg and Kat appeared around a turn more than halfway in.

"Meg, I told you to wait at the entrance."

"But, Your Grace, Kat recalled something to tell you. She says she saw Templar go into the maze when the sun set."

Elizabeth turned toward Kat, taking both of the older woman's shoulders in a firm grip. "Are you certain you know which man Templar Sutton is, my Kat?"

"I saw him at the masque, didn't I? Lord Cecil was nearly

the only one without a mask. But after everything was ended, Master Sutton took his off too, and kept looking around the room."

"Mayhap for me when I took my walk," Bettina put in with a sniffle. "But he'd said he was going straight to bed."

Elizabeth only nodded, but she recalled well that Bettina had said he was already up in bed—reading, though Templar had later remarked that he was working, as usual, on debate topics for his students. No significant discrepancies in all that, she reasoned.

"Exactly where were you to see Master Sutton when the sun set?" Elizabeth asked Kat.

"I was in your bedchamber, gazing out over the grounds and distant river, just enjoying the view. I'd been resting in the trundle bed by yours, though Rosie and Meg had actually locked me in, didn't you, girl?" she asked, turning to Meg with a flash of anger. "But I decided to go out to discover why Master Sutton was lingering at the entrance to your maze—he moved the rope to slip in, too, so I went down to tell him not to."

"But if you were locked in..." Meg said.

"Do you think I can't use the privy escape entrance King Henry put in all his palaces?" Kat demanded. "It's bolted only from the inside and didn't have a guard on it."

Elizabeth realized she'd have to put a guard outside to keep Kat from further wandering. A heavy arras covered that locked doorway in her chamber. She had used it herself, as had several members of her Privy Plot Council in the past, though not for several years.

But when Kat had mentioned Elizabeth's father, her hopes fell; Kat was going to plunge into the past again. "So I went down," Kat continued, "and followed Master Sutton into the maze a ways, just inside the entrance, and saw he was stooped over as if he were looking at each leaf. And he'd just plucked off a small, dark piece of cloth from a branch where it must have snagged."

Elizabeth felt furious with herself that she hadn't thought of searching the hedges so precisely. At least she'd been careful to keep Kat from the distress of knowing her royal mistress had been attacked in that very place last night. Though Kat was not a totally credible witness lately, all she had said seemed probable.

"And then?" Elizabeth prompted.

"I said he had no right to be in the maze, roped off as it was, but he said he was working with you to care for it—that it needed tending, cutting or some such."

Clever Templar. He had not broken his pledge for secrecy and had evidently known not to unsettle Kat.

"There's not much else to tell," Kat went on, sounding suddenly exhausted. "Since he had your permission, I let him walk farther into the maze, and I went back up to bed."

"You've been a big help, Kat, and Meg will take you back to the palace."

"I'm not leaving you, lovey. I never have, and I won't now!"

Tears blurred the queen's vision, and she blinked them back. Kat Ashley had once known never to call the queen her childhood sobriquet before anyone else, but what did that matter now? Elizabeth prayed that, despite Kat's sinking health, she would never leave her, but she knew better and it scared her. Since she'd nearly died of the pox two years ago, the thought of death—anyone's death—frightened her dreadfully.

"Stay tight with Meg and come along," she told Kat, against her better judgment. "Ned, Jenks, on!"

The two men evidently recalled the maze pattern well from their search of it last night, but Elizabeth knew it best. Increasingly impatient, she took Ned's torch and walked just behind Jenks, who displayed both torch and sword.

"By broad daylight tomorrow, you will search each leaf and twig in this maze, as well as look for anything significant which might have been dropped," Elizabeth whispered to her men. "And that includes searching the grass underfoot, though, sadly, footsteps do not make imprints there. Templar must have found a tell-tale piece of cloth, and it wasn't from my costume, not a dark piece. Many at court that night wore some dark garment, but for the ten virgins, and who knows but the cloth wasn't snagged there some other time. It may signify nothing.

"All right, we're nearly to the goal," she announced more loudly, referring to the finishing place at the back of the maze. It was the spot where one knew he'd conquered the labyrinthine paths, but must now turn around to try to find the way out. The compact, square space boasted a stone bench and an old sundial—her father had ordered the latter placed in many a garden—though it only told the time around noon when the sun's rays could reach it within the depths of these living walls.

Nothing unusual in the goal, she thought, when their torch light illumined it. But Kat pointed behind the bench, and sang out, "There he is! I told you he came in here!"

The queen saw the fallen form and rushed to the body.

Templar indeed, sprawled facedown!

"My dearest, my dearest!" Bettina cried, sobbing and throwing herself upon him on the ground. "Templar. Templar!"

The queen knelt beside her and tried to tug her away from her husband. "Meg, you've seen bad falls and sudden paralyzing ailments," Elizabeth said. "Is he badly hurt?"

But as Bettina rolled the old man over and Meg felt for the pulse at his neck, Elizabeth knew he was not breathing. With her index finger she touched his wrist—cold but not rigid. The torches thrust closer revealed a huge, bloody bruise on his forehead, and the queen glimpsed a thick glaze of blood on the pedestal of the sundial.

"He tripped, maybe on the bench foot—and hit his head there," Jenks said, pointing. "I've seen death afore, and he's—bless his soul, he's gone."

Templar Sutton's unblinking stare silently testified to that truth.

Though she hated to do it, the queen finally ordered Ned to lift the sobbing Bettina from her husband's body. She also regretted having to send for the local authorities, because she didn't want anyone else probing this tragedy, nor declaring it a murder—which she feared it could well be. Two attacks in two days in the maze, one on her person, the other fatal. It was certain her attacker had not erroneously believed she was Templar Sutton, then finished the job this evening—nor had Templar, evidently, been strangled. 'S blood, even though she must send for the parish bailiff and coroner, she was going to get to the bottom of this double outrage on her grounds and on her terms!

"Your Majesty," Jamie Barstow cried as he appeared with another torch, "I came when I heard crying in here, no matter what Lady Rosie said at the entrance. I just wanted to help to—oh, no! Master Sutton?" he cried, gaping at Bettina, then the body. His usual calm crumbled; he looked for a moment as if he'd sob right along with the new widow.

"Mistress Sutton, I'm so sorry..." he managed before his voice broke.

"That's right, you've known each other for a time," Elizabeth said, much relieved. "Jamie, escort Mistress Sutton to her chambers. Take Rosie with you and do not leave her. I will be there when I can, but much must be seen to here, including summoning the local authorities."

"But it looks like a dreadful accident," Jamie observed, bending slightly closer to study the corpse of his former teacher. "And since this is on crown property, and you, Your Majesty, are the crown..."

"I do not need your advice on this, Jamie. Master Sutton was my guest and is owed all the legal rights of justice—which he so ably defended and brilliantly taught," the queen managed before her own voice broke.

"I'll not leave him," Bettina said, weakly now, but she made no more protest when Jamie took her arm and coaxed her away. Elizabeth could hear him talking calmly, quietly to the poor woman until his voice faded.

"Ned," the queen said, "the yeomen guard are to surround the sides and rear of the maze until I command otherwise. And put back the rope across the front facing the palace. Call off the search outside, saying we have found Master Sutton, dead in what appears to be an accidental fall here in the maze."

"Accidental?" Ned challenged, in a whisper evidently so Kat wouldn't hear. "Jamie may have said so, but he didn't know—

about the other night. I supposed this could be an accident, but the coincidence of the same setting—"

"Do as I say, and let me do the thinking right now. Then fetch Cecil to meet me here. Hurry up, man. No, leave your torch—give it to Meg." Scolded to silence, Ned turned and hurried away.

"Jenks," the queen rushed on, "tell your master, Robert Dudley, his queen commands him to ride for the parish bailiff and have him summon the coroner. And on your way, escort Kat to Anne Carey for companionship until I return. Take your torch, for this one will serve Meg and me. Before the authorities arrive, we will throw what light we can upon this sad demise of this teacher and preserver of queen's justice."

Mildred listened carefully to what a man—she was certain it was the queen's player who had read the Bible parable at the masque last night—was telling her husband in the hall outside the closed door: Templar Sutton had been found dead in the maze, and Cecil was to come to join Her Majesty there posthaste. The local officials were being summoned.

She stepped away from the door as Will darted back in to seize his cloak and cap. "Templar Sutton's died suddenly, and the queen has need of me," he said only. Grief contorted his expression; tears glimmered in his eyes. "Don't wait up for me," he added and was gone with a bang of the door before she could say a thing.

"Will ye be preparing for bed then, milady?" her girl Johanna asked, poking her head around the bedchamber door. It was obvious that the girl listened far too often at keyholes. Mildred assumed it was Will who had the maid watching her because she couldn't fathom who else would give a fig what she did around here.

"Just turn down the covers for me and take your ease," Mildred told her. "I'm going to read here for a while."

But the moment Johanna closed the inner door, Mildred was out the one into the hallway. She hurried down it, certain of where to turn, where to find a door on the south side of the sprawling palace which overlooked the gardens and maze on the lawns above the Thames.

She saw much commotion ahead, torches, people. Finally, she made out the solitary dark form of her husband heading at a fast pace toward the maze. Stretching her strides, she nearly managed to keep the same distance from him across the dewy lawn. She saw three figures emerge from the black hulk of the maze: the silhouette of the person in the middle was unmistakably that of the new widow, Bettina.

Mildred stopped walking, feeling drowned by the darkness both outside and inside herself as Will, despite his summons from Her Majesty, stopped, evidently to comfort Bettina. He leaned close to speak to her, held her hand, their outlines merging in distant torchlight. Then she saw him hurry on, disappearing into the maze as the couple supporting Bettina brought her this way.

Mildred could not bear to look at the woman, so she cut a broader path to avoid them. The maze seemed to have its three backsides lined by men with torches; only the rope across the mouth of it guarded the front, which was lit by what was now blazing palace light. If anyone tried to stop her entry, she would simply say she had something to tell her husband who was within. Ducking under the restraining rope, she followed the irregular paths until muted voices became clearer amidst the noise from outside. Out of breath, she stopped on the other side of a hedge wall and strained to listen to the inner voices.

The queen: "Cecil, thank God, you're here, as we may not have much time before Robert Dudley rousts out the bailiff, and he sends for the coroner."

Will: "Templar dead? I—cannot fathom it, even seeing him—like this. Dare we believe it is some sort of freak accident—or must we accept the worst?"

The queen: "His head must have hit the foot of the sundial, see? But the question is, on his own or with help?"

"At least he wasn't strangled."

"That is one thing we must find out."

"You have sealed the entrance again."

"Yes, but what good did that do us last time? Lady Rosie was there, but I needed to send her with Jamie Hatton and poor Bettina. I am beginning to believe our murderer comes *through* the maze like some sort of specter. And here, poor Templar told me that evil spirits avoid mazes because they can't turn the corners. . . ."

The queen's usually clear voice snagged before going on. "I am sorry, my lord, that I ask you to do this when your dear mentor and friend lies here, lost to life, but I want you to quickly examine his body for other marks or possibly wounds—especially strangulation ligatures—while Meg and I search for hidden exits in the maze hedges. With rampant torchlight on the sides and rear, we will be able to discern if there is any sort of opening where a possible attacker escaped without coming out the entrance."

"Yes, I see. For decency's sake—and Templar was a thoroughly decent man—I will search him for signs of foul play and tell you what I find."

"Obviously, Bettina and you will have disturbed the way he was found, but we shall simply explain to the officials I've summoned that Templar's body was moved when we turned him over and his widow grieved. And, Cecil, keep an eye out for a bit of dark cloth on his person, which Kat said she saw him find in the maze today. Our murderer might have torn his or her garment the night I was attacked," she added with a huge sigh, "and Templar took it upon himself to help me even more than I had asked. Come on, Meg. All that torchlight outside makes it easy to see through the leaves and limbs, and at least doubles the moonlight in here."

Mildred backtracked quickly, amazed yet somehow not surprised that Elizabeth Tudor herself would spearhead such an investigation. It made her admire the queen all the more, yet fear her, too. Next, that brilliant woman would be probing one's very tortured thoughts. Mildred ducked under the rope at the mouth of the maze and lifted her skirts to hurry away across the dewy grass.

Her finger snagged in the tear on her black gown. For appearance' sake—safety's sake now, too—she'd best don another skirt and cut this one up for scraps.

One thing was certain, the queen reasoned, trying to control her full skirts as she moved through the maze. If the murderer had entered or exited through a thin spot in these back hedges, it could hardly be a woman, at least not unless she was disguised as a lad. She and Meg had discovered two thin-leafed places, though she also surmised that an intruder must bear scratches, too. Now that could be a clue, but she could hardly order everyone to disrobe so she could examine their skin for scratches. Or could such be visible on someone's hands, face, or neck?

"Will we point these bare spots out to the officials as well as look at them better ourselves tomorrow?" Meg asked.

"I intend to let them examine Master Sutton's demise on their own and see what they determine about whether his death was accidental—and discover how good these crown-appointed men are at their tasks. Perhaps they will turn up something we have not, but whatever they decide, I am undeterred about *secretly* tracing my attacker—and, I warrant—tying it somehow to Templar Sutton's death."

"If someone slipped out this way, he'd have ended up in the grape arbors or could have hidden in the stand of trees along the river bank," Meg observed.

"Ah, the grape arbors or those trees—someone who was familiar with the area, or who thought it could hide his dark deeds," she whispered, recalling Lord Darnley's illicit assignation there. She had not shared her real plans for Darnley with anyone but Cecil and didn't intend to. But, if the ruttish coxcomb—who was thin as a rail—had tried to murder his monarch, she'd have a decision to make. She intended to send Mary Stuart a weakling to wed, not someone who strangled queens. The Queen of England would not do that, even to her nemesis, the Queen of Scots.

"Let's go back and see what Lord Cecil has discovered," Elizabeth said, and led the way back toward the goal. "My lord," she called to him across one width of hedge, "is he decent now?"

"Enter," Cecil clipped out, as if he were summoning an undersecretary, but she knew how deeply this had distressed him. "Nothing is decent about this," he muttered when the two women came around the turn to find him slumped on the bench by the body. He had managed to balance the single torch they'd left him on the top of the sundial to give himself good light.

"No, don't rise," Elizabeth commanded, staying him with a firm hand on his shoulder. She was surprised to feel him trembling. "Did you—look him over thoroughly, my lord?"

Cecil nodded forlornly. "I found no dark scrap of cloth," he said so quietly she almost couldn't hear him. She gestured for Meg to leave them, and she instantly obeyed. "I am sorry to ask all this of you, my lord," she told him. She sat down on the end of the bench, so he would not feel compelled again to rise. "I know he was dear to you."

"I was steady until you asked—asked me that way, 'Did you look him over thoroughly...' I was just thinking, the very first day I met him twenty-three years ago at Gray's Inn, after we had talked for a while, *he* looked *me* over thoroughly and questioned me at length. He told me I had great potential, but he would never stand for me doing things half-cocked. Though I was a strong student, I'd admitted I'd left Cambridge when I was close to taking my degree. Master Sutton also said that day," he added and swiped his nose with a sleeve like a lad, "that I must never make slipshod, rash decisions that would errantly affect my life and my career."

"Meaning, like leaving Cambridge too early."

"Also meaning that I had defied my father, who had been supporting me, by passionately, rashly wedding an innkeeper's daughter. 'Be circumspect in all you do, and let not passion be your rule,' Templar said that day, and I've never—that is, tried never to forget it."

"Surely, you have made him proud these last years, my Cecil. You have not been rash or done things in an errant or slipshod manner, I can testify to that. You and the others like Chris and Jamie are the sons he never had, just as Bettina said when—"

"I'm only human!" he cried, lunging off the bench and turning away, evidently to wipe his eyes and nose, again with his sleeve instead of his handkerchief. "Like you, Your Grace," he added more quietly, "the man had a way of looking right through one and knowing everything. I never meant to let him down. . . ."

"Of course you didn't. But, the thing I would know before the parish officials rightfully take this out of our hands—at least I know they will claim Templar's body—is what you found when you examined him."

"No marks around his neck at least," he said with a sniff.

"Thank God for that. What then? Why are you looking at me like that? You don't believe it could just be an accident?"

He shook his head hard. "Granted, a fall into the stone pedestal could have stunned him—I pray God it did. Because on the back of his head, the nape of his neck, he was struck either a second time—or at first."

He stooped to point at the back of Templar's head. Cecil had turned him face down again, but arranged him with cap and cloak covering his neck, much as they'd found him.

"Struck back there by what?" the queen asked, bending over

him, too. "You mean he was pushed or slammed against the bench first, then thrown onto the pedestal?"

"There is not a spot of blood on the bench. I would postulate he was struck on the back of the head by a blow from a brick which sent him into the pedestal. The imprint in his scalp—his very skull—has a definite shape with the mark of a corner."

"The bench has squared corners," she argued.

"But this crumbled material was stuck in his blood at the back—not the front—of his white hair."

Even as they heard the voices of men coming closer in the maze, Cecil pulled something from his padded doublet. In the light of their single torch, he opened and extended to her his clean handkerchief. Bits of bloodied, rose-hued brick lay in it. The queen gasped, rewrapped the cloth, and thrust the handkerchief quickly up her sleeve as Robert Dudley led a group of men into the very heart of the maze.

Chapter the Seventh

 THE MEN'S LANTERNS AND TORCHES LIT THE MAZE SO brightly that the queen and Cecil had to squint at first. Robin had Chris Hatton at his side, which amazed her, since Robin didn't like the younger man. Frowning, Chris bit his lip and shook his head when he saw his teacher's body sprawled beneath the bench.

Jenks and two yeomen guards brought up the rear of the party, but before them paraded three parish officials. Elizabeth was immediately annoyed that, crowding in, they did not give a care to the area in case there had been clues, even though she knew her people had tramped about, too.

Snatching off their caps, the visitors made matters worse as they all bowed. Packed like fish in a barrel of brine, they bumped into each other, sending the largest man of the three into the hedge wall, bouncing the bushes. Robin's knees accidently brushed the queen's skirts when he rose from his bow.

"Your Most Gracious Majesty," he began when she nodded to give him leave to speak, "may I present to you the parish bailiff, Jonah Withers. Bailiff Withers, the Queen's Majesty has personally summoned you as the deceased was an important teacher of law in her kingdom."

Bailiff Withers was of middling height and weight, with hair red as autumn pippins. As he bowed again, Elizabeth noted he'd been rousted out of bed, for his hair stood on end like a cock's comb, and he had sleep wrinkles on one side of his face.

"No doubt the cause is accidental death, Your Gracious Majesty," Withers said, wringing his cap in his hands, "for I hear the departed was frail and of an age. And to be walking out at night alone in a maze—well. But if the coroner suspects foul play, I shall serve any needed writs and carry out immediate arrests."

"I should hope immediate, Master Withers," Elizabeth replied, "though we discovered no one near the body, and no one has rushed forward to be arrested. Say on, my lord Dudley."

"And the coroner," Robin announced, "is Richard Malvern...."

The queen recognized the name as a local family of good gentry stock, so she surmised his progenitors must have held the post, too. Malvern had piercing, dark eyes set in skin white as a toad's belly. His raven hair was cut as if a bowl had been placed over his head, like the friars of old, but with no tonsure. His clothes looked costly, exceedingly so, but perhaps he'd scrambled into his best attire when he'd heard the corpse was at court.

"By your leave, Your Most Gracious Majesty," Malvern said with another bow, "no matter what Bailiff Withers says, we'll need a justice of the peace if we must bind an accused felon over for trial. Ergo, I have taken it upon myself to summon one."

She noted that Withers shot Malvern what could only be called a withering look. Had these men not heard her that no felons had been found? Jenks must have informed Robin that foul play was suspected, and Robin must have told these men. Since the Crown received a portion of a murderer's property, did they think she insisted on a murder? 'S blood, murder it must be, but let them look into it officially while she probed it her own way.

"I charge you, Coroner Malvern," the queen commanded, "to discern exactly what happened here, pure mischance or foul play, then to report to Lord Dudley, who will report to me."

"And finally, Your Majesty," Robin said, gesturing the last stranger forward, "may I present Constable Vernon Wright."

The big man who had bounced the bushes looked more the part of one who abetted rather than apprehended brawlers or drunks, let alone murderers. He reminded the queen of a chipped earthenware jug: brawny with no apparent neck, a scarred visage, broken nose, and protruding ears. And these were the men who administered queen's justice in the surrounding parish to her people? Worse, when she was just about to urge them again to their necessary duties, another official was escorted in by yeomen guards.

"Justice of the Peace Henry Featherstone, at your royal service," the newcomer murmured so quietly she could barely hear him.

"Speak up, man," Robin said, so he repeated himself, including his bow.

The justices were nominally appointed by the monarch, though in actuality by the Lord Chancellor, so the queen seldom had to traffic with them. It was the justices who called witnesses if needed and examined the accused, then committed them to gaol or released them on bail until trial. She sensed none of that would happen here, even if the coroner did declare this a homicide. And not just because these men seemed rustics, for queen's justice of necessity must rely on such men in parishes and shires.

It was rather that the queen finally admitted to herself that she too might not identify and halt the culprit. She was up against a demon, who hated those who were brilliant, admired, and scrupulous, like Templar. Surely the same someone who, for those reasons and others she must divine, hated her.

"I expect each man to do his duty," she concluded abruptly. Feeling suddenly closed in, she pushed through the crowd and maze to the darkness outside.

Though Elizabeth was distressed and exhausted, she felt she must look in on Bettina before retiring. Chris Hatton had followed her out of the maze with her yeoman Clifford, whom she'd ordered to keep close to her person when she left her apartments, so she walked toward the east wing with Chris at her side and Clifford behind.

"How did Mistress Sutton take her husband's loss, Your Grace?" Chris asked. "She's very—well, Italian."

"Only her mother was Italian, but yes, of course, she was

emotional. It was heart-rending. I sent Rosie and Jamie to sit with her until I come."

"Jamie? He'll not lend the sort of comfort she needs. He's a watcher, Your Grace, an analyzer of all things. He keeps somehow aloof from the heat of daily passions."

"From the heat of daily passions?" she reiterated, meaning to argue, before she realized Cecil—and Mildred, for that matter— were somewhat like that. "Perhaps that is no longer true of Jamie since he seems intent on courting Rosie Radcliffe, though she's the sensible sort, too. But the kind of man you describe makes a good lawyer and leader, does he not? And, evidently, he strives to be a good friend."

"Granted, Jamie is a sturdy friend for all seasons to me. As for the law, Jamie sometimes quotes the Lord's word about how it can be useless—the law, not the Lord's word."

"Which biblical quote on lawyers dare say that? The Lord's word and English justice are perfectly aligned, at least while I sit the throne to which He has brought me."

"I'm trying to recall the one I meant." That made the queen recall that Cecil had once said Chris Hatton could win over a jury on his countenance and charm, but no cleverness for legal argument. No matter, for it was loyalty she valued at court, though she did wonder at times how he got even as far as he did at Oxford and Gray's Inn with demanding sticklers like Templar for teachers.

"Ah," Chris said at last, "I think it goes something like, 'Avoid strivings about the law for they are unprofitable and useless.' "

"That only means the strivings are useless, not the law. In

other words, a cold-blooded lawyer is better than a hot-tempered one. Hell's teeth, I could have told you that. It's probably true of monarchs, too," she muttered to herself, "and ones with quick tempers should heed such."

"But as for a friend, Your Majesty," he said, evidently trying to backtrack, "Jamie is a good one, and I know he'd like to be your friend."

"Tell me, Chris, what is your last memory of Templar Sutton? If you saw him earlier today, what did he say?" Meg had told her that she'd overheard Templar scolding him, and she wondered if he'd admit it or explain.

"The same plainsong he ever sang me," Chris said, hanging his head. "That I needed to yet study, to read more to elevate what I know and can converse on."

"Ah," she said, relieved he had spoken the truth, if not in Templar's very words Meg had reported.

She was prepared to let the subject lapse when Chris added, "It doesn't help that Templar rebuked Jamie, too, if for a different reason."

"Which was?"

"Jamie was a fine student but left school early, granted to come to court with me, but Master Sutton didn't like that, for he said more was expected of Jamie than of me. Yet he told Jamie he was as disappointed in both of us, that we should finish law school at Gray's and not just serve a queen in pleasantries at court."

Elizabeth nearly jolted to a halt, then walked on. So Templar blamed her for reeling such young men into her court when they should be about more serious business. Evidently Templar Sutton thought her frivolous and would have liked to scold her, too. And if the man played not just law teacher but judge and jury against his monarch, who else did he censure to their faces or behind their backs? Templar Sutton must have enemies, for surely not everyone he criticized admired him as she herself and his students had. Somehow, she must discover who Templar's enemies were—and so, perhaps, find her own.

"Let's go in this door," she told Chris, though it was Clifford who leaped ahead to open it for them. "The Suttons' new chambers are somewhere in this hall."

"I've been trying to bear up but just can't face it, Your Majesty," Chris blurted, hesitating at the threshold door. She turned around to face him. "Poor Master Sutton and Bettina too!" He heaved a sigh as he finally stepped in. The scent on his breath—gillyflowers? Or was he one of those many courtiers her chief cook had said begged or bartered for breath cloves?

Forgoing to question him about anything else now, Elizabeth walked to the only open door in the hall, one which spilled light out onto the wooden floor. She assumed it was the Suttons' room, but she was mistaken. By wan lantern light, Mildred Cecil sat studying a parchment diagram of some sort just inside the door.

"Oh, Your Grace," she cried, hastily rising to her feet while the parchment rolled noisily closed. "I had the door open for my lord's return—he is all right?"

"He is yet about my business," the queen told her from the doorway. "I fear he will be late, and I am sorry if you are lonely, but there was a good—a bad—cause."

"He told me of Master Sutton's sad demise."

"I have come to see the widow. Your lord moved her chambers into this hall today."

Mildred's jaw dropped, and her eyes widened before she recovered. "It's all right," Elizabeth explained. "The murder took place out in the maze, not in this hall near you, Mildred, so put your mind at ease."

"I—I shall, thank you, Your Majesty. I shall put my mind at ease."

Through the door set ajar, Jenks finally spotted Meg bent over a seething kettle in a small brick garden shed she used for drying herbs. Since the queen had left the maze, Lord Dudley had sent Jenks back to the stables to oversee tending the parish officials' horses, but he was taking the long way around by the outbuildings.

"Meg, you all right?"

She jumped and gasped. "Don't sneak up on me like that! Now I've burned my knuckle, making this tonic."

"I didn't sneak up. Called your name right out."

He stepped into the cluttered place, lit by a single lantern. Hanging bunches of drying herbs bumped his head and swayed. "I see you know those slip knots, too, like what was used on the garters round the queen's neck," he observed, noting how neatly she'd tied each bunch.

"Meaning what? I'll not have accusations I'd ever harm her, not with what all I been through."

"What we've all been through. I missed you desperate bad the years you were in exile for—displeasing her."

"Jenks, has she sent for me?" she asked, fanning the air with her hand to cool her burn.

"It's me wanted to see you."

"You're seeing me."

"I warrant I am," he agreed, and looked her over with a guilty grin. Sure, Meg Milligrew resembled Her Majesty in coloring, size, even in the face, but she was ever her own woman. "Even in the middle of all kinds of things going on," he tried to explain, "I always want to see you."

Her head came up a bit, and her eyes widened. "It's kind of you to wonder if I'm all right. It's just that Lord Cecil mentioned earlier today he'd like something to lift his wife's spirits."

"Anything I can do to help?" he asked and stepped closer.

"Hardly," she clipped out, then looked sorry she'd said that. "I'm using a few drops of this expensive oil of spiknard to relieve Mildred Cecil's downheartedness," she explained, turning away and pointing. She sounded nervous. Jenks shuffled nearer to her and her array of jars and paper packets. "I'm boiling it with borage for courage," she went on, talking faster and faster. "Apothecaries say, it 'purgeth melancholy.' "

"Then I could use a swig myself," he said, his voice slow and soft in contrast to hers. His chest almost touched her back, and he could feel the heat from her as well as her kettle.

"Hm," she said and giggled. "Just don't get it mixed up with the yew juice in this other jug."

"Yew? From those patch-piece bushes in the maze set among the hornbeam? What about yew?"

"And you're supposed to be tending the queen's horses?" she said, her tone teasing as he lightly placed his hands on her shoulders and leaned closer, pretending to peer past her. "Any farmer or forester," she went on, "knows that even a big animal eating yew can be dead quick as quick from a mere mouthful of yew shrub."

"You're brewing up poison?" he demanded, turning her to face him.

"Not exactly. Just like with foxglove and some other herbs, a little is good physic, but too much can kill you. And yew, in the right, spare doses can help with gout, bilious problems, and infections. If I tell you a secret, can you keep it?"

" 'Course I can. You don't mean Her Grace has some sort of infection from that attack on her?"

"Jenks, I swear, you need someone to take care of you," she said, shaking her head and shifting slightly away. "Jamie Barstow has a urinary infection and doesn't want anyone to know. Manly pride, and I guess you know about that."

"Me? Barstow's sweet on Lady Rosie, that's who he doesn't want to know, I warrant. But if a man truly cares for a woman, there comes a time when he lets down his guard. You know, tells her true how he feels."

He carefully took her hurt hand, lifting it to see if there was a burn mark. He couldn't see a thing in this light. But he felt the burning for her, in his heart and in his loins.

"Meg, you been widowed nigh on two years, and I know your union wasn't happy—"

"Like being trapped in hell, it was."

"But have you ever thought of marrying again, I mean someone who served the queen, someone who understood and admired you to..."

"What about the queen?" a deep, distinctive voice came from the door behind Jenks.

Ned. Damn his eyes, Ned!

Meg pulled her hand back as if it was burned for sure. Her expression, which had been wary, lit like a Yuletide candle.

Jenks's hopes fell. He'd practiced aloud what he'd say, recited it to a bunch of horses all afternoon, and now Ned Topside—Meg too—had ruined things again.

"Ned, come in," Meg said. "We were just chatting about this and that."

Jenks pushed past Ned and stormed out the door, banging it so hard the whole shed shook.

Clifford located the Suttons' chamber, knocked on the door, opened it, and announced the queen and Lord Hatton to those within. Bettina had wilted over a table, sitting between Rosie Radcliffe and Jamie Barstow.

Rosie and Jamie jumped to their feet to curtsy and bow, and Bettina, looking dazed, slowly stood and managed a half-curtsy. Elizabeth sat in the chair Jamie vacated, made Bettina sit again, and turned to comfort her.

Jamie went to stand by Rosie and whispered to her, but Bettina stared at the doorway. Thinking Clifford was standing there yet, unsettling her, Elizabeth turned to motion him away, but only Chris waited, hat in hand.

"Sir Christopher Hatton," the queen said, "of course, you want to offer your condolences to your teacher's widow."

She gestured for him to take Rosie's chair, but evidently Bettina didn't see that. She stood and hurried to him, her hands outstretched. "Oh, it's been so dreadful," Bettina cried, "and here, you've lost a dear friend, too."

Bettina, the queen thought, hugged Chris a bit too hard and long, but then grieving widows could be granted some leave for overwrought emotions. She noted that Jamie Barstow, despite the fact that Rosie Radcliffe was hanging on his arm, looked angry enough at Bettina's boldness to spit.

"All of you out now," Elizabeth said. "I need a few moments alone with Bettina."

They cleared the chamber, and Clifford closed the door. "Will you have a place to live—and a means of living?" Elizabeth asked the young widow as she returned to her chair. She gripped the arms of it so tightly her fingers turned stark white.

"I suppose I could stay on at Gray's in some capacity, or go to live with my sister in Kent. Though it would tear me up to do it, I can sell Templar's extensive library piecemeal."

"You mustn't do that, not to just anyone. William Cecil is ever eager to increase his library, and admired your husband, so you must speak to him, or perhaps he'll even donate some of them for the Gray's Inn library. Bettina, as esteemed and well-known as Templar was—do you think he had enemies, someone perhaps who hated him enough to harm him, someone who wanted him out of the way for some reason?"

She stared unblinking at the queen, as if she'd never considered such a thing or that her husband might have been murdered. Yet she did not protest or argue the queen's implications.

"He always spoke his mind," she whispered at last. "He was a demanding, not a coddling teacher and mentor, he said, to prepare his students for the courts and to combat the evils of the world. He often told his students, 'The law is not made for a righteous person, but for the lawless, the ungodly, the unholy and profane, and murderers. . . .' "

Bettina burst into tears and buried her face in her hands. The queen put a hand to her shaking shoulder and waited until she quieted to gasps and sniffles.

"I know this is a dreadful time for you," Elizabeth told her, "but you must immediately make a list for me of names and possible motives of those Templar may have offended. Bettina, I will pay for a fine funeral for your husband, and have him buried nearby, if I have your permission. The coroner should not keep his body long. Shall we send messengers to your family or his?"

"Oh, Your Gracious Majesty," she choked out, "I can't thank you enough. I—looking back now, I had so little time with him, and never was worthy of his standards, his talents."

"I too had little time with him, but I can tell you what I observed," the queen said. "Your bright spirit and faithful heart brought him much joy."

Bettina burst into tears again. Seeing the woman had soaked her own handkerchief, the queen almost extended hers, until she recalled the crumbled brick inside. Templar's murderer could well have been her attacker, someone who sneaked up from behind in the maze to maim or murder.

Hardening her resolve, while Bettina sobbed herself breathless, Elizabeth stood and fetched paper and pen from the sideboard and placed them before the poor woman.

"This is important, Bettina. You have helped me before, and I pray you will help me again."

A half hour later, the queen opened the hall door and called Rosie to come back to spend the night with the grieving widow. She dismissed Chris and Jamie, and, trailing Clifford through the warren of corridors, took the tear-splattered list with her.

Chapter the Eighth

THE NEXT MORNING AFTER BREAKFAST, ELIZABETH MET again with her Privy Plot Council, having them use the back staircase to enter the state apartments. Meg, Ned, Jenks, Cecil—all looked as ragged as she felt.

"While we are waiting to see what the parish officials turn up," Elizabeth began without ado, "we must plunge ahead, assuming that Templar's murderer is my would-be murderer, too."

Her voice caught. Cecil shifted forward, sliding his clasped hands across the corner of the table toward her, almost as if he'd touch her. She wished Kat could be here, but it would only upset and confuse her, so Elizabeth had asked Rosie and Anne Carey to take her outside for a walk—and not near the maze.

"We will begin by reviewing evidences we were examining before Templar's murder," the queen continued. "Firstly, no other gowns the women wore in the masque, except for mine and, of course, Bettina's, bore grass or dew stains on the hems. Nor did I find any hairs but mine snagged in the garters."

She nodded to Cecil. "And I, unfortunately," he said, "did not discover upon Templar's body the piece of black cloth Kat saw him recover. I'm afraid we've been wide of the mark all round."

"Ned," the queen went on, "you said that the handwriting samples did not match the note I received?"

"Not the ones I have already, Your Grace, though quite a few courtiers are yet to give them to me. I could hardly make handing them over a royal command."

"They won't even bother now, I warrant," she said, smacking her palm on the table. "Everyone knows the court must become even more solemn with a death among us and funeral in the offing. Besides, I will not even pretend to be promoting amusements which are not of a religious nature while the plague is still in my kingdom. The ruse of your elaborate play must be put on the shelf for now, Queen's Master Player.

"Jenks, what of your early morning search of split places in the hedges?" she asked. Jenks looked particularly glum this morning. He had hunkered down by himself at the end of the table, away from his usual seat next to Meg.

"Oh, aye, Your Grace. The hedges are old, but big bald spots are few, what with the yew and privet patching. I checked the two thin places you mentioned at the back of the maze and found nothing snagged in them."

"I gave the hedges a good looking over, too," Ned put in, repeatedly tugging down his pleated linen cuffs, "just after Jenks did this morning."

"We were supposed to go together," Jenks muttered. "Sounds like you're just watching what I do and crashing in after."

"The point is," Ned declaimed in his most erudite stage voice, "I observed no leaves or twigs broken primarily in one direction. In other words, the breaks in the hedge could just as well be exits as well as entrances for a thin intruder—or for no one."

"Such brilliant deduction is always of use to us," the queen said, her voice dripping sarcasm. "And this is no time for bickering among any of you." She leveled an index finger at Ned, then Jenks. "My lord Cecil, anything else to report?"

"I believe I found the site from which the fatal brick was plucked," he said, "though I can't actually prove it and didn't find it discarded anywhere."

"Someone probably gave it a good heave-ho into the Thames or the well," Meg murmured.

"The brick entry to the grape arbor behind the maze is crumbling a bit," Cecil continued. "It's the old mortar at fault— and exactly one brick is missing, chipped or lifted out."

"Aha. And the surrounding bricks match the crumbled brick you found in Templar's wound?" Elizabeth asked excitedly. Each time someone mentioned the grape arbor, she pictured the thin, tall Lord Darnley there, the same spoiled wretch who kicked dogs and beat horses—and who obeyed his treacherous mother's every order.

"We could make the match now, Your Grace," Cecil said, "as I have chipped out the brick which was next to the missing one." He reached into his satchel under the table and fetched up a heavy rectangle swathed in a piece of burlap. While Cecil unwrapped it, from her puffed sleeve the queen drew her handkerchief and carefully opened it on the table.

"Templar's blood?" Meg asked, gaping at the handkerchief.

"With bits of the brick in it we believe killed him," Cecil explained.

"Looks like a match to me," Meg whispered. "Don't mean to brag, Your Grace, my lord, but apothecaries need a good eye to match seeds, powders, and petals, sometimes by subtle smells, too. And that reminds me, the new elixir tonic for Lady Cecil's ready, my lord."

Elizabeth first shot Meg a quelling look for rambling off the subject. Yet she understood Cecil's sense of urgency. If Meg had made something special for Mildred's melancholy moods, perhaps she'd better have her mix up something else to try on Kat, though it was hardly the same malady.

"The same, it seems to me," Cecil was saying, "the brick's hue, I mean. Though the rosy colors of Hampton Court's bricks are from different kiln batches and may have weathered irregularly, I say Templar's murderer took his weapon from what was at hand—much as those garters about your neck must have been selected nearly at the last minute, Your Grace."

"And so," the queen said, "are we searching for a culprit who is confident enough to know he can improvise—or one who is rash and stupid enough not to plan ahead but attacks on mere whim—or passion."

"I'd say he—or she—is a confident criminal," Cecil said. "I cannot fathom two crimes of passion with whatever was at hand, though, I must say, garters seem a female weapon of choice and a brick masculine."

"Yet we shall and must proceed as if the attackers are one and the same person," Elizabeth argued.

"At least we know we're looking for a brick—a bloody brick," Ned said. "And we therefore may be looking for possible bruises on hands—and scratches on the culprit from pushing through hedges."

"Lord Darnley's a whit scratched up," Meg blurted. "Saw it yesterday, wrists, hands, even on his face."

"That pretty face marred?" Ned muttered. No one else paid that comment heed, but the queen caught it.

"Before I let you go, as Lord Cecil and I have much of the kingdom's business to see to this morning," Elizabeth said, "I must tell you that Bettina gave me a list of those whom Templar had possibly offended. I asked for an entire list, though the names on it, of course, of people who could possibly have been in the area must be those most closely scrutinized. But, so as not to unnecessarily smear reputations, I will study the list first, then decide who of us must pursue which names. And so, with a reminder to be vigilant for scratches on skin, I dismiss you also with my thanks, all but Secretary Cecil—and Ned."

Ned, she thought, looked pleased. Did he think she would shower him with praise for observations any of them could have made?

"You have a part for me to play to draw close to Lord Lennox now that he is back at court?" Ned asked, jumping far afield when she just stared at him after Meg and Jenks left.

"I have a part for you to play with the 'pretty' Lord Darnley, as you call him. What do you know of Darnley's practices and predilections?"

Ned gaze wavered and dropped away from her steady stare. "He's selfish and rude," he said, sounding not so sure of himself.

"Don't joust with me, Ned. Darnley prefers men to ladies, does he not? And has he approached you?"

For one moment, she feared her favorite actor was at a lack for words, but he did not disappoint her. "He dared," Ned answered, sitting up straighter, "to say he wanted play-acting lessons, not, he said, in comedy or tragedy but instruction in romance. I saw through his gambit and turned him down flat, so whatever you have in mind won't work, Your Grace, as Darnley knows I prefer women."

Elizabeth had never seen her principal player so much as color up before, but he blushed bright as a rose.

"*Prefer*, you see," she parried, "that is the key word. As full of himself as Darnley is, perhaps he'll think—for him—you changed your mind. You are a fine actor, and I'd bet a throne you can convince almost anyone to anything. So you must play the part of getting close to Darnley. I am certain you can string him along and not get *too* close, if you take my meaning. You offered before to spy on my cousin Margaret, and just mentioned cozening the Earl of Lennox. But Henry Stewart, Lord Darnley, will have to do."

"Yes, Your Grace. I can manage it, of course, and get him to sing like a canary—about his whereabouts during your attack and Templar's murder, I assume you mean."

"That will be a start, though you must discern if his parents have plans for him—romantic plans—with Queen Mary."

"Oh," he whispered. "His taste for men aside, you mean you see Darnley as an—an actor of sorts, too. He could obviously dupe and deceive Queen Mary for his own—his parents'—purposes."

"Just do it circumspectly and quickly," she ordered. "You wanted to write an elaborate masque for court, but now you've got one to act in."

"Yes, I see. Of course, there will be naught to it, and I'll report back soon." He bowed himself out so only she and Cecil still sat at the table.

"Who is on Bettina's list?" Cecil asked.

"About every colleague or student Templar ever had," the queen told him with a sigh. "The distraught woman obviously went overboard on this, citing everyone Templar ever so much as scolded or who talked back. I will question her again and pare the list down when she is not so unhinged."

"Then—my name is on it?"

"Templar's berating you was evidently too far back for her to know about. No, it's a list of people with whom Templar had any bone to pick since Bettina was his wife, stretching back about nine years—as long as you've been wed to Mildred—I take it."

"Yes, I see," he said, looking even more unsettled. "Then are Chris Hatton and Jamie Barstow on it?"

"Cecil, don't fret. I can't take this lengthy list seriously. Chris Hatton told me last night that Templar was even angry with me—me!—for 'luring' his students to serve at court. Bettina admitted she never could come up to her husband's lofty standards either. By the way, did you hear her speak of him in the past tense last evening when she simply told us he was missing? 'He loved this maze,' she said."

"I did. But she's hardly a killer, and why would she do it at court, even if she wanted him gone for some reason?"

"Maybe she thought, since she'd helped me, I'd help her, even if she came under investigation. Hence, after someone attacked me, she could kill Templar with impunity because we would assume it was the same attacker. I just don't know, but I—we—must reason out something soon, besides just keeping everyone out of the maze, before this phantom assaults someone else."

"May I see the list then?"

"We've much of royal business to do, is that not so?" she asked, rising. "As I said, I'll winnow the list down, and we shall concentrate on persons we consider our best bets."

"All right then. Let me summon my secretaries to bring in the warrants and such for us to go over."

As he turned away, the queen was glad she'd not brought the list with her, or she might have given in to his entreaties to see it. No good to vex him that, for some odd reason she would ferret out without upsetting him, Mildred's name was on it.

"But did your sister say why she wanted to leave court—leave me—so suddenly?" Elizabeth demanded. "Robin, I invited Mary here for a fortnight, and she begs my leave to go after but three days?"

"You know she covets your company, Your Grace," Robin assured her, "but she knows you've been busy."

It was true that she'd spent scant time with Mary. She must feel she was being neglected, perhaps because she'd refused to be in the masque. Though Elizabeth and Robin now stood in her presence chamber surrounded by her women, the queen slowly steered him toward the seat set in the open oriel window so they might have some privacy. She sat, then indicated he might, too.

"The thing is, Your Grace," Robin went on, leaning close, "Mary misses her home and children. Lord Cecil's son Tom is visiting there too, but even the Sidney sons bear watching."

"Mm, I'll warrant they do, but why by Mary? Oh, 's blood, never mind. I know she feels trapped in her rooms, even if she does go abroad at night, which is doubly dangerous now we've had this dreadful murder."

"And shall I tell her she can go?" Robin pursued. "Besides, she says Queen Catherine Howard's rushing about outside her door is keeping her from getting any sleep at night...."

Elizabeth gaped at him, ready to take his bait when she saw his smug smile. He had no notion, of course, that she actually thought she had sensed a ghostly presence in that hall.

"I am not in the mood for games and teasing, my lord," she said and smacked his arm. "Damn, but you'd think a queen could have things the way she wants at least. I cannot make my dear Mary stay with me, and I must needs make my treacherous cousin Margaret Stewart stay!"

"The word's out you changed your mind to let Lennox and Darnley go to Scotland soon. People are wondering why."

She nodded, frowning. She wished she'd told Ned to find out if Darnley had had any sort of conversation with Templar since he'd been at court. The convoluted possibilities of this puzzle were driving her to distraction.

"But as you have said, Elizabeth," he whispered her name as he used to so her attendants would not hear, "you are queen. You can command my sister to stay at court, and you can command anything of me."

With one hand on his gartered knee and the other on his heart, he gazed expectantly at her. She felt the treacherous embers of her buried love for him kick into sparks, but fought her feelings.

"Good," she declared. "Then I command you to be prepared to go to Scotland yourself someday soon, and with a royal suitor's pleasant manners—and with the title I shall give you this autumn, of course."

"But if you are letting Darnley go, I thought that meant that you had given up on your earlier idea of my courting her," he protested. "Your Gracious Majesty, I will not allow whatever legal minds you bring to court—those who would like to get rid of me—Cecil, Chris Hatton, Jamie Barstow, too, for all I know, tell you what to do about—"

"*You'll* not allow?" she began, then bridled her temper. "And Templar Sutton?" she probed. "Do you believe, my lord, I brought Templar Sutton to court to advise me on how to most effectively, legally, force you to do my bidding to court and perhaps wed Mary, Queen of Scots?"

"Of course not. You don't mean you suspect that I had aught to do with the man's death?"

"No, I don't," she said, flopping her hand helplessly in her lap. She nearly blurted out to him that she'd been attacked but held back. Always she held back from Robin, fearing she could not trust giving in to him. But who else in the bosom of her court should she not trust? "It's only," she tried to explain, "because I have no one certain I suspect of Templar's death that I am sadly suspicious of far too many."

"What made you change your mind—about acting lessons for some sort of romantic play?" Lord Darnley asked Ned as they slipped away from everyone and strolled out toward the grape arbor. Ned had thought it clever to try to steer him out here, even to the very spot from which the brick murder weapon had been taken, but Darnley himself was the one who'd suggested the route.

"I heard rumors you might be leaving court," Ned answered, with a slight shrug, "and just couldn't let you slip away." He felt nervous, very nervous, and that wasn't like him.

"Those are not rumors," Darnley told him with a lewd wink, "though I know I often arouse them."

At that sly turn of phrase, he leaned closer to Ned to bump his shoulder and displayed a bright, hopeful smile. Ned's first instinct was to smack the sot silly, but he followed Darnley into the shadow of the heavily laden, arching grape vines.

"What happened to your hands—and what's that mark on your face?" Ned asked, deciding those questions gave no cause for suspicion.

"Oh, that. I got so angry with my mount the other day when it got all skittish and ran me through the trees that I plucked off a branch and switched him good. The poor dumb brute looks worse than I!" he added with a sharp laugh.

"Can you get out at night for assignations?" Ned asked Darnley. "Away from your parents and staff, I mean?"

"I can and do, but why wait for night?"

"Surely, not now," Ned blurted a bit too loudly. "We can meet out behind the maze, I suppose."

"Not such a good site as it was once, is it?"

"It will do as long as the queen or her watchdog Cecil don't catch on or, worse, catch us."

"As long as my mother doesn't find out," Darnley countered with a snicker, "though she'd get over it. She has before. She needs me more than any land or fortune."

"I suppose you detest Cecil for refusing to let your family return to Scotland all this time—and if you detest him, you'd probably hate those he was close to."

"His wife Mildred? Or do you mean the queen? Surely, not the poor, departed Templar Sutton, an outsider who got the queen's ear immediately when my poor mother, of royal Tudor blood, never could? Ah, Topside, you'll never get me to say a word against our Gracious Majesty, not at least since she's said father and I can go to Scotland to pursue our family's destiny."

"And before Her Grace changed her mind? Did you use to resent her power over you? Granted she can wield it with a heavy hand."

"You know I'd like to play along with all this, Topside, because I still fancy you," Darnley said, propping his beringed hands on his hips. "I've adored watching you up on the dais or stage, with your fine face and turn of leg. I'd almost risk much for a roll with you, but you're too close in Her Majesty's affections to find a place in mine, clever Ned. Best stick with that stupid skirt of a red-headed herb girl who's always making cow eyes at you no matter how many times you lie in some other maid's lap."

Darnley shook his head ruefully and walked away. Both relieved and disappointed, Ned watched the whoreson codpiece run his hand over the spot where now not one, but two missing bricks made a gap-toothed hole in the arbor's arch. Darnley eyed the double space there—perhaps he'd been expecting only the first brick he took to be gone.

Ned watched Henry Stewart, Lord Darnley, swagger toward the back of the maze. He fancied for one moment he'd actually walk through it like some sort of specter, but he turned and disappeared around its leafy corner.

Ned was furious. He'd never failed Her Grace before, not in being asked to play a part. And how dare Darnley call Meg a stupid skirt and in the same breath imply she was enamored of him? After all, most wenches were.

Two days later, standing between Kat and Rosie on the warm, windy walkway atop the palace's Great Gatehouse, the queen watched Templar Sutton's black-draped funeral barge rowed into the main current of the Thames. William Cecil had donated a grave plot at St. Clements Dane in London where his infant son was interred. But the queen couldn't spare Cecil to attend, nor did she want her people back in her unhealthsome capital. Sir Christopher Hatton and Jamie Barstow, chief mourners accompanying the coffin, were under orders not to enter the city but to wait for the returning barge at Chelsea.

Spouses by tradition did not attend funerals or interments, so Bettina had kept to her chamber, still induced to sleep by a potion of mullein and rosemary which Meg Milligrew had brewed. The widow had not even come to the funeral feast. All during the repast, Elizabeth had been as distracted as Kat and nearly as despondent as Mildred. There, the queen thought when Templar's draped coffin was carried to the barge, but for the Grace of God go I, murdered in a maze.

Now, she startled as Robin Dudley approached her on the parapet. He spoke loudly to be heard above the flap of royal pennants just overhead.

"The coroner's report has come at last, Your Majesty."

"And why did it follow long hours after the body was returned to us?"

"They said they wanted to be thorough."

That only bolstered the queen's belief the parish officials were bumbling rustics, for a coroner's inquest consisted only of a thorough external examination of the corpse. A civilized Christian nation would never pronounce it legal or moral to dissect a dead body, as a doctor in rare instances might a pauper's or criminal's corpse. She noted that Robin, too, looked sorrowful, though he had not even known Templar Sutton. No doubt he was still saddened by his sister's precipitous leave-taking in but an hour.

"If their examination of the body was complete, good," Elizabeth said, walking him a bit apart from the others. "Let me hear their verdict, my lord."

"Coroner Malvern's ruling is one of deliberate mischief—"

"Mischief? Murder, he means!"

"Yes, Your Grace. Deliberate mischief resulting in a murder, a homicide, were his exact words, though I warrant you could have told him that."

Robin bit his lip, as if afraid to go on; the queen realized his emotions could be colored by the wrenching investigation into his own wife's sudden death four years before, a death for which many had blamed—still blamed—him. *Fatal mischance*, the verdict had been in the inquiry over Amy Dudley's mysterious death, with the further explanation: *No one person is deemed directly to blame.* But if Templar's murder went to a trial, she would never allow that judgment. Murder most foul had been committed and by someone who had threatened—perhaps yet did—the queen's own sacred life.

"Say on, Robin," she said, narrowing her eyes against the sun to watch the funeral barge turn the bend of river.

"Without witnesses, of course, the parish officials ordinarily could not proceed, but since this occurred at court and caused the loss of a royal subject of importance to both you and Lord Cecil, the coroner and bailiff are bound to investigate and will report anon to me on your behalf. Servants and courtiers alike must be prepared to answer questions put to them."

"Fine. And they must keep us apprised of their progress."

Let them turn something up if they could, she thought. Yet she believed there would be no progress because she had not made any when she had done more than the traditional search for witnesses and turned up naught.

"Look, Your Majesty," Kat's voice interrupted as she came over, pointing into the distance. "Isn't that the funeral barge returning in great haste instead of stately manner? Why, you'd think Templar has risen from the dead."

"Robin," the queen said, "go see why they are returning and—and what Hatton and Barstow are shouting."

She could see them windmilling their arms, but the west wind pulled their impassioned words away. Elizabeth waited nervously, her fists bouncing on top of the gatehouse wall under the flapping pennants. Word of the barge's return evidently spread, for Cecil and Mildred came up on the gatehouse walkway. Cecil held his wife's arm while Mildred's black skirts flapped like ravens' wings.

"Something's amiss," the queen cried to them and pointed below.

They watched Robin ride out of the gates beneath them and pound across the wooden bridge over the moat, then gallop down to the barge landing as the queen's oarsmen put the black-draped barge back in.

But even before Robin nodded and rode back toward the palace, she knew it was dreadful news of some sort. Her stomach knotted tighter than those garters had to cut off her breath. Though she had told no one, since that moment she'd been fearful of foes and fierce death.

Robin reined in on the bridge below and cupped his gloved hands around his mouth to be heard. "Plague, the black death!" he shouted to them. "It's come upriver but a few miles away!"

Chapter the Ninth

AFTER GIVING THE ORDER THAT SHE WOULD LEAVE for Hatfield House with a train of courtiers and guards the next morning, Elizabeth made her way to bid farewell to Mary Sidney. Now her friend's sudden departure seemed only wise.

"Wait here in the hall for me, and do not leave under any circumstances," she told Clifford, but she took Kat inside Mary's chamber with her.

"Dearest Mary," she greeted her friend, "I shall miss you and regret if I've made a shambles of our time together here."

"I know it is ever court business for you, even when we should simply be enjoying midsummer madness," Mary said, hugging Kat after bobbing the queen a quick curtsy. "Your Grace, I hear you'll be leaving, too, thank God. How close has the plague come?"

"Within a few miles. You must not allow your bargemen to put in anywhere along the river until you are well past London."

Mary sniffed so hard behind her veil that it bobbed. "Do you think I would take that chance, since I have cheated disease and death once? Though, trapped as I am with this body and face, I sometimes think I might have as well have died then!"

The depth of fury in Mary's voice surprised the queen, for she usually seemed so stoic. Had she gravely misread her friend? "It will be good for you to be home again," she assured Mary. "At least Robin said you rode out at night—but alone?"

"Yes, rode, walked. At home I am oft surrounded by people, but here—in the midst of your busy court—I feel even more alone."

A rebuke? An accusation? Elizabeth almost argued with her that she had tried to lure her out among company, but she decided to shift the subject. "Mary, Robin was teasing me, was he not, when he said you've heard Catherine Howard's ghost in the hall?"

"I have heard—things, but then I've been so overwrought these last few days it might have been the raving in my own head. It is here I was admired, courted, and beautiful. I almost take leave of my senses sometimes to think how things once were. And now you have everything at court, and I have nothing, and I wish I could do something to make you understand."

Mary choked back a sob and turned toward the window. Her shoulders heaved once before her hands gripped the sill as if she could control herself that way. Though Elizabeth could not see her ravaged face through that veil, she fancied she could—and the ravaged soul, too.

Yet it could not be, the queen thought, that her dear friend was the one who wrapped the garters—where would a recluse get those garters?—around her throat and threatened her life to teach her how vulnerable and alone one could be. Or for revenge: Elizabeth had survived the pox with but a few marks while Mary caught a more virulent form while nursing her.

"I shall visit you when I can at Penshurst," Elizabeth promised, on the verge of tears herself. She wanted to hug Mary farewell but could not. "Meanwhile, God keep us both safe. Come, Kat. We all have much to do to leave this place."

Kat followed to the door, then hung back. "I hope you liked the new scarves, stockings, and garters I sent you, Mary, the riding gloves, too," Elizabeth overheard before Kat closed the door.

"What garters did you send Mary?" she demanded in the hall.

"A whole array of them just to lift her spirits. But I fear they didn't help one whit, for catastrophe still clings to her."

Kat went blithely down the hall while Elizabeth stood stunned. Those last portentous words described not only Mary but herself.

An hour later, the queen paced back and forth, fanning herself in her withdrawing room while her court churned in chaos around her. She kept the windows closed with the plague so close, but she could still hear voices and noises. In her own state apartments and throughout the vast hive of the palace, courtiers and servants packed in a panic. When the queen traveled, her furnishings, hangings, plate, wardrobe, and closest servants traveled with her. Her Controller, her Cofferer, and the heads of her twenty household departments scurried to report to the Lord Chamberlain that they would be ready to depart at first light on the morrow.

The queen would move in public procession to her manorhouse at Hatfield, farther from the great liquid highway of the Thames where the plague could spread at will. Because Hatfield House was dwarfed by Hampton Court, only fifty of her chosen retainers and thirty servants would go with her, though her guard would be doubled en route. Some courtiers were preparing to return to their country houses, or, if they were very necessary or ambitious, to find accommodations near their queen. Hatfield was thirty-eight miles away, a three-day trip, so couriers had been sent out to arrange for two nights' royal accommodations.

"It would not be three days if you'd agree to travel mounted with a band of my men, instead of in that jolting bucket of a state coach," Robin had groused earlier. "We could make it in one long day as we could cover nearly eight miles an hour in this good weather, and you, my queen, are the most eminent of England's horsewomen."

"You might as well go prate to Cecil—and then listen to his arguments against me," she'd told him.

"Cecil and I agree on this?" he'd asked, amazed.

"He simply feels these are not the times to go in open progress among my people. But they are my people, and they must see their queen and know she is not made fearful by the Black Death, nor anything else any villain this side of hell can devise!"

Word had spread that the queen was as bold as ever, even if she would be visiting her shires of Surrey, Buckingham, and

Hertford earlier than she'd originally planned. If she surprised the good people of her realm in a premature visit, that was life—for lately, life had surprised her, too.

The sudden move also played havoc with the murder investigation the local authorities had planned, but the queen could not ask her people to remain here to be questioned as the plague approached. Templar was already dead; others might soon be if they did not flee. Besides, she had the desperate feeling that Templar's killer and her attacker would find her again—or even be traveling with her. She would be ready, no matter how upset Cecil was that an enemy along the route of her cavalcade could shoot a long bow or firearm at her. This murderer, she was certain, preferred more intimate encounters.

"The people must see their queen—serene and in splendor, Cecil, and that is that!" she had shouted to end all discussion.

Now she waited for her guards to announce various people she had sent for. "Ned Topside, Your Majesty," Clifford called out from the door set ajar, and swept it open for Ned to enter.

"Ned, I have not sent for you."

"But I needed to tell you—about Darnley," he ended in a stage whisper as he rose from his bow. "And I told your guards you had sent for me."

"All right then, tell me quickly of Lord Darnley. Did you meet with success?"

"For the first time in my six years of serving you, Your Grace—well, I told you it wouldn't work."

"'S blood, nothing is working as it should!" She whacked her fan against the wall, so hard she broke its ivory ribs, then went over to slam the door herself.

"Yet, Your Grace, though he didn't fall into the snare we planned for him, I learned, I believe, all I need to know."

"Stop making contrary speeches, man. Spit it out!"

"Though, thank the Lord, I didn't have to prove it, Darnley definitely desires men, if any of that is of interest."

"Of interest, yes, but hardly news."

"And he seemed shocked to see that two bricks instead of one were missing from the arch in the grape arbor."

"Now that is useful—perhaps. That means either he is guilty of pulling out the first one, or that, since the arbor is his evident assignation spot, he merely noticed a difference. Anything else?"

"He said his mother has caught him at his—ah, preferences before, but she needs him for her plans, so abides his behavior. And, oh yes, he admitted he has easily gotten out alone at night."

"So weapon and opportunity, even motive when it comes to attacking me, but why kill Templar? Ned, I believe you have managed more than you realized. Even when we think we are in a dead end, there is yet another turn to come."

"Your Majesty," Clifford's voice boomed out through the door, "you have summoned the Countess of Lennox, Margaret Stewart, and she awaits without."

"Go, then, Ned, with my thanks. I will need you, Meg, and Jenks to keep close to me on the way. Remember, but for the few on my Privy Plot Council, no one else knows that I too have been attacked—except for the one who did it."

Elizabeth threw her broken fan into the empty hearth and stiffened her backbone as her cousin Margaret swept into the room, arrayed in black brocade despite the heat of the day. As

Ned ducked out behind her, she looked taken aback either by the stifling room or the queen's expression. Now, as Margaret curtsied, then rose, the queen's gaze skimmed her gown, looking for snags or tears.

"Your Majesty," Margaret began when the queen nodded her permission to speak, "I am eternally grateful you will allow the earl and Lord Darnley to go to Scotland to reclaim our lands, and what better time than now when you are reducing the size of your court for a country respite and haven from the plague."

"The earl may depart when he will, but Lord Darnley may go later. Even as I am loath to part with your company, cousin, I find it difficult to let our charming Lord Darnley depart. When his father is certain that the tenor of the times in Scotland is safe for your heir, he may join his sire."

"But just the other day, you had changed your mind to let them depart anytime. Why not our son now, too?"

"Shall I change my mind again to let none of you go—or to return you to house arrest at Sheen, where I am sending poor Templar Sutton's body to be buried since London is now off limits?"

"I—no, of course not," she faltered, obviously taken aback by the outburst. "Your wish is indeed my—our command," she said, but her olive-hued complexion blanched white as almond paste.

Elizabeth and Cecil had argued late last night over her keeping Darnley around too, but she had cited two reasons, neither of which she would share with this snide harpy. Firstly, it was ever her practice to keep high-placed, hostile courtiers under her nose to better smell out their reeking, treasonous plans. Secondly, even before Ned's report, Henry Stewart, Lord Darnley, had been on the list of her possible attackers, though she had several other candidates, too.

"You must excuse me for I have important people to see," the queen informed Margaret with a dismissive nod.

She could tell the woman took her ambiguous comment with the intended barb. Margaret dropped a jerky curtsy and huffed her way to the door, nearly colliding with Mildred Cecil, who waited just outside to be announced. Ordinarily, the queen would have been appalled to see that Mildred barely moved aside for a woman of royal blood, but it perversely pleased her to see Margaret thrown off balance in more ways than one.

"The countess believes I'm as mad as Tom O'Bedlam anyway," Mildred said in feeble apology as she rose from her curtsy. "After all, she was at the baby's christening where I—I shouted at you and should not have, Your Grace."

"But you were ill then, still recovering from childbirth, and are obviously better now. Sit with me here," Elizabeth invited, indicating two chairs. She looked Mildred's black skirts over too as she turned, sat, and arranged her gown, but saw no snags or tears. "You are not mad in the slightest, are you, Mildred, however sad or fretful sometimes?"

"Only mad at myself for not meekly accepting whatever burdens our heavenly Lord would allow. After all, He gives us strength to bear up under—and fight back against—all our earthly trials."

Her voice was so keen-edged that Elizabeth paused before observing, "Your lord loves you very much, you know."

Mildred nodded stiffly; tears glazed her eyes. "I thank you, Your Majesty, that you are keeping me with your court to go to Hatfield, though, of course, my lord and I can move immediately into our nearby manorhouse at Theobalds to give some-one else a chamber. My lord husband said that he would rent no one chambers at Theobalds to keep it as a retreat for you, and he wishes to show you the new property and his grand schemes for it."

"I certainly want to see Theobalds too, but will need Secretary Cecil with me at Hatfield until then. And you are welcome to stay also."

"But I—I hear you are keeping Bettina Sutton with you."

"I can hardly cast her off now, especially since we have heard that the plague is spreading in London as well as creeping up the Thames. And, frankly, Cecil says he wants to counsel her on financial affairs. As busy as he is, it is good of him."

"Oh, yes, very good."

"I sense you do not like Bettina."

"It's only that she saw my outburst at the christening. No, Your Majesty, it is not only that," she corrected herself, sitting up straighter and gripping her hands hard in her lap. "It is that I have gathered from some of the current law students my lord has sponsored, who have dined at our table, that Bettina Sutton is a bedswerving lightskirt, and has carried on as such under poor Templar's nose!"

The queen sat back in her chair. Now that, if it were fact, led to many new ramifications. And Mildred had never been the sort to gossip.

"Current students?" the queen queried. "But Bettina would be much older than they are."

Mildred tried to stifle a sniff. "She's trifled with current—and former, I'm afraid."

"Such as Christopher Hatton?" Elizabeth asked, recalling how Bettina had seemed so smitten by him. "Or Jamie Barstow?"

"I don't know for certain, though it would not be for her lack of setting snares, I take it."

"Mildred, did you try to talk to Templar about this and have words with him? Could Bettina have known you told him such, and perhaps feared . . . But I am getting ahead of myself."

"I only know what I overheard and believe to be true. Will you dismiss her from your presence now?"

"Not until I know the facts. I do know a woman's sullied reputation can be a fragile thing. But you have helped to open my eyes to new possibilities. I am glad to see you calm and much yourself again."

Mildred rose as the queen did. "Yet my lord always says that I am not myself, does he not, Your Grace?"

"He worries for you. He is very proud of you and the children," Elizabeth assured her as she nodded her leave to depart.

"*Some* of the children," Mildred muttered as she curtsied and hurried out the door.

Jenks had to admit Meg Milligrew sat a horse well, especially for a girl who'd been reared in London. Her deceased husband had once been a bargeman and had taught Meg to row and swim, not ride. Jenks himself had made her a middling horsewoman, about the same time Ned taught her to read and say her words better and not slouch. So why did Meg have to choose Ned Topside over him when Ned hardly knew she was alive, not as a desirable woman anyway?

Jenks rode up to Meg's place in line on his way toward the vanguard of the growing array of riders and wagons which would follow the queen's guard and coach. Her Majesty always felt better if he and Lord Dudley rode near her, especially when the Countess of Lennox and her son, Lord Darnley, were riding right behind.

"Nice weather at least." Jenks tried something safe with Meg.

Still unmounted, she was struggling to balance two bulky, sweet-smelling burlap bags on her horse's rump, so he reached over to help her.

"It is that," she agreed, "though any day's a good one for fleeing the plague. You just keep a sharp eye out for varlets who might try to harm Her Grace."

"Folks already gathered at the palace gates waiting to cheer her on. She'll be fine now we're leaving that cursed maze behind, and Hatfield's got nothing like."

"Not unless you count that knot garden I put in six years ago, the year she became queen." Meg shook her head and frowned, but he figured it wasn't at him this time. "I haven't seen it since then, so unless the caretakers of the manor tended it, the pretty twists of shrub hedges will have gone to rack and ruin."

"Your touch will mend them fast."

She smiled up at him, right into his eyes in the slant of morning sun. "Jenks, I don't want hard feelings between us."

"Not on my part, Mistress Milligrew. Come on then, I'll give you a boost up," he said, and quickly dismounted.

She seized her reins, and he laced his hands to take her foot and hoist her into the saddle. She settled her skirts as he remounted.

"Jenks," she began, then bit off what else she'd say as the cries "Forward! Forward! Make way for the Queen's Majesty!" sounded over the hubbub in the waiting line.

"Tell me quick, though I'll see you along the way," he said.

"I do care for you and always will."

"But not the right way?"

"I can't explain about Ned. God knows he doesn't deserve my care and concern..."

"He doesn't and I do, but you still want Ned," he said, his voice harsh when he'd meant to sound sweet. He'd been carrying around for days a pair of riding gloves he longed to give her as a courting gift and here she was getting ready to explain why she loved Ned.

"The plague," she whispered, leaning closer to him and reaching out to touch his hands gripping his reins, "and the threat of death to us, the queen's being attacked too, all make me think about what's important, and—"

"What's important now is getting this progress on the road," he said and doffed his cap to her as he might to a fine lady. "Facing death from the plague or from loving someone you can never have—hell, I'm just sticking to serving the queen, because it's all too much for me."

Cutting off what else she would say, he spurred his mount around those waiting to move and caught up with Robert Dudley directly behind the royal coach.

The shortened royal entourage stretched nearly a mile instead of the usual four. One would have been deaf and blind to miss the grand procession, and people responded with wild adoration of their queen.

On earlier progresses, the queen would ride a white horse, but she'd left Fortune behind with her new foal. Elizabeth had been known to recline against cushions in an ornate litter carried by men or pulled by a team of white mules. But today, she waved from her open-sided coach, drawn by matched horses with their manes and tails dyed orange. Accepting numerous nosegays and even petitions, she waved and smiled until she thought her arm would drop off and her face would crack. At least no one had had the forewarning to be able to prepare the usual delaying speeches and pageants.

When they passed a stretch of open fields with scattered shade trees, she finally stretched and stared straight up at the carved and plumed roof of the coach. The interior was richly upholstered in scarlet cloth, dripping gold and silver lace. Despite its splendor, even pillowed and padded, the damned thing rested on two hard axles and jolted her nearly to death.

"Stop at once, Boonen!" she shouted to her coachman. "I need to stretch my legs before your driving these pitted roads turns me to mincemeat!"

Robin appeared immediately to help her down. Already behind her, word of a respite had spread, for others dismounted or jumped from wagons to stretch or tend to privy needs. Elizabeth did not want to catch Margaret Stewart's eye and have her come traipsing over to join her, but she noted she was huddled with her son.

As the queen drank the proffered goblet of ale, men quickly erected her small, crimson-cloth pavilion. She paced back and forth, but when she finally glanced past Robin's shoulder and saw Bettina Sutton on the road behind, she sent Jenks to fetch her. As the woman came closer, the queen noted that she looked quite sober and dry-eyed for the first time since Templar's death.

"You are not sending me back, Your Majesty? I'm afraid to go back to London right now," she cried as she rose from her curtsy.

"Why would you think that? Have I been anything but kind to you?" Immediately, the queen regretted her baiting tone. Mildred's casting suspicion on Bettina had changed her attitude toward the new widow, and that was unfair, at least so far.

"You have been so gracious I cannot fathom the depth of your care," Bettina gushed and blinked back tears as Elizabeth indicated she might join her in the small pavilion. They sat on low, folding camp chairs on a Turkey carpet spread over the grassy fringe between the road and the fields.

"You've been riding with Chris Hatton and Jamie Barstow today," Elizabeth said. "Since you've known them for quite a while, I thought they might be of some comfort and you could talk of old times. Because Templar kept close relationships with his students, I'm sure you had some intimacy with them, too."

For one moment, Bettina blinked at Elizabeth like an owl. "Oh, yes, I knew them all."

The queen merely raised her eyebrows, hoping Bettina would feel the need to elaborate.

"One can't help but feel sorry for young men away from home," Bettina went on, shifting slightly so her wooden chair creaked. Each time she sighed, her breasts heaved. "At our dinner table, Templar questioned and bullied his pupils to become better orators or to learn to discern truth through their disputations. Of course, I was hostess for those events."

"Discern truth through their disputations," the queen repeated. "I also recall Templar liked to retire early to bed to read, you said, though he later mentioned it was to plan questions for his pupils—as he did the evening of the masque. So the way you described it was close to the truth, yet slightly askew."

Bettina had looked merely uneasy, but at that salvo, her bewilderment seemed to shift to bravado. "Yes, as Templar said, he retired early the evening I found you nearly dead, Your Majesty."

The queen fixed Bettina with a steady stare and let silence hang in the air between them again.

"Templar cared deeply for his work and his students, yes," Bettina said, her voice almost breathless.

"And did you care for them deeply, too?"

"Of course, I did. But—you mean Christopher, do you not?"

The queen threw the rest of her ale out the tent opening and tossed her goblet on the carpet. "Tell me about your relationship with him then."

"There is naught to tell, Your Majesty. He was charming and handsome, and I delighted in his company, that is all. What red-blooded woman would not respond with warmth to that particular young blood, as they call the Gray's Inn students. You no doubt noticed I was happy to see him here again. I am proud that he is doing well in your eyes, that is all. I warrant the fact I favored him among my husband's students was not one whit different from the way he was—and is—treated by any woman, however highborn, with two eyes in her head, Your Grace."

Elizabeth almost slapped her, but she was forced to admire the woman. She might look like a coquette, but she could probably sway a judge or jury like any good lawyer. The queen decided to switch tactics.

"Of course your skills as hostess would be a great help to your husband and solace to yourself," she said, forcing herself to sound pleasant. "And I can only imagine that living with someone as brilliant and demanding as Templar was not easy for you."

"No, Your Gracious Majesty, it was not, when all I wanted was to be as loved and cherished as were his precious law and his books."

A flood of new tears. At least Bettina had not denied her mingled feelings toward her husband or her attraction to Chris Hatton. Despite wanting to harden her heart against this young woman, Elizabeth understood being lonely—the swirling desire to be coddled and cherished when important men seemed ever busy with other things.

"But, Your Majesty," Bettina plunged on, evidently not knowing when she was winning, "if you think I had aught to do with harming Templar, I swear to you by all that is holy that I did not, could not! And I don't know what you're implying about my relationships with my husband's students, but I feel much maligned. Ask Chris and Jamie if you don't believe me—send someone to Gray's Inn to ask anyone!"

"Impossible now with the plague there, as you know. But I assure you I will speak to Chris and Jamie. Then tell me why you put Mildred, Lady Cecil's name on the list with all those men."

"Just the other day she argued with Templar and tried to turn him against me, and now she's turned you against me too, has she not?"

"Turn Templar or me against you how?"

"The question is *why*, Your Majesty. Mayhap she thought I was always part of the camaraderie between Templar and his students, including her own husband. Templar and her lord remained close over the years, and Templar preferred him to visit us instead of the other way round, and Lord Cecil always loved coming back to Gray's. That day Templar became godfather to the Cecils' new child was an exception to the rule. Since Lord Cecil was busy at court and then spent time with us, perhaps Lady Cecil became jealous of or hostile toward me, especially if she is of unstable temperament of late."

"So, you are surmising that Lady Cecil was jealous of you for merely being part of—a close witness to—Templar's and her husband's friendship, for helping indirectly to keep Cecil away from her, so to speak?"

"Your Majesty, from what Templar told me, she was of a jealous nature, not so much of me but of another woman—a dead woman," Bettina declared with the look of one who had just thrown her trump card.

"What? Of whom?"

"Of Lord Cecil's first wife, the mother of his heir Tom. I take it she haunts Lady Cecil like a ghost."

"Like a gh—jealous of a woman long dead? Explain," Elizabeth demanded, leaning forward.

"I don't know more than that, I swear it, but something has driven Lady Cecil to distraction. Maybe she saw me slip out the night of the masque and thought she was strangling me—until she saw it was you and, of course, stopped. Then the day she argued with Templar, mayhap she saw he was walking alone, trying to find who attacked you, and decided she must stop him at any cost."

Elizabeth gaped at her. All that was completely outrageous, and yet it made as much sense as some of the other paths she'd been down.

"Bettina, say nothing of this to anyone. Mildred Cecil absolutely cannot be guilty of such atrocious deeds."

The rest of the journey, Elizabeth of England smiled and waved, but she was shaken by much more than the jolting, rocking coach.

Chapter the Tenth

 WITHIN A MILE OF THEIR DESTINATION, WHEN THE forest road turned achingly familiar, Elizabeth halted her entourage. "Bring me a horse, Robin," she commanded. "I want to ride into Hatfield as I used to. There is no one here anymore to impress in this damned coach."

After he had brought up her horse and checked the sidesaddle straps, he helped her mount. Suddenly, her guards rode closer to surround her—the nervous Cecil must have put them up to that—but she motioned for them to move back.

"Jenks only with me, just as in those difficult days," she announced and motioned for her stalwart guard. "Everyone else may follow," she called over her shoulder and spurred her horse.

Just as in those difficult days. Her own words echoed in her head in rhythm with her horse's hoofbeats. Did she not think the times were troubled now? But she ripped off her hat and let her tresses bounce her hairpins free. It was her first visit to dear, old Hatfield since she had learned here she would be queen. Now, if only for one mile or one moment, she would ride free from fear and whatever dangers and destruction threatened.

"Remember when we rode so fast 'The Pope' could not keep up with us?" Elizabeth called to Jenks as he kept his horse nearly abreast hers. Her sister Queen Mary Tudor had named Thomas Pope her guardian but in truth he'd been her gaoler.

"Aye, Your Grace! And how you outfoxed him more than once to get us away from those Catholic household spies."

The queen looked back to see Robin riding a short distance behind with Chris and Jamie in his dusty wake. The moment of exuberance and defiance ended; Elizabeth reined in to a trot as her burdens leaned hard upon her heart again. And she had a murderer to find, perhaps one who was part of the royal retinue strung out behind.

The central single tower and two stories of the russet brick building burst into view through the protective arms of old oaks. Three roe deer on the lawn bolted for the cover of surrounding forest. She was evidently heard or seen by humankind too, for the skeletal staff which had been sent ahead emerged from the arched entry and lined up to greet her.

She saw immediately why the deer had been on the lawn. It had not been cut—sheep used to graze on it—nor had the shrubs been kept in trim. The intricate knot garden Meg had labored over the last autumn she, as Princess Elizabeth, had lived here in forced exile had run riot to weedy tangles. So, she thought, by coming a bit early she had caught the simpletons who were to keep the place up.

The queen dismounted with Jenks's help and briefly greeted the waiting staff as Robin caught up to her. On the journey, she'd given much thought to what she must do next to try to find the maze murderer before she was buried in courtiers and cares again.

"Robin," she said, tossing him her reins as Chris and Jamie dismounted, "please see to these horses. Sir Christopher, Jamie, Jenks, come with me while I tour this old place, once my shelter and now, I pray, so again."

Robin looked utterly dismayed, but she swept in the front door. Memories assailed her again, but she kept going, past the wide, worn oaken staircase she'd traversed a thousand times, down the corridor to the vaulted and beamed great hall where she had held her first council meeting after she had learned her sister was dead. Her booted footsteps echoing, she strode the entire length of the long, narrow room to the dais, and sat in the chair at the end of the raised table.

The three men trying to keep up with her halted, uncertain whether to sit or stand. Chris looked around jerkily as if he expected someone to leap at them from the afternoon shadows which hovered here despite the high windows.

"Jenks," she said, "guard the door and see that no one enters until I say so. Sir Christopher, sit here," she added pointing to the chair on her immediate right, "and Jamie, on my left."

Jenks did as he was told without question, though both her legally-trained courtiers looked as if they'd like to argue or at least cross-question her. Both chairs scraped as they pulled them out, sat, and scooted them in.

"Have we unwittingly vexed Your Grace?" Chris asked, sitting ramrod straight. Were they guileless or guilty, she wondered, watching how they seemed to avoid looking at each other.

"Not at all. I merely wanted to tell you about this room, since neither of you—unlike Jenks, Lord Cecil, and my dear Kat Ashley—were in my service when I last was here, before I went to London to be crowned queen."

Chris heaved a sigh of relief; Jamie still sat like a deer scenting the hunter, but then, however alluring Chris looked, it was Jamie who had the brains. If it ever came to keeping just one or the other of them about, she'd be hard-pressed to pick, for they each had their strengths and uses. But if one of them was a murderer, what, in God's name, could be a motive?

"This chamber," she went on, not looking around but at one of them and then the other, "is where my parents used to entertain in their happy days, before everything went so wrong and my mother was tried and executed. Imagine, even someone who had climbed so high in the monarch's favor could tumble from that lofty position."

Chris still looked raptly interested in her mock history lesson; Jamie took her point and started to fidget.

"This is also the room where, in my initial council meeting, I first felt my father's power which had been weakly held by my poor, ill brother and had been abused by my sister Mary. It is a room in which I feel I must do right by myself and my people, especially to help those who have been harmed and to punish those who do not deserve my good trust."

She looked into Chris's green eyes; he nodded and a tight smile lifted the corners of his mouth. She turned to stare Jamie down. He looked intently concerned; his gaze did not flicker or waver.

"Though we have been forced to flee the site of your dear mentor Master Sutton's murder," she continued, "I shall not let it go, and will speak to anyone who knew him to ferret out the identity of the murderer. That includes especially those who knew him well and spoke with him mere hours before his sad demise. He had promised me he would 'tell me tales out of school' about those he had mentored, and that includes both of you."

"Secretary Cecil too," Chris put in, "though afore our time."

"Let me worry about Cecil," she clipped out. "Now, Chris, you have told me how Master Sutton berated you for not using your skills and for following a frivolous path to come to my court, so Jamie, I would hear the Templar tales as they impacted you."

"First of all, I'd debate the assumption that coming to court is a frivolous path," Jamie said, shifting forward in his seat. She noted again how agitated he was acting, despite his calm voice. "Of course," he went on, gesturing, "I concede there are indeed entertaining benefits to courtly life, but from the source of such power as you wield, Your Majesty, there flows national duty, pride, and power—hardly frivolous things in life."

"Well said. But I believe Templar also berated you about your choices and decisions, Jamie."

"He did."

"And? Say on, man."

"Forgive me, Your Majesty. It is just that I feel I'm testifying at the bar now, and any lawyer worth his salt tells witnesses to answer simply only what was asked and not expand."

"'S blood and bones, I'm your queen, not some lawyer!"

"But you do sit in the lofty station of judge and jury, Your

Majesty. Master Sutton said I had risen far for nearly a self-made man. You see, Sir Christopher's father, who has wealth and position, had sent me, in effect, his servant's son, with him to Cambridge and Gray's, so I had the runoff of some benefits."

"So far, so good. Go on," the queen prompted.

"Indeed, Master Sutton felt Chris should not have left Gray's early, but he was adamant it was foolish for me to do so. He felt that, if I fell out of favor with Chris or with you, I'd be out on my hind end, I believe he put it, with no calling to earn my bread, whereas he believed that Chris was cut out for court life and, though a second son and not his father's heir, could make his way here. Master Sutton claimed I could not stomach the stratifications and niceties of court life and, quite frankly, would be bored to death."

"Bored—to death. And have you been?" the queen queried, even as Jamie shifted in his chair again.

"Never, Your Gracious Majesty. Not at your court where great decisions are made and wit wins many a battle and—"

"Wit, yes, you've got that, doesn't he, Chris?"

"I can't ever thank Jamie enough for how he's served me through thick and thin, been my valet at times, if need be, my groomsman—and my tutor when Cambridge and Gray's were overwhelming."

She glanced from one man to the other, wondering if she'd been wrong to question them together. She had wanted to see how they played off each other, and if there could be some conspiracy of silence between them. She did not believe so, but she had one more card to play.

"I also need to know," she said abruptly, "whether your relationships with Bettina Sutton were entirely proper."

That appeared to jolt them both. Damn, Elizabeth thought, it must be true that the little half-blooded Italian had betrayed her husband. And if so, would she in passion strike him down to preserve her secret licentious practices?

"Chris may answer first," she said, holding up a hand to stop his keeper Jamie from coming to his rescue with some well-honed excuse or diversion.

"I know you are strict with your ladies' reputations, Your Grace," Chris began, gripping the edge of the table. "And, of course, your own."

"What does that have to do with the price of pigs at market? I'm asking about a woman who is not one of my ladies, one you have both known for years. Did either of you ever play your teacher and mentor false with his wife?"

"She—she tried," Chris said, frowning. "I know that sounds pompous and craven, but I'm used to it—women's attentions, I mean—and swear I don't take advantage of that. No, she tried to entice me once. Remember that, Jamie, that autumn night our first year at Gray's, after Master Sutton retired to bed, but I said no and she backed off and never so much as hinted at such again, I swear it."

"You must have been terribly convincing," Elizabeth said in mocking tones, then realized it all sounded completely plausible. As far as she'd seen, Chris Hatton had been the very picture of male virtue at her court, and had seemed to be swayed only by her favors and no one else's.

"Perhaps I was the one who was convincing, Your Majesty," Jamie said as he slid to the edge of his chair. "I warned Mistress Sutton to keep away from Chris, however much the Adonis he looked. I've protected him before like that, not that he's been a saint on his own——God's truth, neither of us are that. And she never approached me, not a poor *pleb. fil.* there at Gray's on charity. And that lowly status, of course, is also why I've hesitated to beg your leave to truly tell Lady Rosie how I feel about her. May I have your permission to speak of this at some later time, Your Majesty?"

Elizabeth's mind was in whirls. She had not realized this young man was so clever and skilled at persuasion and influence. Because he seemed to stand in Chris's shadow, he had somehow faded from her notice. James Barstow, a plebeian's son or not, should be working for Cecil——or her. He could be trained to be an envoy or an ambassador's aide someday, even a spy.

"Speak of your intentions for Lady Rosie now," she commanded.

"I know Rosie Radcliffe could make a hundred better matches than I, Your Majesty, but I throw myself at your feet, imploring that you will not ask me to forsake the firm relationship the two of us are building. And I swear by Almighty God that no one could respect or admire her more or love her better."

'S blood, Elizabeth thought, Robin should take wooing lessons from this man. No wonder her sensible, spinster Rosie had been swept off her feet by Jamie Barstow, despite his lack of station and income, both of which everyone knew the queen herself could amend if she so desired. And she was starting to want to, despite the fact Jamie kept shifting in his chair as if it were a hot seat.

"Forgive me, Your Majesty," he blurted, "but it's been a long ride since our last stop, and I need to excuse myself for one moment."

"Of course."

His usually steady gait was nearly a sprint to the door.

"Speaking of telling tales out of school," Chris said, leaning forward confidentially, though no one but the two of them were now in the vast room, "the thing is, he's suffering from a problem in physick. Can't hold his water, but he's taking tonic for it."

In that moment, Elizabeth could not decide whether to laugh or cry. At least it explained why Jamie had acted as if he were on pins and needles. But now there was another complication, for she was certain, when Chris leaned so near, she could smell gillyflowers on his breath.

"I smell a sweet scent," she said.

"It's either all the flowers gone to riot outside, I'll bet, or the cloves I chew."

"Does Jamie chew cloves, too?"

"Doesn't like them but fetches them for me. He told me once cloves were too expensive for someone of his station to chew and spit as I do."

It amazed the queen that her convoluted interrogation had come round to this trivia. She couldn't fathom that these two friends were guilty of anything dire, but she refused to let her heart rule her head again, not after what she'd been through with Robin. It was only fair that she authenticate her young courtiers' stories. Rosie's future hung in the balance as did her own safety. The problem was that the queen could hardly trust Bettina or even Mildred's gossip with so much at stake. And the witnesses she needed to substantiate Chris and Jamie's stories were probably battling the Black Death back in London.

———

Later, the afternoon they arrived at Hatfield House, Elizabeth summoned Cecil and took a proprietary stroll around the immediate grounds with him. He assumed, no doubt, she needed to discuss the Mary, Queen of Scots marriage problem again, but she had in mind his own marriage dilemma.

"You are certain Mildred's headache will go away if she simply rests?" she asked him. "I can send Meg to her with some soothing tonic or even summon a doctor if that's needed."

"No, she said a nap will restore her. Besides, it looks to me as if Meg has her own task for the day."

Despite the warmth of the sun, Meg Milligrew had waded into the midst of the unruly knot garden and, with long-bladed, rusted clippers, was madly hacking at leggy rose bushes. Her skirt snagged by thorns, knee-deep in hedges that should be close-cropped and shaped, she did not see them standing nearby.

The varied interlacing sections of woody shrubs had been set out, trained, and trimmed in the shape of a great, intricate knot. Within its whorls and turns could be placed colored gravel, herbs, or flowers—in this case, apothecary roses. Such ornate designs had originated in France, but the English had elevated knot gardening to an art with the varied hues and textures of boxwood, yew, rosemary, and other woody herbs.

"Meg," Elizabeth called to her, "you must fetch someone to help you."

"Oh, Your Grace, Lord Cecil," she said, arching her back and shading her eyes. "I can't abide that it's run riot. I'll have it looking like a fine embroidery knot again and not some wilderness. Nothing can bloom aright in a mess like this," she added, throwing up her hands so fast the gap-jawed clippers went sailing into the green tangle and she had to search to retrieve them.

"Of course you'll get it back to rights," the queen encouraged her, "but don't overtire yourself. And remember to take the Countess of Lennox those strewing herbs for her chambers." Elizabeth and Cecil walked on toward the cooler shade of the huge oaks.

"Meg is not the one you have watching Darnley and his mother, is she?" Cecil asked.

"In part, for I would not expect Margaret to trust my herb mistress. I have also put my guard Clifford in the hall by their rooms to keep a good eye on her and Darnley, especially Darnley."

They stopped, as if by mutual consent, under the oaks which lined the lawn. "The six years I've reigned have flown by," Elizabeth admitted. She reached out to touch the very tree under which she'd been standing when Cecil and Robin had ridden from London with a party of men to bring her the coronation ring from her dead sister's finger.

At that memory, the queen shivered despite the heat. Someday the gold and onyx ring—she glanced at it on her hand—would go to someone else . . . when she too was dead and buried in Westminster Abbey, but not yet, pray God, not for many years. Not unless the one who attacked her tried again, even here in this secluded haven in the heart of her England.

"I said, Your Grace," Cecil was evidently repeating to snatch her back from her woolgathering, "speaking of setting traps, I wish we could actually lay one to entice Darnley, or whoever is our quarry, to come to us—but not with you as bait. The last time we tried that, you almost lost your life."

"But I didn't, and we caught a killer. My lord Cecil," she added, strolling deeper into the forest, "I was wondering if you'd considered buying Bettina's books, those from Templar's private library back at Gray's Inn, that is. I suggested to her that you might be interested."

"Indeed I am, both to honor him and help her. I shall speak to her about it."

"Fine. But because Bettina is under a cloud of suspicion too, I asked Chris Hatton and Jamie Barstow to describe their relationships with her. They have admitted that she was not adverse to being overly intimate with some of her husband's students, even ones younger than she. And your Mildred said the same had been bandied about your dinner table when you hosted Templar's students from time to time."

He frowned, looking off into the distance. "And you're wondering why I didn't tell you?"

"I realize you are not one to credit rumors or besmear a reputation without proof."

"Your Grace, when you appointed me your principal secretary here at Hatfield, you challenged me always to give you truthful counsel, and I have done that. So I must admit that I believe there is a basis for such rumors about Bettina."

She stopped walking and swung slowly to face him. That had been carefully couched lawyer talk indeed. "Then, yes, my lord, why did you not tell me?"

"I cannot fathom she would have aught to do with murder. True, Templar was not the best husband for a woman of her youth, temperament, and needs. But she would never strike him down with a brick from behind in some cold-blooded, calculated murder, not Bettina!"

"You speak passionately in her defense."

"She is a passionate woman, to her shame, I warrant, at times, but, I repeat," he said, seeming to stumble for words now, "not a murderess, Your Grace, and never one who would try to strangle her queen."

"I must tell you too that Mildred seems to resent Bettina so that I believe your wife is almost jealous of her. Perhaps, Bettina tells me, it is because you used to visit the Suttons often when Mildred herself had not seen enough of you because of the demands of queen and kingdom. Cecil," she said and gripped his forearm, "forgive me, my friend, for asking this, but in these tenuous times, I must. Tell me straight you have never betrayed your marriage vows."

His brown eyes widened under his high, furrowed brow. The corners of his mouth tightened, and for one moment she believed he would refuse to answer or confess the impossible.

"No, Your Grace, I have never betrayed my marriage vows."

"Thank God, for I needed not those sort of complications in this—or to think ill of you, my bedrock advisor and ever my friend. I charge you to be certain Mildred knows that truth, for she evidently had harsh words with Templar the day he died. The reason I have not shared Bettina's list of possible culprits with you is that I am discounting one name on it—and if I do that—all the other names on the list are suspect, too."

"One name. What name?"

"Mildred's, my lord. It is obvious to me that, though the two women have seldom met, they dislike each other, and that can't be helped. I'm afraid it is rather like me and Mary of Scots," she said with a forced little laugh.

Cecil was not laughing, for tears matted his lashes before he blinked them away. Elizabeth had meant to corner him on Mildred's possible resentment of his first wife and of his heir by her, but the queen could not bear to see her Cecil cry.

When William Cecil hurried back to be with his wife, the queen tarried again at the knot garden. Though it was nearly dusk, Meg's bodice was soaked through with sweat.

"Since when have you decided not to heed my orders?" Elizabeth asked her. "It is high time to leave off that task."

"Aye, Your Grace, I'm quitting for now. I'm going to take a plunge in the pond beyond the trees to cool off, too, or the Countess of Lennox will smell me coming, strewing herbs or not."

The thought of immersing one's self in the spring-fed pond sounded both alluring and daring to Elizabeth. Meg Milligrew was the only woman she knew who could swim. Surely the bathing tub the queen's father had installed at Whitehall Palace would be a far cry from drifting free in a rush of living water.

"I believe I'll go with you, though hardly to swim," she told Meg as her herb mistress held up her skirts and made great giant's strides to escape the knot garden. Meg bent to hide the clippers in the thick foliage before they walked on. "Perhaps to dabble my toes and let the fish nibble them."

Suddenly, Elizabeth felt lighthearted at the mere thought of bathing outdoors. No doubt because Meg resembled her—and was used upon rare occasions to stand in for the queen when she was endangered—she sometimes also mentally put herself in Meg's place, wondering what it would be like to go shopping on the London streets, or to go unguarded about one's business, to run an apothecary shop, or even to swim.

"But I was going to strip down to my shift and then where will your guards be?" Meg asked.

"I shall be your guard, and you'll be mine," Elizabeth declared with a laugh but then sobered. "No, since I was attacked, I'll not risk that even here where I feel quite safe. We'll stop by the stables and have Jenks come along and stay well back."

The queen studied Meg's face as she mentioned Jenks's name. Though looking much overheated already, the young woman blushed.

"If we're going by the stables, I suppose we could pick up Lord Robin to watch out for someone who might sneak a peek at us, too," Meg teased and could not stifle a giggle.

Once the queen might have boxed a servant's ears for such impertinence, but she only laughed again. Hallowed Hatfield seemed a haven, and she'd fear naught here.

Chapter the Eleventh

"SO, MEG, ARE YOU AND JENKS GETTING ON WELL?" the queen inquired in a soft voice. "I've seen some friction between you, and I can't afford that with my servants—or my Privy Plot Council members. Yet I was beginning to believe he would follow you anywhere instead of me."

"His first love and loyalty, and mine, will always be to you, Your Grace. But lately he's been more than protective. He's been attentive and painfully intent. I suppose I've been a bit hard on him of late."

"Ah," Elizabeth said only, as they saw the pond through the trees, but she was thinking *poor Jenks.* She had sent him to fetch Kat, and she and Meg had the older woman in tow, whereas Jenks trailed a good ways behind as ordered. The queen turned back to gesture to him to stay where he was unless they called him. Robin had not been at the stables to double their guard, but that was just as well, she thought, perversely amused that the trials of queen and herb girl could be at all similar when it came to men who were passionate yet problematic.

"I shall dabble my feet while you swim," Elizabeth said.

"I too," Kat spoke at last, though she'd seemed to be enjoying the walk. "I always used to test the water in your bath when you were young, lovey, to be sure it would not burn you."

Kat and the queen followed circumspectly while Meg scrambled toward the end of the small, oval pond where bramble bushes hid the grassy bank. "Shall I help you with your shoes and stockings then, Your Grace?" Kat asked.

"Do you think I am some ninnyhammer who's forgotten how to undress herself? Ah, Kat, do you recall how we used to make do with old-fashioned, darned garments and few enough of those last time we were here at Hatfield?"

"Of course, I recall. I always vowed that should you become queen," Kat said, plopping down beside her on the bank, "you would have the most beautiful gowns—and someday you shall."

Meg was so used to that sort of past-and-present scrambling that she didn't even look up as she stripped to her shift and waded in while Kat and the queen pulled off shoes and stockings. "Oh, it feels delightful," Meg said and flopped belly down in the pond to paddle like a dog. Elizabeth was transfixed with envy.

"Quite unnatural and unladylike," Kat muttered, swishing her bare feet in the water, "but you do make it look like fun, Meg."

"I've a good nerve to get in, too," the queen declared, smacking her hands on her full skirts, "but these petticoats would pull me under."

"You'd have to take them off, that's for certain," Meg said, not even sounding out of breath. "Watch this, Your Grace."

To their amazement, Meg sucked in a big mouth of air, pinched her nose, and disappeared under the rippling surface. Kat and Elizabeth held their breaths too until Meg burst upward again in a fountain of bubbles. To Kat's obvious dismay, Elizabeth stood and began to strip off layers of petticoats from under her gown.

"You don't mean it," Kat cried. "I'll not allow it."

"I'll stay near the bank, and I don't take orders from you as I did once, dear Kat. I must try it. No one will know, and I may never get such a chance again. Just look how easily Meg goes under and pops back up."

"Everyone will say you fell in when they see you," Kat protested. "Your father will blame me."

"He's given me permission," Elizabeth declared.

Meg stood awed in the pond as the queen, clad in bodice, sleeves, and now drooping outer skirts, sat again on the bank and carefully edged into the water. "Like a big washtub," she said, "but ooh, it's slippery underfoot."

"Just moss and mud," Meg said, coming closer to help. "Here, dip down a bit like this." She bent her knees and blew bubbles when the water covered her mouth, then put her nose in too and snorted like a horse.

Despite her fears, Elizabeth laughed and followed suit. Doing something so curious and bold bucked her up. After all, the queen set standards. No one could tell her she could not do a simple thing one of her servants could, even if it were an outrageous practice. Imagine, swimming like a dog or fish!

Her air-filled skirts buoyed her up at first, but soon went

sodden, like heavy plaster around her legs. The weight of them pulled her down the moment she lifted her feet from the slanted bottom of the pond. She tipped sideways and lost her bearings. As she sputtered and coughed, Meg helped haul her up and steady her.

"Had enough, Your Grace?" Meg asked. "Best get out now."

"Not until I've mastered it."

"But I've been at this for years."

"You both climb out of there right now!" Kat ordered.

But Elizabeth gasped in a great breath, held it, and plunged under, nearly sitting on the pond bottom. The shock of being completely encased in the press of cool, heavy water stunned her. Currents of her own making tugged at her hair and swayed her heavy skirts. But she held her breath, then blew out tickling bubbles that raced up her forehead. She felt defiant and free until she recalled how she could not get her breath when the garters were around her neck, stopping her air, strangling her in the maze.

She choked and snorted out, then in. Water slammed up her nose and made her head sting. She tried to find her feet again, to rise above the surface, but she slipped in the grasp of her skirts.

Get air. Stop the strangler. Her hands clawed wildly in the dark maze of heavy water.

Her head popped up, slicked with her sopping hair. Hacking, she gasped in breath after breath as Meg helped her to right herself.

"We'd best not tell anyone you did this on purpose!" Meg said.

"I'm not taking the blame from your father or his sneaking, snippy, young Queen Catherine Howard!" Kat insisted.

"Hush both of you—and go to the house together—to fetch me dry clothes," Elizabeth gasped, sitting exhausted and angry on the bank. "Meg, you send Lady Rosie out with the dry things so Kat doesn't need to come back. And send Jenks to wait here with me. I daresay he's seen me in worse straits."

Both women hurried to obey. Jenks came running, his eyes wide when he saw her.

"No, I did not fall in," she told him, "and if you laugh at me, I shall ship you off forthwith to Scotland. I just had to try it."

"Sounds like me with Meg, Your Grace," he said, not daring to so much as smile. "I'd try anything to please her, but it all goes wrong."

"You offer her that power over you, and she's afraid of it, that's all. Command is not an easy thing to wield over others, but the most sobering, awesome responsibility, especially when one cares for the well-being of the other," she counseled, wringing water from her skirts and hair.

"I can't come up to her standards—that's more like it," he muttered.

" 'S blood and bones, Jenks, you are a good, brave, and deserving man. I just wish I had someone as loyal as you who would ride into hell—or at least plague London—for me. I need some answers from Gray's Inn about Jamie Barstow and Sir Christopher's reputations, not to mention Bettina Sutton's. But that dread disease sits in Londontown like a big, bloated poisonous spider, so that's the end of that, just like this is the end of my swimming."

She'd been nearly shouting, but it did feel good to get that all out, and she could always trust Jenks. "Here, help me up, my man," she said, more quietly, as she offered him her hand. "London is out of the question, so we'll simply have to make do with what we can here to flush out the maze murderer."

Her first night back at Hatfield, despite how exhausted she felt, the queen couldn't sleep. It almost seemed the place was haunted, for memories marched back and forth in her brain about the good times and the bad. From here she'd been ordered to the Tower and feared she'd never return. She'd been questioned here for her parts in Protestant plots; she'd been ignored and afraid and yet hopeful too that someday the throne could be hers, that a woman could rule alone. At dear, old Hatfield, she'd learned to survive against all odds and that was just what she meant to do again.

She must have nodded off because when she woke a woman in white was standing by her window. Her heartbeat jumped to a pounding pace. Surely, not a spectre, but . . .

It was Kat in her nightrail. She'd been sleeping in the truckle bed with Rosie against the wall of the queen's chamber, but now she walked toward the door to the hall. Rather than bothering Rosie, who was breathing heavily in sleep, Elizabeth got up, wrapped herself in her damask robe and shoved her feet in her flannel mules. She'd bring Kat back to bed herself and bother no one else.

But her old friend had quickly, quietly opened the door to the privy chamber and then to the dimly lit hall. "Just changing rooms," Kat whispered to the guard—Stackpole, not Clifford, who was down the way by Darnley's door—and the beef-wit let her pass. Granted, Elizabeth had not wanted to tell the guards how unhinged Kat could be, but she could have slapped him for letting her out in the dead of night.

Yet Elizabeth merely held up her hand to silence him and went out, too. Tomorrow would be soon enough for new commands and reprimands for her guards. At least Hatfield was far smaller and safer than the great palaces where Kat had wandered off before, but Elizabeth still could not bear to order her to be restrained or confined.

Somewhat unsteady in her bare feet, Kat went down the corridor toward the smaller, servants' rooms under the slant of eaves. Perhaps Kat was going to find Meg, for Elizabeth was not certain which chambers her people, or her cousin Margaret's, were in.

Elizabeth was just about to call to Kat when she opened a door and stood in shadows thrown by a single lantern lit within. Through the thin linen of the nightrail, the queen could see how thin and frail Kat looked, for full skirts and sleeves oft hid her shape.

"I overheard the two young men talking about you and wanted to warn you," Kat said to someone within.

"What? You are the queen's old nurse, are you not?"

Bettina's voice. Elizabeth had no notion Kat knew where to find Bettina or had business with her.

"Yes, I've been with her a long time," Kat said, her words not quite as angry as Bettina's strident tones.

"Why are you here at this hour? She hasn't sent for me? And what young men were talking about what?" Bettina demanded, her voice rising.

"The Princess Elizabeth has naught to do with this warning, but everyone will be talking soon. You've made your own bed and you must lie in it. Did you think it would be easy to wed an older man yet carry on with younger ones?"

"I—do you mean you overheard Chris Hatton speaking with someone?" Bettina stammered. "I'll get him for that."

Elizabeth pressed herself to the wall, wanting to pull Kat back, yet mesmerized by the disjointed conversation. Bettina must have come closer to the door, for her voice grew louder and her shadow leaped onto the hall floor. Wherever the confused Kat was going with this, perhaps Bettina would give something away.

"You do know that the penalty for adultery by the monarch's wife is treason and the punishment death, do you not?" Kat cried.

"Monarch's wife?" Bettina demanded.

"Your royal husband has already executed Anne Boleyn on trumped up charges of adultery, but you have truly betrayed him, so you will surely die!"

"Go away!" Bettina screamed. "Are you demented to come in here like this and—"

"Catherine Howard," Kat cried, "your ghost will haunt the castle!" The disheveled but fully dressed young woman appeared in her door and tried to shove Kat back. "And you'll deserve your fate," Kat carried on, "for taking younger lovers and cuckolding the old man. . . ."

"Kat," Elizabeth whispered, stepping forward to seize her arm, "quiet now. Sh! Back to bed."

As shocked as she already looked, Bettina gaped to see the queen. "She sleepwalks and has delusions," Elizabeth explained to Bettina, putting her arm around Kat to pull her away. Unfortunately, two doors nearby opened and faces appeared in them. One was Meg's. Elizabeth gestured to her, but saw she must be sleeping naked with a sheet wrapped under her arms, so she motioned for her to stay back.

"Come, Kat," Elizabeth coaxed. "Come with me. She's confused about Catherine Howard's ghost at Hampton Court," Elizabeth whispered to Bettina.

"But probably not confused about Chris Hatton speaking ill of me!" Bettina said in a stage whisper. She dared to pursue the queen as she hustled Kat down the hall. "I swear I'll speak to them—Sir Christopher Hatton—about this!"

"Catherine Howard," Kat muttered to Elizabeth as she huffed along, "is also the one who's been listening at keyholes, because I've seen her."

"You mean the woman you were just talking to?"

"Yes, lovey, Catherine Howard, the one I saw kissing Nicholas Culpepper in the maze back at Hampton Court."

The queen just shook her head. Nicholas Culpepper had indeed been Queen Catherine Howard's long-time paramour and had also been beheaded for treason years ago. On the scaffold Queen Catherine had made a defiant speech that she would rather be the wife of Culpepper than queen of England, the little fool. But this latest obsessive dementia of Kat's was too much for the queen to bear. It was getting so difficult to keep others from knowing how ill Kat had become.

"You mean," Elizabeth said as tears blurred her vision, "you saw that very Catherine Howard behind us in the hall"—here she turned and pointed at Bettina—"listening at keyholes?"

"That's what I said. It's not right. She should be punished and stopped."

"Whose keyholes? When?"

"Well, why don't you ask her?" Kat said sassily, pulling free from the queen to point at Bettina, who stood, hands on hips, at the turn of the hallway about ten paces back.

"You deserve a good thrashing, you strumpet!" Kat shouted at Bettina. "But as I said, you'll soon enough be executed for your sins, and we'll see who has the last word then!"

Bettina turned and fled toward her room. Numerous doors in the hallways opened, then slammed, though several faces peering out briefly registered on the queen: Mildred Cecil, Robin, Lord Darnley, Chris Hatton.

For days, the queen had fought both hysterical laughter and tears, but once back in her bedchamber, she gave in to both.

"Mildred, it is good to see you," the queen greeted Lady Cecil the next morning after breakfast as the Cecils joined her in the small, oak-paneled room she was using for her presence chamber. "My lord Cecil says you insist on leaving for Theobalds at once. Since I shall go over soon to see the site and my lord must needs stay here for now, cannot you wait a few days?"

"He's always wanted me to take a part in planning Theobalds's great house and grounds, and now I shall," Mildred replied as she rose from her curtsy and sat next to Elizabeth on the window seat as she had indicated.

"But there is nothing yet for you to do there," Cecil said, brandishing a large, rolled document as if it were a sword. "I'm having the old manor cleaned for our arrival and the plans for our future are all here."

In truth, he had come straight to Elizabeth even before breakfast, vexed that his wife had taken the sudden notion to move on to Theobalds, or if he refused that, to Stamford where the younger children were staying. Ordinarily, he would have promoted that, but had admitted to Elizabeth that he felt uneasy about Mildred's temperament and tendencies. When the queen had explained to him the upheaval with Kat and Bettina last night, they commiserated over the behavior of their loved ones even more.

"I can't believe I slept right through that row between Bettina and Kat," Cecil had said, shaking his head.

"Mildred poked her head out the door, so she heard it," the queen had explained. "I'm surprised she didn't tell you first thing this morning, as Lady Rosie says it's been noised high and low already. You don't think—is there anything about Bettina or even Kat's acting like that which would make Mildred want to flee?"

"Not that I know," Cecil had said with a slump to his shoulders that frightened her. "But then, I'm only her husband, so what do I know?"

"And I am but the queen. Indeed, I'm starting to long for the mere trials of some political revolt or international outcry to tend to instead of all these domestic worries on top of Templar's murder and my attack."

"My lord husband," Mildred said to bring Elizabeth back to the present, "Her Grace has not yet heard another reason I would leave for Theobalds. I know your dear Katherine Ashley has become dim of wit, Your Majesty, and I could take her with me and watch her closely."

Elizabeth dared not look at Cecil. The last thing on God's green earth they needed was for Mildred to tend to Kat or vice versa—or would that be good for both of them? No matter, the queen thought, she could not bear to part with Kat.

"As is my custom all these years, dear Mildred, I will keep Kat close to me," the queen explained. "Since she becomes confused in familiar surroundings, I fear how she might react in new ones. However, I would deem it a great favor if you would help to keep Kat calm, to spend some time with Lady Rosie Radcliffe here as she tends Kat. And in a day or two, I shall take a small party to accompany you and your lord to see the site on which great Theobalds will stand and—"

Someone rapped loudly on the door. "I've sent a guard to fetch Bettina," she explained to the Cecils, "and he's been overlong."

"Then I shall be on my way to see Kat," Mildred said, rising as Cecil answered the door. The yeoman guard Stackpole entered, which reminded Elizabeth she would rid herself of him the moment they got back to London.

"Beggin' your pardon, but Mistress Sutton's gone, Your Majesty," Stackpole blurted.

"Gone where?"

"Don't know, Majesty. Could be out for a morning walk, but your own strewing herb mistress says she don't think she even went back to bed last night after the set-to everyone's talking about."

"Then send Meg to me—and find Mistress Sutton!"

Meg soon appeared of her own accord. "I heard Bettina's

gone missing," she said as Cecil closed the door so the three of them were alone. "I don't think she ever went back to bed."

"But she headed down the hall that way."

"After she carried on so, I thought I'd better keep an eye on her," Meg explained. "Just in case you sent for me to help with Kat, the state that she was in, too, I got garbed and sat in the hall, nodding off 'til dawn to see if Bettina came back, but she didn't. That's what I'm telling you."

"One step forward, then two back in this—this labyrinth," Elizabeth muttered as she began to pace. "What I like least of all is the way Templar went missing the same way Bettina has, and you know how we found him. Yet I trusted Templar, and I do *not* trust Bettina."

Both Cecil and Meg stood back, silent, as if waiting to see which way the royal wind blew. The queen stopped, whirled, and sat.

"Meg, fetch me some sort of calming herbs for this headache I'm getting. Cecil, send someone to fetch Jenks to me so I can have him search the surrounding roads for Bettina. She protested that I not send her back to London, but that, despite the plague, could have been a diversionary tactic. It is where her home is, where she could gather up Templar's books to sell so she could flee, especially if she's guilty of something dire."

"I didn't have the chance yet to tell her I'd buy his library *in toto*," Cecil explained as he headed for the door and Meg darted out. "When I mentioned helping Bettina that way, Mildred wouldn't hear of it, not with the coming expenditures to make Theobalds a fine place."

"Such uncharitableness is not like her. Cecil, wait," the queen insisted as he put his hand to the door latch. "I must tell you something that Bettina said about Mildred's problems, but it really begins with you."

He froze, his hand outstretched. His eyes widened, then narrowed. "With me, Your Grace? And what could Bettina know of Mildred's problems?"

Elizabeth walked closer to him, studying his face in the slant of morning light. "She said that Templar had mentioned Mildred was somehow jealous of your first wife—and her son Tom, your heir."

"Nonsense. A bright, sensible woman like Mildred, jealous of a long-dead woman? Now, the part about Tom, I understand, because Mildred's been at sixes and sevens since *her* firstborn surviving son was such a delicate child. She frets for his bent back, and the way his legs are a bit uneven."

"And don't you, too, my lord?"

"Of course, I'd like him to be hale and hearty, but he is my son with my dear Mildred, and I fully intend not only to provide for him, but richly too, beginning with Theobalds being his inheritance someday. And," he added, finally dropping his arm from its stiff stance, "I've learned with Tom that the strong outer trapping of a fine-looking lad can belie the weak character within. I have vowed to myself that I will spend more time with Robert than I did with Tom—perhaps that was what he needed, not just my carping at his flaws."

"And have you told Mildred about your love for her son and her?"

"It's something she surely knows," he insisted. "As for the notion she's jealous of my first wife, that is daft indeed, though that's how Mildred's been acting lately. I shall think on it and speak with her, come hell or high water," he promised as he opened the door and went out to fetch Jenks.

His last words echoed in the queen's mind. Lately she'd known a bit of hell and high water herself.

Jenks set out on the road to London with orders to turn back if he did not overtake Bettina before the capital's outskirts. Elizabeth's guards and servants searched the grounds and surrounding forest for any sign of the woman, though the queen knew everyone was murmuring that the last time they had searched for a Sutton they had found a corpse. Like a ghost into thin air, Bettina seemed to have vanished.

At noon, Elizabeth gave the order for the search to cease and for everyone to return to their duties. The scent of the lavender and violet water with which Meg had bathed her forehead had somewhat soothed her, though each time she frowned, she felt her head pain again.

"I'm more sure than ever now that she was guilty of Templar's death," Elizabeth told Cecil as she finally settled down to signing warrants and state papers. "And perhaps even of the attack on me, which must have been a spur-of-the-moment decision when she saw me in the maze where she had gone to be alone—or to meet someone." The scratch of her quill pen on parchment seemed incredibly loud now that the hue and cry outside had ceased. "If she dares go back into London to abscond with Templar's books and perhaps head for a ship to flee to the continent to sell them, she deserves the plague if it seizes her!"

"I still cannot believe she murdered Templar," Cecil said, shaking his head as he handed her the next document. "She obviously had the best of both worlds, her adoring law students and Templar's support, so why eliminate him?"

"Because, my lord, she must have found someone she wanted more, someone who would have her if she were free. And then, when Kat exploded at her like that last night with such accusations, which though demented were yet close to the mark, Bettina must have decided to flee. I really think—"

A scream shredded the silence outside. Elizabeth leaped to her feet and headed for the door with Cecil right behind. "That must be Bettina," Elizabeth said, yanking open the door before her guards could. "Jenks has brought her back against her will."

Forcing herself to walk circumspectly, the queen descended the great staircase, cursing because the short, slatted gate which kept the larger dogs on the ground floor was latched. Cecil scrambled to get it open, and they went outside even as voices and hubbub filled the air again.

Elizabeth squinted into the sudden sun. Meg stood again in the center of the knot garden, which she'd partly tamed since yesterday. She had no clippers in her hands, but was pointing down into the central hedges which still looked thick and ragged.

The queen came closer as Cecil and guards fell in around her. Darnley and his mother, Robin and others, Lady Rosie without Kat or Mildred hurried toward the knot garden, too.

"I—I found her," Meg gasped out, wide-eyed when she saw the queen. "Just lying here . . . like she's asleep—Bettina, but she won't wake up. She could be drunk, but I think she's dead."

Chapter the Twelfth

"KEEP EVERYONE BACK," THE QUEEN ORDERED ROBIN, but did not protest when Cecil waded with her into the knee-high knot garden.

Bettina lay on her back, her hands crossed over her breasts, her eyes closed and features slack as if in untroubled sleep. Her usually olive-hued skin was as pale as purest candle wax. Neatly aligned in a twist of yew and rosemary shrubs, she was only visible head to waist with her lower torso greatly obscured.

"Meg," the queen managed to choke out, "see if she's dead."

Meg bent to feel for a neck pulse. "Dead and starting to stiffen. Beginning rigor mortis, so that means she's been gone at least an hour, maybe as many as six. And so cold, even though the day's warming fast."

"I warrant she's been here at least since before dawn," Elizabeth surmised, "perhaps since she may have chosen to walk outside last night after Kat threatened h——"

Elizabeth bit her next words off; her stomach cartwheeled. Dear God in heaven, surely those who had beheld Kat's berating Bettina in the hall last night would not take the old woman's rambling warning to heart. Although only Elizabeth had heard Kat say that Bettina should be punished for listening at keyholes, surely every eavesdropper had overheard Kat's threat that Bettina would soon be executed for her sins.

To convince everyone that Kat thought she was addressing a woman beheaded nearly twenty years ago might help people to excuse Kat's behavior, but it would also be admitting Kat should be locked up as being *non compos mentis*. Worse, her courtiers might think dear old Kat should be punished for this young woman's death. And if they thought Kat had killed Bettina, would they wonder about Templar's demise, too?

Standing in the heart of the knot garden, Elizabeth suddenly felt exposed. Beyond agonizing about Kat, she had a second slaying on her lands, in her living labyrinths. The murderer was making a mockery of her attempts to solve a crime and to control her court and kingdom. She felt taunted and threatened, but she intended to fight back.

"It appears that Mistress Sutton has died but how is the question." The queen raised her voice to the circle of curious courtiers and servants. Her eyes skimmed the crowd; some gasped, some elbowed each other and whispered. Margaret and Darnley had appeared, looking smug as usual. Ned was here, but she didn't see Kat or Mildred, only a dismayed Rosie, now accompanied by Chris and Jamie. Both young men looked shocked.

"Guards, fetch a winding sheet, and keep everyone well back," Elizabeth commanded.

"Shall I summon the local authorities again, Your Grace?" Robin called from the shrub border.

"Of course, we must ascertain the exact cause of Mistress Sutton's death, but I shall tell you when we need the authorities. Send someone immediately to find Jenks on the London road where he has gone searching for her. He has orders to ride no closer to the city than Moorgate." Robin hastened to obey.

"Your Majesty," Lady Rosie said, leaning on Jamie's arm as the guards began to urge the crowd away, "it can't be the pestilence which has killed Mistress Sutton, can it?"

Everyone froze, poised as if to flee.

"Set your hearts at ease for that," Elizabeth assured them. "Though some victims of the black death seem quite well until they suddenly die, the plague is not in these parts. As for the more blatant form of the pestilence, we have all seen Mistress Sutton with us lately, not showing any signs of fever, spotting, or black buboes. With her husband newly dead, she may have died of a broken heart, for she was much distraught. I charge you to pray for her soul. We will arrange a formal inquiry of this matter." Seemingly calm and assured, she stared them down until they moved away again and began to disperse.

"Now *that* was a politic answer," Cecil muttered. "Surely, we can link this to her husband's death and your attack. I cannot believe the audacity of someone to leave bodies in your mazes as if daring us to solve the puzzle."

"It is someone," the queen added, turning to look down at poor Bettina again, "we have brought here with us. Hell's gates, even Hatfield's too large to oversee with too many folk!"

"Since we can't go to London or back to Hampton Court, we could leave even more of your entourage behind and move into the manorhouse at Theobalds to defend ourselves better, Your Grace."

"I shall think on it, but we have much to do here first. Meg, get that sheet the guards brought out and hold it up to block out prying gazes from the upper windows. Meanwhile, before she's moved inside, we must see if there are clues at this site. As for her body, I see no strangulation marks on her throat or evidence she's been struck with something heavy, though we will completely examine her inside."

Elizabeth stooped amidst the interlacings of shrubs and roses to push the growth farther back from the upper torso. Indeed, no wounds, no blood visible at first glance, at least not on the front of Bettina nor staining the soil around her. And no scent of death yet, only the faint odor of the roses—or was it cloves?

"See why I thought she might be drunk, Your Grace?" Meg interrupted her agonizing. "There's that goblet rolled a ways from her left elbow as if she put it down when she was finished drinking."

For the first time, the queen noted a plain pewter goblet on its side in the soil. Elizabeth pulled her handkerchief out and carefully lifted it. "Lest it be a weapon with blood smears from the back of her head or such—or in case we can tell what was in it," she said, tilting the goblet so the morning sun lit its depths.

"Whatever it was, it has run out and left neither stain nor scent," Cecil noted, peering into it over her shoulder. She handed it to him; he wrapped it more completely and stuck it by its thick stem in his belt.

"I don't believe," the queen continued, "she merely fell drunk among these shrubs and died, for none of them lie under her and all above, as if they were arranged to hide her after she was laid here."

"Which means," Cecil surmised, "she could have been murdered elsewhere and then, in the dark of night, her body arranged to give some sort of misdirection or, as we surmised earlier, a message from the murderer."

"More specifically, an insult, a challenge, or a threat." As she spoke, Elizabeth parted the shrubs and thorny roses covering the lower parts of Bettina's body. The queen gasped, and Cecil swore. Meg jumped so in surprise she dropped the sheet.

The corpse's skirts and petticoats were hacked off thigh high to expose her bare legs, and the hedge clippers were stuck into the ground between her splayed knees.

Jenks had not seen anyone resembling Bettina, or even the horse which was missing, along the London road. He'd stopped at two inns to see if she'd gone in for refreshment, but no one recalled her.

"An' we would a 'membered her if'n we'd a seen her," the keeper of a flea-bitten Rose and Crown on the very outskirts of the capital told him. But what Jenks had liked about the place was that the horses in the stables were better cared for than the people. The burly innkeeper was a man after his own heart and would do well to abet his plan.

"Aye, the woman is a bit of a looker," Jenks admitted, trying to jog the man's memory and get in his good graces. "Built pigeon-breasted, she is, with a ripe body."

"Naw, that's not why I would a 'membered her, not in these times," the man protested. "She'd be stupid as a cow, if she's heading *toward* London 'stead of *'way* from it, that's what I'd a 'membered. 'Fore folks were halted by a new ord'nance closing the city gates to outward traffic, people be only hustlin' out, not in, man!"

"The gates have been closed?"

"God's truth, they have. City 'fficials tryin' to keep the pest'lence bottled up inside best they can. Thank God Almighty I don't live or work in there."

That settled it, Jenks thought. At first he'd meant to leave his horse here so he could tell Her Grace he hadn't ridden farther than Moorgate, as she'd ordered. But now, no way was he taking the fine animal into plague London where people could actually be hungry enough to eat a horse.

At all costs, Jenks was determined to help the queen find and question Bettina Sutton. But in case he failed at that, he meant to search her chambers, and somehow discover whether or not Her Grace could trust Chris Hatton and Jamie Barstow. She had said plain out she needed someone to go to Gray's Inn and get information on those two. Besides, with Meg not wanting him, he'd dedicate his life even more to serving the queen's every need.

"I need to board my horse here for a few hours, maybe a day and be sure, when I come back, he's still here, been fed and watered, too," Jenks said, taking an entire crown from his purse. "And they'll be more of this for you if it's like I say."

"Sure, if'n you're not goin' into the city, then coming back out. Don't need no one here could be carryin' plague."

"Just looking for the lady outside the walls and gates, because

I know she'd not go in," Jenks lied without blinking an eye. Ned would have been proud of him and dubbed it merely play-acting.

"Hey, just don't try handin' me that coin straight out," the innkeeper protested, jumping back. Several louts standing around leaped away, too. "Don't care if you claim you been out in the country, can't trust touching coins might a been in the city. Drop it in this here pot of vinegar, case it's got the plague on it."

"Right," Jenks told him and dropped the coin in the sour-smelling pot the man held out at arm's length. "You just can't tell who's been where."

"We must discover as much as we can from examining her body, then properly reclothe it before we summon the authorities," the queen told Meg. "These hacked-off skirts are shameful and insulting."

Cecil had left the first floor withdrawing chamber where her guards had laid Bettina on a long table, so Meg and the queen were alone with the cadaver. Since it was a room with little light, the queen had ordered lanterns placed at the woman's head and foot. They flickered to throw the body into shifting shadows, as if Bettina yet breathed or moved.

"Kat used to help with things like this," Meg murmured, looking suddenly squeamish as she repeatedly wiped her palms on her skirts.

"At least," Elizabeth said, clearing her throat, "she wasn't cut or stabbed with the clippers, though that's what I expected when I saw them stuck like that—there."

She pointed to Bettina's spread knees, which had gone rigid. Had her legs just relaxed in death like that, or had her murderer spread them to leave some message or threat beyond the hacked skirts? If they could find the several circles of material cut off, they'd have their man—or woman.

"If all her layers of skirt and petticoats were cut off with those hedge clippers, someone's used to handling those big, awkward things," Meg said, "and it's not me."

"I suppose those ragged sliced edges of material could have been done with a sword or knife. Now, enough of avoiding what we must do. Let's be quick but thorough." The queen forced herself to touch Bettina. "No bruises or scars on her legs anywhere I can see," she observed.

"Nor here," Meg said as she unlaced the points which attached her sleeves and bodice to bare her white arms. "She's so stiff we'll have to turn her completely over to see the backs of her arms. And to unlace her bodice itself—if you think we should. You don't really believe she could have died of a broken heart, do you, Your Grace?"

"I've heard of it—or perhaps she died of fright, of being swiftly, suddenly seized. I thought my heart could beat right out of my chest when I was attacked."

They worked to turn Bettina facedown. "What is all that?" the queen cried, darting away in alarm from the purple bruises on the backs of Bettina's thighs. "Not the beginning of the black plague swellings!"

"No, for I've seen this before. I still may not remember some of my past, but I recall helping prepare my grandmother for burial, and she had these marks. *Livor mortis*, it's called, where the blood pools and settles in the lowest parts of the body once the heart stops beating."

Holding her breath, the queen came closer to examine the discolorations of Bettina's pale skin, along the backs of her thighs, even on her back as Meg unlaced her bodice.

"So it's natural, you mean?" she asked at last.

"Natural if one's dead and lay in a face-up position right after giving up the ghost. And I see no other kind of marks on her back under this bodice, or in front," she said, holding Bettina's shoulders up to peer at her chest. "Well," she muttered, "she's not gone stiff there anyway."

"I can't fathom being so large-breasted, not when I—you and I—are both so small," Elizabeth whispered.

"I can't fathom her getting in the flat-fronted gowns everyone wears. She's built so unstylish, but I think men like it better, no matter what women think. Oh, pardon, Your Grace."

"I think with Bettina they liked it better, and she took advantage of that," the queen said with a sigh as Meg relaced Bettina's bodice. No use putting a new one on her, though they had sent Cecil to get a skirt of Mildred's to cover poor Bettina so they could hand her over to the local coroner. The queen could hardly take one from Meg, and her own garments and most courtiers' clothes were too richly woven for Bettina's burial.

"So," the queen said, helping cover the corpse with the sheet again, "what could she die from if there is not a foreign wound or mark on her?"

"Poison's all I can think of," Meg admitted, "and she did have that goblet."

The queen shuddered as her gaze snagged Meg's wide stare.

In the year Elizabeth became queen they'd faced a poison threat here at Hatfield. That murderer was long dead, yet the mere memory haunted the queen.

"If it was poison," Elizabeth whispered, "that could mean we are indeed looking for a murderer of random advantage, one who changes weapons at will, using whatever person just happens to be in his or her path to murder for the mad thrill of it. But I think not. There is method to these attacks, especially to use some sort of maze. What frightens me is that we have someone who perversely plans—*and* enjoys the thrill of the kill, because of some deeply harbored hatred—perhaps hatred of me."

"Any way we reason it out, the maze murderer's outfoxing us so far."

Unfortunately, Meg was absolutely right.

He was no numbskull, no matter what people thought, Jenks told himself. So, though he had now followed Her Grace's orders to ride clear to Moorgate to try to find Bettina on the main road from Hatfield to the capital, he was not going through the plague city. Thank God, the Inns of Court were on the northern edge of London, and Gray's the farthest out with fields and hills beyond, so he could go in that way and avoid the worst. Traveling afoot, he'd be in and out quick and safe with nary a brush with the Black Death.

He walked westward through fields and down deserted lanes with the sinking sun in his eyes. He'd have to put up at Gray's for one night and head out at dawn after talking to whomever could tell him about Bettina, Chris Hatton, and Jamie Barstow.

Nothing complicated in that, he tried to buck himself up. All would be well.

From this view on slightly elevated ground, it was hard to believe the city suffered. Yet he could see that the usually heavy traffic on the distant Thames was near nothing. As he looked down Chancery Lane toward Holborn, he paused, one hand on his sword. So few were in the streets. London lay before him like a ghost town.

Still, he hustled down the lane toward Gray's, blessing his lucky stars again that he need not go into the city proper. But nothing looked proper about London today. The few folk who scurried by glanced back over their shoulders as if someone were stalking them.

More than once he almost turned to flee, though folks had said the pestilence this year was not as bad as last. That was not saying much, since over twenty thousand deaths had been recorded in London last summer. And anyone who caught the death had a less than half chance of pulling through.

He told himself he would not fear, for he was on a crusade for the queen. Besides, if he took sick, suffered, and died, maybe Meg Milligrew would finally realize how much he should have meant to her. But he had things to do for the one woman who did appreciate him.

Of course, he'd have to find a way to report what he learned here without actually approaching the queen until a proper period passed so he knew he wasn't carrying the pestilence. Good thing Her Grace insisted everyone on her Privy Plot Council must know how to read and write. That bastard Ned had taught him when the queen commanded it, one of his few kind deeds ever. So Jenks would only go so far toward Hatfield and send a note in with his horse. Once that smart stallion got close enough to the royal stables, he'd find his way. With a tight smile, Jenks pictured how heartbroken the queen—and maybe Meg—would be when his mount came back without him.

"Now," the queen said as she assembled her already decimated Privy Plot Council, this time also without Jenks, "we must investigate Bettina's demise without panicking anyone about a murderer loose in our midst."

"That will be a good trick, as I'm starting to feel panicked," Ned said. "I can't believe Jenks hasn't hightailed it back here yet when he didn't find Bettina."

"I'm sure he has a good reason," Meg piped up.

"Lord Dudley has sent a man after him," the queen explained, "but he has not returned yet either. By the way, I am considering bringing Lady Rosie Radcliffe into our midst at the next meeting, if there are no objections."

"To replace Kat?" Meg asked.

"No one replaces Kat, or ever could."

"Then Kat hasn't become suspect?" Ned asked, putting his hands up as if to ward off an attack from the queen. "I mean, I realize you said at an early meeting to 'leave Kat out of it,' Your Grace, but I'm not sure we can now. She admitted she sneaked out at night to speak to Templar in the maze, evidently just before he was murdered, then she threatened Bettina and *voilà*—"

"Ridiculous," Elizabeth cut in. "She was in bed in my chamber during the time Bettina must have been dispatched and placed in the knot garden."

That settled that, she thought, but she knew full well, though she'd put Kat to bed last night, she'd finally fallen asleep only to find her dressed and having breakfast when she and Rosie awakened. At night, the hall guards changed and even nodded off at times. But Elizabeth knew deep down, despite Kat's dementia, she would harm no one. It was Mildred Cecil she was starting to suspect.

"My Lord Cecil, I hope Mildred slept through all of this, so as not to upset her."

"She was still asleep this morning, Your Grace, so I haven't even had the opportunity to tell her this tragic news."

Steadily, almost defiantly, his eyes met his queen's stare. They both knew Mildred did not like Bettina. Perhaps, Elizabeth thought, as she broke their gaze first, if Mildred was dangerous, she should send her to Theobalds as she'd requested. Had she actually asked to go because she wanted to flee a murder she knew about before anyone else? But to think that the staunchly moral Mildred would harm someone was as insane as blaming the befuddled Kat.

"What did the local authorities say when they came to claim and examine Bettina's body?" Meg asked.

"I meant to begin with that but was distracted," Elizabeth said.

"I'll bet they declared it murder outright," Ned put in, "especially when they heard her husband was recently dispatched in a maze, too. And if they knew about your attack, then—"

"I did not tell them any of that. Besides, we don't know for certain," Elizabeth challenged, "that Bettina *was* murdered or that it was *in* the knot garden, and it's not quite the same as a maze."

Everyone's heads had snapped toward her, even Cecil's. Ned's jaw dropped before he closed his mouth. Obviously, they were surprised, but once again, she had not been impressed with the rural bailiff and his men. Nor did she want it noised far and wide that she had been attacked, probably by the same murderer. And truth be told, she'd do anything to protect Kat from being questioned.

She was beginning to panic. She was going to lose control. Even to be considering those dearest to herself and Cecil as people with motives to eliminate the chatty, promiscuous Bettina terrified her.

"I want an independent investigation of Bettina's body," Elizabeth explained further, "without the authorities being swayed by what happened to me or Master Sutton. We must see if they can discern a natural cause of death, or if it must indeed be poison. I gave them permission to bury her in St. Alban's, and they will report to me soon, but I—we—cannot wait for their findings.

"So, let us turn our thoughts toward the relationships between Bettina and her husband's former students—his younger students, I mean, of course, my lord," she added with a nod at Cecil.

"I believe," Cecil put in, "other than Lord Darnley, Chris Hatton and Jamie Barstow are our best bets for a culprit."

"You are no doubt right," Elizabeth said. "In the hall last night, Bettina immediately blamed Chris Hatton for gossiping about her and even declared she'd get him for that. Perhaps she went looking for him, they argued . . . though I cannot believe it of him."

"But he's ever with Master Barstow," Ned put in. "And it's

obvious Barstow's been his guard as well as valet and tutor at times, so he's probably the man to question, too."

"I am suspicious of the young men," Cecil said, "Darnley too, because of the cut-off clothing and the clippers stuck in the ground as they were. It seems to me to be the work of some randy young man who wanted to insult Bettina for her carnal and seductive nature. Not that I believe her murderer actually ravished her, for then, why bother with that bold display?"

"So you aren't implying she was ravished?" Elizabeth asked.

"I certainly have no way of knowing that. It could be that the mere message of the clippers and exposed legs *were* the assault on her person."

"Then that hardly rules out a woman murderer," Ned said. Elizabeth saw Cecil glare at him, though she too would have liked to order Ned from the room.

And, Elizabeth thought, though she agreed with Cecil's smooth reasoning, the sexual innuendos from the way the corpse was displayed hardly pointed to a woman assailant—unless it was a woman who wanted to publicly punish and shame Bettina for her promiscuity.

Across the table Meg hugged herself and shuddered. "At least the murderer didn't cut the poor thing up with the clippers. If I only hadn't left them there the day before . . ."

"Don't blame yourself," Elizabeth said. "But, needless to say, we are looking for the bottoms of Bettina's skirts. They may be merely hidden or someone may have kept them for a sort of trophy. Meg, I want each inch of that overgrown knot garden searched for them."

"We can at least trace this," Cecil said, producing from his satchel the goblet they'd recovered from the murder site.

"But it's plain—commonplace," Ned observed, "like a hundred others I've seen. Maybe it was even Bettina's. Have we considered suicide? I mean, she was emotionally volatile, bereaved, and then made distraught by Kat's claims which shamed her with courtiers and her queen looking on."

"I believe she was too strong and clever to take her own life," Elizabeth said, though she realized that solution would solve so many problems. "But, if that goblet did hold poison, I vow I will find whether it was hers or someone helped her die. Her room has been sealed, but tonight—when a hundred eyes won't watch me—I will search through the few possessions Bettina brought with her to Hatfield."

"Well," Meg said, "I can't see the Countess of Lennox or Lord Darnley having a goblet plain as that, though that hardly lets them off the hook."

"But I can still see this whole thing amusing Lord Darnley," Ned said. "He's wily and slippery as an eel, and I believe it pleases him to play games. Perhaps, like Templar used to, he fancies puzzles or conundrums."

"He has not half the wit Templar Sutton had, though he'll be thoroughly questioned again," Elizabeth declared, hitting the table with her fist. "I've had my yeoman guard Clifford watching him, and he says Darnley took an evening stroll late last night, after the hubbub with Kat and Bettina."

"Though," Ned added, "with Darnley's proclivities for late night assignations, he may have been meeting a man."

"But," the queen countered, "if Bettina was out wandering the grounds and Darnley ran into her, he could have killed her to plague us all again. 'S blood, I didn't mean to say it like that."

"Clifford didn't follow Darnley when he went out?" Cecil asked.

"I had told him to stay put in the hall of their wing and note all their comings and goings, which he did faithfully."

"I will do anything I can to help," Cecil said with a fierce frown that contorted his features, "but if I begin to interrogate courtiers, it will get out we're investigating on an official level." He looked so tired and careworn that Elizabeth's heart went out to him despite her own inner chaos.

"And, I suppose," she added with a deep sigh, "if I go after everyone broadside, they will whisper that I am trying to pin both Templar and Bettina's deaths on someone else to protect Kat. But we must persevere, and I am the one most able to get away with an inquisition, at least of Chris, Jamie, and that damned Darnley. I swear, as soon as I can discern Darnley is not a murderer, at least, he's going to be sent straight to Scotland!"

She sighed again as everyone headed for the door. "Did you reclothe poor Bettina properly?" Elizabeth asked Meg, the last one to leave the room.

"Yes, Your Grace, with an extra black skirt of Mildred Cecil's her lord brought me. One Lady Cecil won't want, he said, as it was stuffed in a rag bag, but he had their servant steam it out. It's a good, somber black, not fancy but of good stuff. It had some snags in it, a hole too, but I made sure that was under her. You know, maybe it would be best if the coroner declares she took her own life, though that's a vile sin and..."

But Elizabeth had not listened to Meg after she mentioned the hole in Mildred's black gown, one she'd evidently hidden away. Yes, without telling Cecil the real reason, she must send Mildred, as she'd asked, to Theobalds, then go there herself to question her forthwith.

Chapter the Thirteenth

 "BUT THAT'S DREADFUL ABOUT BETTINA," MILDRED told her husband as they ate a private dinner together. "First Templar, then Bettina. Who could have held such a grudge against the two of them, my lord?"

"All I can say is that the local authorities have been summoned. As for grudges . . ."

His voice trailed off, though Mildred could tell he had something to say. Her stomach in knots, she bided her time, forcing herself to keep eating the fine pigeon pie which might as well be filled with sawdust.

"Grudges," Will began again, "especially those that are long-festering, can come out in strange ways, I warrant. Mildred, I realize that since Robert's birth you've been fretting about how he compares to Tom—"

"Fretting? More like foaming at the mouth, like some sort of mad dog, isn't that what you really think?" she challenged, clinking her spoon against her pewter plate. Yet she was relieved the conversation had not taken another turn, for this was familiar jousting ground.

"And I was wondering if what might be bothering you, too, could stem from the fact that I wed his mother in the rashness of youth, when it was ill-advised, yet I persevered."

"Indeed you did," she said, rising and walking to the window to gaze out over the sunny grounds of Hatfield. "Your tutors at Cambridge were appalled, I hear, that their brilliant student was ruining his reputation, and I know your father nearly disowned you."

"True—that's true. Because I went through such a bad streak, you think I'd countenance Tom's caperings, but I've been so hard on him, not wanting him to make the same mistakes."

"Caperings? Seducing virgins from respectable families and stealing from his tutor's money box when you sent him to study on the continent is mere caperings?"

"Do not sway from the subject at hand this time. I'm admitting I made mistakes back then. But can it yet vex you that I wed Mary Cheke against all odds?"

She knew she would lose control, but she couldn't help it. "Does it bother me that I know full well she was the great love and passion of your life?" she screeched.

He looked astounded and appalled. Had the man, one of the most able in the queen's kingdom, never considered that his love for his beloved first wife produced a strong son and his mere duty with his second respected wife a dead son and then a sickly one?

"You are much mistaken, Mildred, but I—I see your reasoning," he stammered at last.

"It's not reasoning, my lord, as educated as I may be. It is my heart talking, not my head. How you yet must long for her, the woman who—though she was an innkeeper's daughter—made you risk your entire future for her."

"But Mildred," he said, getting up from the table so fast his chair knocked over onto the floor. He left it there and came toward her, arms outstretched, palms up. "Mildred," he began again, "all I knew was a wild beating in my blood then, and the foolish defiance of my youth. I may have lusted once for Mary but it is you I chose with much forethought, you whom I respect, honor, and deeply admire."

"Respect and honor, even admire?" She smacked her hands on her skirts so hard they bounced. "Templar supposedly had all that from you, too, and Bettina had—"

She bit off her words and raced to the door before she could say more. But when she opened it to run out, the queen's fool and principal player Ned Topside stood there, hat in hand.

"Pardon my lord and Lady Cecil," the actor said, sweeping off a plumed cap. "Her Majesty has decided that Lady Cecil may go to Theobalds if she wishes, and she'll provide an escort. But she needs you, my lord, to stay here on state business."

Mildred noted that Ned lifted his eyebrows as if in some signal to her husband. "Though it pains me and my lord to be apart," she said before Will could get a word in, "tell Her Grace that I shall gratefully obey and be gone within the hour. No doubt, my lord, Her Majesty has need of you right now."

"As a matter of fact..." Topside said and gestured toward the hall.

"It heartens me you will have some time there to appreciate the place and to see that the manorhouse is in order for the queen's visit," Will said as he grabbed his satchel and his hat. He was no doubt relieved to ship her away so there would be no more outbursts. That suited her, for she wanted out of here.

"I'll be over to Theobalds to see you as soon as possible," Will added, "and I'll bring the building plans."

Mildred could see his usual cool control was ready to boil over. "By all means, bring the building plans," she said, and closed the door a bit too hard behind him.

But he opened it again. "I forgot to tell you that we needed a good but sober black skirt with which to clothe poor Mistress Sutton to face the coroner and then for burial, so I took a black one you had evidently cast off. I didn't think, since the poor wretch was dead, that you would mind."

Fortunately for him, he closed the door quickly, because she heaved a pewter plate at it as hard as she could. But when she realized which black skirt he meant, she shouted for her servant and began to pack in earnest.

Jenks's hopes fell. The Inns of Court looked as deserted as the rest of the city. Worse, just a few doors beyond the sprawl of Gray Inn's buildings and courtyards he spotted a tell-tale bundle of straw hung from a window to signify an infected house. Quickly, he ducked down an alley that ran beside the main building of Gray's. A black rat darted across his path, then veered back toward him. He kicked at it, then turned through the first door he found open into the paved central courtyard.

"Halloo! Anybody here?" he called out only to have his voice echo off the walls. "Halloo!"

The silence and solemnity of the place impressed Jenks. The Inns of Court, including Gray's, Lincoln's, and Middle and Inner Temple, were collectively called the Third University of England for the learning of law. Twice he'd been with the queen's party when she'd been entertained at Gray's, one the day she'd plucked Chris Hatton out of his student life here. The place was usually aswarm with students. He couldn't believe they'd all fled since it seemed so safe and sheltered here.

As the sun set, he found a lantern, but not a bite of food. He wandered through the wilderness of brick or timber-and-plaster walls, his feet echoing on slate, stone, or oaken floors. He looked in the dining hall, the chapel, and the library, wondering if Templar Sutton's books were part of this massive sea of them, maybe half a hundred, all told. He felt crushed he'd not find anyone to question and no food either but at least he had a light.

As he headed out of the library, a dark figure blocked his path. Tall, thin, the man raised a cudgel.

"Hold there!" Jenks cried, crouching to spring or flee.

"State your name and business," the crisp voice cracked out.

"Ned Jenkins of Norfolk, a friend of former student Chris Hatton. He told me I could put up here while passing through."

Jenks amazed himself. It was always the clever actor Ned who invented people and played parts, but it was too late now to take the straight and honest way.

"Passing through plague London?" the man challenged. Then he added, "Certes, I remember 'Handsome Hatton,' as they dubbed him." He stowed his cudgel back in his belt. "Name's Hugh Scott, night porter here, pretty much the only one left to keep an eye on things with bands of thieves and ransackers about and all. So, how's he doing at court—and that friend of his went along, too?"

"Jamie Barstow, you mean?"

"Aye, Jamie Barstow. He was more my style, one foot firm on the servants' rung of the ladder, but the other leg up. Hey then, I was about to go mad as a Bedlamite, alone in this big rabbit's warren of a place, so what the deuce, I'll put you up one night."

Maybe there was some benefit to lies, Jenks thought. This man might not have believed him if he'd said he came for the queen, and in a way, he hadn't. Elizabeth Tudor would have his head for sure if she knew he'd disobeyed her to come into off-limits London—unless he could get what she needed out of this man.

"We don't know exactly what we're looking for, do we?" Meg asked the queen as they searched Bettina's goods in her tiny, slant-ceilinged room under Hatfield's eaves late that night.

"Another wretched surprise, I suppose," Elizabeth muttered as she ransacked the single, small coffer while Meg stripped the bed down to its web of supporting cords so she could probe the mattress and sheets.

"I hate to say this," the queen admitted, "but I'd give a country castle to turn up a suicide note, saying she murdered her husband and couldn't live with the shame so she killed herself. But not with those hacked off skirts and those clippers, she didn't, and the murderer wanted us to know that. He—or she—lives by his own set of perverse rules, as in some hide-and-seek-in-the-maze game we're supposed to be playing.

"Look," she went on, delving deeper into the coffer. "She brought Templar's garments and goods here with her. I should have known she had a certain affection for him—unless she just kept them to sell later." She flipped through a law book in Latin in case something were secreted within; she couldn't believe her good fortune when a piece of paper fluttered out.

"I don't think she's the bookish sort," Meg muttered. "That's probably Templar's notes."

"No," the queen said as she skimmed it, "it's a note to Chris Hatton, and, I warrant, in Bettina's hand. It must be very recent or at least she's hidden it here recently. Otherwise Templar could have found it."

" 'I never meant to shame you or tarnish your new path here at court,' " Elizabeth read. "So, she wrote it either here or at Hampton. 'But I cannot keep from wishing you would smile on me, instead of her—Her Majesty, I mean.' "

"So she did have a motive to attack you," Meg cried.

"Enough of one to strangle her sovereign? I wonder why she didn't send this note, or if this is just a copy or draft. That is probably the case as there is no more, and that can't be the end of it."

"Mayhap the end of it was that she decided to eliminate you in some sort of demented jealousy over Lord Hatton's devotion to you. Or she meant to make you grateful to her by appearing to help you after she's the one who really hurt you. Once she kills poor Templar, she hopes you'll keep her at court in gratitude and sympathy for your own salvation, where she can pursue Lord Hatton. But when she tells him or gives him such a note, they argue and he—"

"Meg, you leap too far afield. If it is Chris Hatton who killed her, it must have been an accident, for I cannot believe it of him. And then there is the problem of Jamie, for he's ever protective of his friend."

"Look, Your Grace, Bettina had this tiny filigreed box of cloves, and it is Lord Hatton who uses those."

"With about half of the court," the queen clipped out and turned back to the coffer. The maze murderer simply could not be Chris, and not only because he seemed so loyal and honest: truth was, he didn't have the wit to pull it all off—did he?

Meg's gasp made Elizabeth look up again. "What now?"

"Your Grace, there's gillyflower petals in her pomander. See? Smell it?"

The moment Meg thrust the netted pomander on its waist ribbon toward the queen, the scent brought so much back, including that day in the haunted gallery at Hampton Court when she fancied Catherine Howard's ghost passed by.

"But the Suttons had barely arrived at court that day someone might have eavesdropped at Mary Sidney's keyhole to hear I was meeting Robin in the maze," Elizabeth said, reasoning aloud. "Surely, Bettina had not found her way to me through that vast palace so quickly, even before I walked them through the maze. It cannot be. But I am going to face down Chris Hatton first thing in the morning with this note—and without his watchdog Jamie."

"Lady Rosie would be devastated if Jamie had aught to do with this," Meg reminded her. "How can you bring her into the Privy Plot Council if we'll be discussing whether Jamie or his friend is to blame?"

"You're right about that," Elizabeth said, closing the coffer lid. As she had surmised, neither of Bettina's two remaining skirts were good enough to bury her in, and neither of them had been black or even dark-hued. So far, though it was the flimsiest piece of evidence, it was Mildred Cecil's discarded gown that matched the one for which she'd been searching. After seeing Chris Hatton, she was riding to Theobalds without Cecil's knowledge, to speak with his wife alone.

Jenks could not believe his continued good fortune, even if he was spending the night in plague London. Hugh Scott had shared some bread and cheese with him, moldy though they were. Hugh loved to talk and had been downing mug after mug of his own store of sack, which only made him talk the more. Jenks was wishing he'd slow his drinking so he could assure Her Grace that his source of information had been sober.

"So you really liked Jamie better than Chris," Jenks tried to get him on track again.

"What the deuce, wouldn't you?" Hugh challenged, reaching over to slap Jenks's knee where they sat in the large window bay of the library. "Barstow came from the workaday world like you and me, while most lads here was in on their sire's pedigree and purses. 'Sides, it always riled me how Handsome Hatton had to beat the maids off with a stick—e'en though no wenches were 'round here much but the cook, scullery maids, and the lecturer's wives."

"You mean like Mistress Sutton? Chris mentioned her," he lied.

"I'll bet he did," Hugh said with a snicker. "She was hot for him, and no doubt, other way 'round too, a pretty pair they'd make, eh?" he added, sitting up straighter with a hiccough. "But if she thought her late-night activities was secret, she was cracked. Students like to compare notes, if you get my drift. Aye," he went on importantly, "I might have been only a watchman porter, but my eyes and ears took in a lot, I'll tell you that. Hey, bet Hatton wouldn't want none of that 'bout him and 'the mistress' noised 'round the queen's court, but you can tell him I won't let on," he added, guffawing and slapping his own knees this time.

"So you heard Mistress Sutton bedded with some of the students here?" Jenks asked, then repeated the question more loudly. "What about Jamie Barstow?"

"Barstow? No—all business, that one, just trying to keep his footing around his betters, like I said. 'Sides, I swear your friend Hatton kept him too busy—you know, under his thumb or Barstow could have got the heave-ho. But since you asked about others, what the deuce, come on and let me show you something—my little secret," Hugh said and got unsteadily to his feet. "Bring that lantern, Ned, my man."

Jenks had to admit that Hugh Scott, beslubbered or not, knew his way through the tangled halls at Gray's, probably just as he knew all about the teachers and students here. Now Jenks had a firsthand report to give Her Grace, so she'd have to forgive him for coming into the city. Despite how much she favored Chris Hatton, she'd best consider him hostile to the Suttons. And poor, hardworking, base-born Jamie Barstow sounded like a good man to have in anyone's corner, because he knew well how to serve another.

"Over there," Hugh said, pointing out a casement across a corner of a courtyard at rows of black windows, "Suttons' chambers. Now, over here, just down the hall a ways . . ."

Jenks followed him around two more turns to what appeared to be a dark pigeonhole of a closet until Hugh took and thrust their lantern in. Shelves with ink jars, stacks of parchments— and a long bench with a padded seat.

"So?" Jenks asked, though he was starting to catch on. For one moment, he even wondered if Hugh was going to brag that he'd bedded Bettina, too.

"This is where she met or brought them, one and all—one at a time, a course—while the old man did his preparations or turned in early."

"You looked in here?"

"Not 'xactly, but all the queen's men couldn't put Mistress Sutton's reputation together again," he said and howled at his own humor. "Even her top man . . ."

"What top man? Whose?"

"The queen's, you pukewit!"

"What?"

"Cecil, man! I'm talking 'bout Lord William Cecil, the queen's high-and-mighty advisor or whatever he is."

"No, you're sadly mistaken and better keep that flap mouth of yours shut," Jenks said, getting more vexed by the moment. "Lord Cecil'd never have any truck that way with Mistress Sutton, and he was gone from here before her time."

"Cecil—came—back—to—see—Templar—Sutton," Hugh said, drawing out his words as if he were talking to an idiot.

"Not only that, but Cecil's lady come looking for him and saw him a-kissing Bettina good-bye, like I saw it right here with my own two eyes."

"I can't believe it. And there was a huge row?"

"Naw. 'Fore the two of them saw her, Cecil's woman run off real downhearted. I let her out into the street myself, since I'd locked the door where she came in. Guess she was thinking she'd surprise her lord to spend some time with him and the Suttons, but was she surprised. Cecil, he once came often, and maybe not always to see his old mentor, know what I mean?" Hugh said with a roaring laugh.

Jenks leaned shakily against the door to the small, dark room. He'd found out more than he meant to or wanted to. The queen might not lose that Tudor temper of hers for his disobeying orders, but she just might kill the messenger of such news.

From a distance, Elizabeth stared silently at the piece of parchment nailed to her "accession oak," as folks had begun to call it, on the grounds of Hatfield House. The stiff paper shifted and rattled in the early morning breeze. She had just summoned Chris Hatton to her chambers when Ned had run in breathless to tell her about this—and that the handwriting looked the same to him as the note they had saved as earlier evidence, the one telling Stackpole to leave off guarding the queen in Mary Sidney's room.

"I didn't want to remove it," Ned Topside explained as Elizabeth strode closer, "that is, before you saw it just the way it was posted, Your Grace."

"Has anyone else read it, besides the blackguard who put it here, I mean?"

"Not that I know of, or I think it would have been fetched to you."

"Draw your sword," she ordered. "The trees get thicker here and someone may be lurking, hoping I would come."

The scraping of sword on scabbard made her shiver. She stepped close to the parchment and read:

> *"Therefore, behold, I will hedge up your way with thorns,*
> *And wall her in, so that she cannot find her paths."*

"What does it mean?" Ned asked, so close behind she jumped.

"It is from the Bible, but I cannot offhand recall what book. It may refer to Bettina's body being left in the knot garden, but more likely it is a challenge and threat to me. Pull this nail out so I don't tear the note, and bring it along."

Elizabeth strode toward the house with Ned soon hard on her heels. "Should I go fetch Cecil?" he asked.

"He'll know soon enough." She spun back to take the note and the nail from him before they re-entered the building. "Tell no one of this. I must speak with Chris Hatton, and then I'm riding to Theobalds. I'll take you and Robert Dudley with me, since Jenks is not here—and Clifford, all of you armed, so go fetch him out of the north hall. And Cecil is to be told I'm merely venturing out for a ride."

"I hear Sir Christopher has the gripes this morning, so he won't be available," Ned called after her.

"The gripes, is it?" she threw back over her shoulder, wondering how he managed to get a bowel complaint when no one else at court was sick. "I don't care if he has the plague or even the pox," she added, leaning over the banister to Ned, "he will see me and now."

Chapter the Fourteenth

NED WAS RIGHT, THE QUEEN THOUGHT. CHRIS HATTON looked sick.

"I regret to hear you are somewhat indisposed, and I will ask you to stand back a bit," she greeted him in the room she was using as her presence chamber at Hatfield. Elizabeth had sent everyone out, because she needed to proceed with care. She didn't even want Cecil in on this, since she was beginning to believe his wife could have something to do with Bettina's—and perhaps Templar's—demise.

Chris grimaced in pain, even as he rose from his bow. Amazingly, he looked as handsome as ever. Even his mussed hair and pale face did not detract from his allure. Rather, it made her want to comfort and protect him. Had Bettina felt that way?

"Jamie and I are a bit the worse for wear, Your Grace."

"He still has his disorder?" They spoke louder than usual since they did not stand close.

"Your herb woman's been dosing him. When he heard Mistress Milligrew was providing tonic for both Lady Ashley and Lord Cecil's wife, he asked for something from her. I daresay he's a bit better, and I shall try to follow his lead."

"Then this will be quick. Did Mistress Sutton come looking for you or vice versa the night she died?"

He looked surprised, but recovered quickly. "Absolutely not, Your Grace. I went to bĕd early as I was starting to feel the effects of this malady."

"I saw you poke your head out into the hall when she and Kat Ashley had their row."

"Forgive me, Your Grace, but it seemed one-sided. That is, Bettina was beside herself, but Lady Ashley was cutting into her with a vengeance."

Elizabeth sat up even stiffer. Perhaps Chris was not as wanting in wit as he pretended. How adroitly he had deflected her attention from himself, and how, though knowing such, she went for his bait. "Tell me then," she said, leaning forward, "do the others think badly of Kat, too?"

"The word's out that she's become a bit—ah, deranged," he admitted, evidently choosing his words carefully. "But yes, some say she could have been jealous of your kindness to Bettina, and to Master Sutton, too. Some say Lady Ashley could have tried to harm them since she's in such a lunatic state at times."

"*Tried* to harm them?" Elizabeth repeated, rising. "Kat Ashley is merely senile and would never hurt another person. What else are they saying?"

"My repeating such does not mean I agree with it, Your Gr—"

"*What* are they saying?"

"That Lady Ashley should be at least—well, detained and examined somehow by the local bailiff or some such."

Elizabeth fought to keep control. Never would she let that happen. "Let's get back to you, Chris. Although you were in your chamber when Kat and I were in the corridor last night, and though you are ailing, did you see or meet clandestinely with Bettina at any time after that—between then and when her body was found, let us say?"

"I did not, Your Grace. I swear it. Though I should not speak ill of the dead, I tell you Mistress Sutton used to favor and fancy me much more than I did her, as I did not care for her that way. And now since I know you, Your Majesty, and am blessed to live in your court, I admire and adore only you."

He went down on one knee, but she noted he kept an arm wrapped around his belly. That's the way she felt, too—sick to her stomach. She still could not fathom that Chris was guilty of anything, and she could not bear to think ill of Kat. Though she fully intended to question Jamie Barstow and to rake Henry, Lord Darnley over the coals of her questions, she must question Mildred Cecil next.

Jenks was deeply shaken when he heard Hugh's testimony that could implicate Cecil in adultery and Lady Cecil in Bettina's murder. He started drinking Hugh's sack with him, and their conversations slowly collapsed into sodden sleep on pews in the back of the chapel.

Just after dawn, sounds—voices—from the library nearby roused them. Hugh whispered that he thought some student had wandered back in, but Jenks was certain it must be Bettina, maybe come with friends to take not only her husband's books but all those others, too. They got up and stumbled down the hall.

Several men were ransacking the dim room. Too late, Jenks realized he'd left his sword behind.

"What, ho!" Hugh cried. "Halt and give your names!"

"Not likely," someone shouted with a sharp laugh.

"Thieves!" the still besotted Hugh cried. And then all hell broke loose.

Jenks cursed himself for not being sober and alert. As if caught in a nightmare, he felt leaden-footed and heavy-handed. The onslaught of blows had already sent Hugh to the floor. Jenks cuffed and kicked his first assailant, but another of the blackguards jumped him. Still, he swung hard, giving nearly as good as he got until a third man leaped on his back.

Someone, something hit him over the head and the whole world went black.

At mid-morning, Elizabeth spurred her horse away from Hatfield with Ned, Robin, and four armed guards in her wake. She was riding east on the road that would take her the nine miles to Cheshunt, a former nunnery where she'd also once been imprisoned. Theobalds was only two miles south of that, so she'd question Mildred Cecil, then be back by nightfall with hard riding. It was the speed at which Robin had wanted her to come to Hatfield, so at least he was keeping up. Ned and the guards hung back a bit, and she felt a flicker of annoyance that Jenks had not returned.

But where the road crossed the first small brook, she reined in.

"What is it, Your Grace?" Robin cried, halting his horse so hard the big beast reared. "Did your mount balk?"

"No, I did," she said, and amazed her entourage by spurring her horse back toward Hatfield.

She had almost made a dreadful decision. William Cecil had been with her since before the days she was confined at Cheshunt, Hatfield, and in the Tower of London. At age fourteen, she had written Cecil a letter of thanks for his aid and signed it, *"Your friend, Elizabeth."* He had given her advice, and more than once stuck by her when he need not. All he had and would ever be hung on serving his queen, and Elizabeth knew that well. It would be traitorous of her to question Mildred without him.

"Besides," she whispered aloud, "if I first saw his precious Theobalds without him, he'd never get over it."

"Your Grace," Robin shouted, riding abreast of her again, "what did you say? Did you forget something?"

"Indeed I did!"

She was going to level with her Secretary of State, her chief minister, she vowed. Though she didn't trust many—actually any—men, Cecil came as close to perfect as the so-called stronger sex would ever be.

Jenks heard voices but he couldn't place them or unscramble their words.

"They both look dead."

"This one who challenged us is, I think."

"The Black Death could have killed them anyway. Can't see worrying 'bout two more corpses 'midst the hundreds. Lem, you load up the books and whatever decent plate or other goods you see. In case there's more guards than these two, we'll toss their bodies somewhere."

"Wait 'til after dark, you mean?"

"Holy hell, we're not waiting 'round here all day, you numb-skull. Maybe we can find a handcart to put them in, then plant them in one of the gardens."

Jenks's head hurt horribly, but he smiled inside his mind as dreams drifted by. Meg had looked so fetching going from garden to garden with her handcart of plants and herbs, stooping over to plant them, busy, intent, happy. When he could, he watched over her, though she didn't know it. He'd almost died when he'd learned she was married—with her memory loss and all, she'd been shocked, too. Now Meg was patting him all over, her hands ungentle in her desire for him.

"This brawny one's got a full purse," a sharp voice said.

Jenks heard coins jingling like bells, bells like Meg wore that time a lot of the queen's servants were playing hide-and-seek and he caught and kissed her. He had hoped that she had wanted to be caught, but he'd never had the nerve to ask.

Someone prodded Jenks with a boot toe. Pain shot through his ribs, so they must be broken. But he felt so exhausted, so—floating—he didn't or couldn't move.

"Hear that bell?" someone shouted.

"That's just these here coins—"

"No. Listen!"

"Bring out your dead! Bring out your dead!" a new and distant voice buzzed through Jenks's brain.

"That's perfect! The death cart's coming. Let's put both of them in it. The cart oafs never look too close and just dump them in a mass grave."

Jenks tried to tell Meg he wasn't dead, but he felt as if he were. Every limb hurt as he was lifted and moved. Even his eyelids wouldn't open, his jaw wouldn't move.

Jenks was jostled, swung, bumped.

"Hey, ho! Wait there! Got two here, law students from Gray's!"

"Two less lawyers sounds good to me. Wrap'm up and toss them up!"

Jenks hoped that Meg was wrapping a sheet around him, some sort of herbal plaster. Maybe she even got in bed with him, because he cuddled against her side under the sheet and slept the sleep of the dead.

"Cecil," the queen said with a wave to summarily dismiss his three scribes who were clustered around a paper-littered table with him, "I want to go to Theobalds today."

His face lit until he evidently saw the expression on hers. "Do you mean immediately, Your Grace?" he asked, sitting again as she indicated. Elizabeth sat facing him in the vacated chair next to his.

"Yes, and perhaps we should take a small party. How many can you house there?"

"Ten or twelve in beds, with your guards in the stables or

in tents. As I said, it's a small manorhouse. Your Grace, forgive me, but you changed your mind abruptly about Darnley being allowed to go to Scotland and then that he could not yet go. You said we would not visit Theobalds and now we are, just after you reversed your decision to allow Mildred to go there. Each time you change your mind, it is never a woman's whim but to advance your plans or lay a clever trap."

"Even when we've been at odds, my Cecil, I've always told myself you were the best bet for a clever man to help me run my realm."

"I feel that we are fencing. Tell me straight out what you're thinking—I beg you, Your Grace. It's something about the maze murders, isn't it?"

"Cecil," she said and rose to look out the single window, "my courtiers are whispering Kat had something to do with Bettina's death, and it won't be long before someone gossips that she talked to Templar and then struck him from behind. Because Kat is not well lately—and I have such a care for her—I must flush the murderer, and my attacker out now, at any cost."

"And, by implication, because Mildred is not herself lately and I have such a care for her, I must help you at all costs," he said, rising.

"Then you have thought that Mildred might know more than she says about something?" Elizabeth parried.

"Perhaps. About something."

"My lord, can more be bothering her than a misshapen son and your first wife bearing you a strong one?"

"I fear so," was all Cecil could manage before his voice caught and his eyes filled with tears.

How deeply he feels for Mildred's agony, Elizabeth thought,

and admired him all the more. She was going to find a way to make Mildred tell all she knew about Templar and Bettina, she assured herself.

"I was going to stay at your Theobalds a short while," she told him, "but I'd best arrange for some people and goods to go along. I hate to move Kat again, but I think it best."

"I had said we might fortify the manor and pare down our numbers there until we settle who is behind all this," he reminded her. "Will you take Darnley and his mother?"

"I'll keep him under watch here and summon him when we are ready. You see, I had even thought we might set a sort of trap for the murderer, in the place he or she is evidently drawn to—a maze, this time your water maze at Theobalds."

"Your Grace," Cecil called to the queen as their entourage rode the last mile toward his new estate under graying clouds, "I must tell you something before Mildred does. I would hate for us not to be completely clear with each other."

Her head snapped around so quickly the plume on her hat whipped her eyes. "Something important to our investigation you've been holding back?" she demanded.

"I know we're close to Theobalds and it's likely to rain, but could we take a respite and have a privy talk before we arrive?"

"Have everyone halt here for a moment!" the queen called to Robin.

Robin did as she commanded, for once without an impertinent question as to what was going on. He helped her dismount, then skewered Cecil with a sharp stare. "I'll keep the company back, but I'll be within the sound of your voice," he told the queen as he turned away to tend to the others. She had brought Kat and Rosie with her, but left Meg, Ned, and Clifford behind to watch Darnley and his dam, as well as to keep an eye on how Chris and Jamie were faring. When Jenks returned, she'd told everyone, he was to ride to Theobalds forthwith.

The queen and Cecil left their horses and walked a slight distance to face each other across a fallen tree trunk where a cluster of chestnuts screened them from the road.

"Do not mince words, my lord. Did you see Kat or Mildred in some sort of awkward situation concerning Bettina?"

"The awkward situation I need to tell you about is mine."

"You?" she cried and grasped a tree limb sticking up like a lance from the trunk. "Cecil, you haven't somehow played me false in all this?"

"I have not lied but did allow you to be misled about something."

"A lawyer's answer. Say on."

"Three days ago you asked me if I ever betrayed my marriage vows."

Her fingers laced, she clenched the tree limb in gloved hands as if she could strangle it. "And you said no."

"It was the truth, but there is another truth. One I am starting to fear Mildred has ferreted out. Though I never told her, perhaps Bettina did."

Elizabeth wrenched the limb so hard it snapped off in her hands, and she heaved it to the ground. "Stop treading a fine line. Just tell me," she ordered.

"Upon one occasion—I swear to you it was just one, which does not excuse it..." His voice began to trail off, but he plunged on, "I bedded Bettina, or vice versa, but I swear to you it was a fortnight before I wed Mildred."

The queen's eyes widened then narrowed. She pressed her thin lips into an even tighter line. "But you were betrothed to her?"

"Yes, while working day and night for your causes while your sister yet was queen, about nine years ago."

"In London, at Gray's Inn," the queen summarized for him, "two weeks before you wed your Mildred, while Bettina was recently wed to Templar, you cuckolded your admired mentor and teacher with his young wife?"

"It was wrong, a sudden sin I've long regretted—suffered for, though I don't think Bettina did. I swear to you, she instigated the act, though that does not excuse my part in it. At least she did not hold it over my head, never mentioned it again to me when she saw how regretful and self-loathing I was. Of course, I reckoned it didn't mean that much to her when I heard she bedded others, but I did fear she'd boast of it or try to blackmail me some day as I rose high."

"And did she?"

"She did not. I don't expect you to understand, Your Grace. I just—"

"You don't expect me to understand?" she cried, her voice rising. "It's the very sort of lewd, immoral, and evidently natural behavior I expect from men, including my father, that traitorous Tom Seymour, King Philip of Spain, Lord Darnley, and the list goes on ad infinitum!"

"I am without excuse. I lost my head as I had years before with my first wife, Mary. There is—was—something of Mary in Bettina that momentarily swept me away. I had no notion at the time it would become common practice for her to take lovers, Bettina, I mean. I swear to you I have never done such with another! I can only throw myself upon your mercy for not explaining sooner, but I desperately needed you to trust me for all we've faced together. It—this grievous misjudgment on my part has appalled and haunted me, especially lately."

He heaved a huge sigh, snatched off his hat, and went down on one knee on the ground before her. She stared at him, but marveled at herself.

Mere weeks ago, before someone tried to strangle her, she would have thrown a raving fit and let her infamous Tudor temper punish and banish this man, even if she forgave him later. But she needed him now, and, more importantly, she still esteemed and trusted him. He had not been wed at the time of his liaison and had not directly lied to her earlier, considering the way she'd couched her question. As for losing one's head, she had nearly done so four years ago over Robin Dudley, and Cecil had counseled her and stuck by her.

"Can Mildred know of this?" she asked in a steady voice.

She saw that he'd braced himself for an onslaught. He looked astounded she was so calm. "Not unless Bettina told her—or Templar found out and told her, but whyever would they have? It's been my worst nightmare that *he* would discover what I'd done, but I swear, I never fathomed Mildred might find out."

"I'm afraid we must ask her—tell her so we can discover if she already knew—and perhaps reacted somehow."

"She cannot be a murderess, Your Grace, even in her present distracted state. Moral, pious, even puritanical, it cannot be my Mildred we are seeking. She knows the Bible like a cleric, can quote it, believes it, too. And I fear telling her all this might send her off even more into the deep end of her melancholy."

"Even after getting away from the demands of the children for a while, she's been acting bizarre?"

"It seems at times she cannot abide me. Since little Robert's birth, I have nearly despaired I was losing her, even as she seemed to have lost herself...."

His voice broke. She leaned down and put her hand, still in its suede riding glove, over his, trembling on his sword.

"Because of Kat, I understand that, too," Elizabeth told him, tears in her own eyes. "But I ask that you, even at the possible cost of discovering Mildred has committed some foolish or malicious act, let me question her alone. Perhaps without you there, she will be more forthcoming. And you do realize that what you told me just now could provide a motive for *your* doing away with Templar and Bettina—to keep them from telling Mildred or me or to keep Bettina from blackmailing you."

"But—"

"Rest assured I know that, each time you've been with Templar or Bettina, you have suffered for your immoral act. I've seen it on your face, but never understood it until now. Besides, I believe your only motive for murder would be to hide that which you freely—if tardily, my lord—confessed to me today.

"And so I ask," she went on, tugging him to his feet, "after I speak with Mildred, you help me set a trap for our maze murderer and strangler, even if it is someone dear to us."

Jenks jolted from his dream and from his bed with Meg. Either Meg was crying or it was raining. But it felt good on his head and face.

"How many this time, then?" a voice asked.

"Fourteen. You still burying them six feet under?"

"God save us, not with the rise in numbers. 'Bout two, three feet has to do. I see you got a peeled onion 'round your neck. What you got in it to keep the death from creepin' up your nose?"

"Stuffed with rue, figs, and treacle. Damned dear the treacle was too, but beats garlic carried in the mouth all day."

"We been burning old shoes to purify the air at home. You think treacle costs a pretty penny, I know a man puts imported mummy in his ale."

"He still healthy?"

"Think so. The likes a you not carted him to the likes a me yet."

"What's been really rattling me is the shapes of the clouds, like they say, conjunctions of the planets in a malignant manner and all that."

"God save us, you seen om'nous ones?"

"One rain cloud earlier like a huge axe hanging over St. Paul's and one shaped like a hearse 'bout an hour ago."

"You're all the hearse these poor souls be getting, so let 'er go then, and I'll mark fourteen more."

Jenks jerked, fell free, then slid down, down. He landed hard with someone right on top of him. It wasn't Meg because she always smelled like the sweetest of her herb gardens, and this bedfellow just plain stank.

Chapter the Fifteenth

CECIL'S HOPES TO GIVE HIS QUEEN A FIRST VIBRANT view of Theobalds went for naught as a warm rain began to fall. Still, he hoped she could see what a fine flow of land it was, joining the small manor with the rising ground where the house would stand someday.

"The great house will go exactly where, my lord?" she called to him as if she'd read his mind. They halted their horses, though Elizabeth motioned for their entourage to ride ahead.

He reined in as the others passed them, grateful not only that she hadn't dismissed or berated him for his confession about Bettina, but that she seemed genuinely interested in Theobalds. He'd been so hungry for shared excitement about the building project with Mildred, but he had longed for it with his queen, too.

"About three-fourths of a mile to the northeast. There!" he

cried and pointed through the silver mists. "Gardens will stretch out there and there, ornamental lakes and walks. Someday, Your Grace, God willing, Theobalds will greet you at its gates with a grandeur that signifies your beauty and might—and my devotion."

Their gazes met, though they both blinked in the increasing raindrops. "God willing, once we rid ourselves of all who would harm such dreams," she whispered and spurred her horse again.

He followed, reveling in the view, even though he'd not yet changed one thing here. The rain was turning the dove-gray of the moated manorhouse to shiny pewter. Thick ivy knit its green fingers up the walls to frame mullioned windows. Cecil wondered if Mildred would be shocked to hear the royal party clatter into their cobbled courtyard. He was thankful he lived in the modern age when homes no longer needed thick walls, small windows, and moats to defend themselves, but could expand to embrace and enhance the surrounding countryside. It was essential that the queen's kingdom remain strong to allow such safety, so they must ferret out this murderer who mocked and threatened her power.

"And where is this unique water maze of yours?" the queen asked as she halted her horse again on the bridge over the moat. She turned in her sidesaddle and craned her neck to look back and out.

"Over there," he told her, pointing again, "fed by the same stream as the moat, sitting in that low-lying water meadow. It's a quickset white thorn maze planted in weighted barrels one can row a boat through."

"Ah, good. A thorn maze adrift in water which is deepening even more in this weather," she called over her shoulder as she headed into the courtyard. "But we shall learn its secrets and conquer it anyway, my lord."

He took her meaning. Elizabeth Tudor was determined to set a trap in his new maze. But the thing that scared him was what she planned to use as bait.

A trickle of water on his face woke Jenks. But when he realized he was thirsty and painfully tried to lift and cup his hand, both his palm and mouth filled with wet soil. He could not even budge.

He gagged, panicked. Where was he?

With a fierce effort he dragged a hand free and began to scrape soil away from his mouth and eyes. He was in some sort of air pocket under debris and—dear Jesus, help me, he prayed—under a cold, stiff body huddled next to him.

He half twisted, half clawed his way out, upward, toward the light. But there was no light, only blackness thick as fear. Had he died and gone to hell?

He shoved someone's leg, then a body aside to lift his head, sucking in great gasps of air. A pit. He was in a burial pit with corpses. Spitting soil, he dug and pushed and broke free.

He squinted through the grit in his eyes. It wasn't night but it was raining, with gunmetal clouds darkening the day. He lifted his face to let the rain wash his eyes.

In pain, trembling, he tried to climb a steep dirt embankment, but it was slick mud, running with rain. He heard cannon fire and ducked. Had he fallen off his horse and tumbled into a trench in some sort of battle? Were these fellow soldiers? The rumbling came again. He realized it might be thunder.

Then he remembered. He was in London in time of plague. With Hugh Scott, he'd been attacked at Gray's Inn. But after that, what?

He began to shout, though he wasn't putting out much noise. So weak, his body aching, every which way he turned or moved. What if he'd caught the pestilence?

But he quelled his panic as remembrance returned. The thieves who'd jumped them had put them in a cart, and now he was in a mass grave . . . a plague grave.

"Let me out of here! I'm alive! Help! Help, ho!"

It seemed ages before he heard a voice. His heart pounding, he stopped to listen, then cried out again.

"I don't have the death! I'm not sick. I'm down in this hole. Help me-*eee!*"

A man's head popped over the edge above him. He dangled a lantern. Even that dim light hurt his eyes. He could not see more than the silhouette of a head.

"Help me, man! Thieves attacked and threw me in here, but I swear by all that's holy I'm not sick."

"You might be now," the fellow told him. "It's not my fault. I just dig the pits and cover what the dead carts bring me. Hang on, and I'll fetch something to get you out."

Elizabeth wondered if there was a way out of these complications with Mildred. She could tell the woman felt extremely nervous as she showed her monarch the accommodations that afternoon and they sat alone in the solar, mistress of the manor and mistress of the realm.

"These lovely grounds and a new home will be a fine heritage for your son Robert," Elizabeth assured her, raising her voice to be heard over the patter of rain on the oriel window panes. "I mean for him to be my man someday, just as his father is."

"It would be a great honor for my son and our family to continue to serve you into the next generation, Your Majesty." Mildred forced a tight smile; her posture was almost as stiff. "But I have noted that you favor fine-looking folk about you, and my dear Robert may never be that."

"I favor above all else those who are loyal to me. Besides, have you not noted that when someone lacks certain physical attributes, he or she oft makes up for that by being especially clever or talented?"

"And vice versa, I warrant," Mildred said. "Such as Chris Hatton or Bettina Sutton—pretty people but perhaps not so clever or talented."

"You saw Bettina as someone who was physically attractive but not clever or talented?" Elizabeth had been looking for a path into this necessary conversation, so this might work well.

"I regret to speak ill of the dead, Your Majesty, but Bettina was clever or talented at things I do not consider strengths. I realize she was much more comely and winsome than me, but her wit—and her moral underpinnings—left much to be desired. And yet," she went on more quietly, almost as if she were speaking only to herself now, "she was desired."

"I assume you are referring again to her seducing Templar's students, rumors you heard from those to whom you extended your hospitality?"

"Yes," Mildred said only, looking a bit alarmed, as if she realized she'd talked herself into a corner.

"And yet, I never took you for one who would judge others

on hearsay, as the lawyers put it. I took you for one who follows Him who said, 'Judge not,' for one who knows and can quote the Bible well," she added, thinking of the note tacked on the oak. "Therefore, I believe you must know more of Bettina's behavior than what you have overheard in mere gossip to dislike her so."

"When I visited Gray's Inn years ago, I myself saw her inappropriate and overly familiar behavior with someone other than Templar, that is all," Mildred blurted.

"And was that someone other than Templar the man who was to soon become your husband?"

The woman rocked back in her chair as if she'd been struck. "I—how c-could you—know—to ask that?" she stammered.

"Perhaps Bettina told me."

"She didn't see me, though the Gray's Inn watchman could have told her. I know my lord didn't see me either. . . . Oh, now I've told you," she muttered as tears filled her eyes.

"He himself confessed to me his one-time sin with Bettina, and how he rued it. I merely guessed just now that you had somehow learned of his grievous fault. To have seen him thusly must have been a shock. And yet you wed him a fortnight later when he had hurt and disappointed you."

"I loved and wanted him, Your Majesty."

"You speak in the past tense. Do you not love and want him now? I believe he's been loyal to your union since and loves you deeply. But it seems knowing this about him all these years—as well as fretting about his first wife and her son—has been festering inside you. And with the birth of little Robert, such a delicate child when you longed for one robust, the infection has burst out into your behavior."

"Does my lord know all this—and put you up to this?"

"No one 'puts me up to' anything!"

"Forgive me, Your Majesty, I didn't mean to cast aspersions, not on you, that is."

"He's a man, Mildred. Addressing Parliament or the stubborn Scots in treaty-making or counseling his queen, he is brilliant. I am ever amazed at the scope of his knowledge and advice. But have you yet seen a husband who can come off so well at close range with his wife?"

Mildred almost smiled. "Though you are unwed, you know men well, Your Majesty. And I find you, not men, a continual wonder."

"But you must solve something for me," Elizabeth said, deciding to press her advantage. "Did you resent Bettina, or perhaps even Templar, enough that you wanted to harm them?"

Panic lit her eyes and froze her features. "You don't mean—could I kill them?" she gasped. Her hands fluttered to her throat, a move so unlike Mildred that it was not lost on Elizabeth. She could yet feel those garters choking life from her.

"That wasn't what I asked," the queen countered.

"No, Your Majesty. If I ever did want to harm Bettina, it would be not to punish but to keep her from telling anyone how my well-respected husband betrayed his mentor and me once."

"Then you never so much as thought of harming the Suttons?"

"Never, though I've come dreadfully close to doing damage to my husband more than once," she admitted. The queen could tell she was not jesting. Something strange and almost frightening flickered in Mildred Cecil's hazel eyes, then faded. Elizabeth knew she would have to warn Cecil, tell him that his instinct to remove Mildred from her family was sound. And she must warn him to be even more watchful for himself.

Still stunned, Jenks realized he'd been resurrected from the dead. Though pain racked him, he stood on firm soil, grateful to be surrounded by mere gravestones instead of plague corpses. He had no idea what were his odds of getting the pestilence now, but he was probably a walking dead man.

"You all right then?" the fellow who'd put a ladder down to him asked as he backed away. "You look a fright. You got a home to go to, or they got the plague there, too?"

Jenks didn't answer but moved slowly away. He was certain most of his ribs were cracked because each breath pained him. One ankle must be sprained, and his back felt wrenched. He'd give anything for his horse—and for Meg's healing touch.

He shuffled through the graveyard, dragging his bad foot, forcing himself on. He recognized where he was, Bowe Church on broad Cheapside, a street nearly deserted now.

He leaned against a building, wanting to suck in great gasps of air, but even that hurt him. Besides, it could be heavy with the miasma of pestilence. He had to get back to Hatfield. Or at least, before he was stricken by the plague as well as weakened further by his injuries, he'd get close enough to shout to the queen what he'd learned about Chris Hatton's needing a good watch. He supposed he'd somehow have to get the word to her about Lord Cecil and Bettina too, though he dreaded that. But in this shape, he'd never make it clear back to his horse in the stables outside Moorgate.

Then he realized he was much closer to the queen's London residence, the now empty Whitehall Palace, than to his horse. And a few mounts would be there. Robert Dudley always left behind the horses which were hobbled or needed tending.

He pictured Meg's healing hands again, longed to feel her palm on his hot forehead, the way she leaned against his bed when she'd nursed a fever out of him last year. To help the queen and see Meg again, he had to make it back, or he'd die trying.

"I want a dramatic line of buildings against the sky," Cecil told the queen the next morning after breakfast as, ignoring the wet grass, they walked the grounds. "Once one rides in the great gate from the main road, the view must be arresting."

The rain had stopped, and this day was breaking clear and cool for late July. "Tall pavilions, cupolas, a pinnacled belfry," he went on as they moved away from the manor toward the maze, trailing two guards.

"And a forest of chimney stacks venting from mantled hearths in nearly every room," she added, as she caught his excitement. She could see it all in her mind's eye. When she was out on summer progress in years to come—when there were no lurking murderers or plagues to ruin sweet summer days—her long entourage would come winding up a fine gravel lane to visit this lovely place. "And what colors on the exterior?" she asked.

"A rose brick facade trimmed with white stone," he said instantly. "Blue slate-hung turrets with gilded weather vanes, like the ones that sing in the wind at Richmond Palace. And fresco-painted open loggias."

"A touch of Italy, but the architecture and art must be of the England we will build together, my Cecil. And don't think I won't have an idea or two for Theobalds, if you will allow a modest opinion."

"I would not have it any other way, for your taste and style are greatly valued. It is one reason I am pleased to have you here, Your Grace."

"And another is that on this site we will catch our criminal," she declared with a single sharp clap of her hands. "We must snare him or her in this curious water maze the previous owner built," she went on as they neared the water meadow in which it sat like a great, green sculpture. She picked up her skirts to avoid the puddles and increasingly spongy ground.

"Someone else may have designed it, but I shall reshape and expand it," Cecil said, hurrying to keep up with her long strides.

"Where are the boats to navigate it?" she asked impatiently, even as he indicated which direction to take next.

"Over here, Your Grace, this way."

The water maze was a quarter mile from the manor, screened from it by a small orchard of heavily laden apple trees. Even from this distance, it looked more intriguing than any labyrinth she had ever seen. Its thorny maze was tall and thick and seemed to grow directly from the shallow lake in the center of the meadow. Fed by the same sturdy stream as was the moat, the little lake, now swelled with rain, reflected the blue morning sky like a mirror.

"Here, Your Grace," Cecil said, pointing at a line-up of six small, short rowboats roped to posts.

The queen saw each craft could seat two, but only one person could row. "The paths of the maze have grown so wide that two boats can barely go abreast," he explained as she climbed into one without waiting for a hand in. She pulled her skirts tight to give him room to get in and row. "That width is also needful," he added, clambering in behind her, "should a single boat need to pass another or turn out of a dead end."

"I fully intend to turn out of the dead end this diabolical maze ghost thinks he has trapped us in."

"Maze ghost?" he said with a tight smile as he cast off their rope and fitted the oars into the locks. "Because he seems to appear and disappear at will? That's not so hard in a maze, I warrant."

"But even when my people surrounded the one at Hampton Court or searched within or looked for exits—nothing. And Bettina's body being deposited so brazenly like that in the knot garden, as if her murderer had been invisible . . . And speaking of ghosts, my lord, I forgot to ask you the story of the one you say haunts the manor here. I heard no moans nor rattling of chains last night, and I'm afraid I was awake for a good deal of it with my mind churning."

"You're worried about Jenks."

"Indeed, among other things such as attacks on my subjects—and myself."

"And you're deeply fretful about Kat."

"Kat, yes," she said, her voice breaking with emotion. "Your Mildred too, for, as I told you, I feel she teeters on the cusp of violence she almost cannot control. Not to mention I've been vexed that Chris and Jamie and that damned Darnley could be involved. And my cousin Mary of Scots is likely to take a husband to make my head spin if I don't get Robin Dudley or Darnley to her, when I can't stomach sending her either of them," she groused, smacking her hands hard on her skirts.

"Then you still intend to tempt Queen Mary to wed that sadistic milksop by dangling him in front of her while pushing your supposed favorite for her—Dudley? Talk about mazes..."

"Yes, mazes. I intend that we assemble here at Theobalds all those we suspect as our murderer and lay a snare."

"You mean to include Mildred and Kat?"

"I will not and cannot suspect them of such dire deeds, but yes, they will be here, too. We shall explain the gathering as an opportunity for those traveling with me to Hatfield to see and enjoy Theobalds and to glimpse the grandeur you will build here. We will have to house them in pavilions, make it a festive occasion where we eat outside, weather willing."

"Of course, we can house the Countess of Lennox inside and let the men and most servants stay outside."

"I regret to allow even this much gaiety in plague times," she admitted as he rowed them through the mouth of the maze, "but it must be done." She noted her two guards had climbed in separate boats, but stayed far back as she had asked.

"Cecil, I believe our murderer—that God-forsaken strangler, brick basher, and poisoner, if that's how Bettina died—will be unable to resist the challenge of this maze."

"Surely not with you in it as bait, Your Grace!"

"With you, I think, my lord."

He stopped rowing, going momentarily still as a statue, his eyes wide. The prow of their little boat bumped a barrel; they nearly grazed the prickled leaf walls.

"Better me than you, Your Grace," he said, recovering his

aplomb and pushing them away from the hedges with an oar. "And I have a feeling, the 'ghost' will not risk everything unless there is a grand prize."

"We must not spring our trap until our guests have had a chance to see and study the grounds and the maze. We must allow them to walk and row to their heart's content. Perhaps, by keen observation, how much time each person spends doing so will tip us off early concerning whom to watch later."

"Then you do intend to have certain people followed or guarded?"

"Only if it is possible without showing our hand. Our ghost must feel confident in this strange maze, and I warrant the idea of drowning his or her next victim will be an enticement, too."

"Drowning? And by the next victim, you mean me."

"We shall safeguard you at all costs. But variety is the spice of life—or death—that's what our murderer believes," she argued. "Perhaps there is no motive beyond the mere challenge of it, but I believe something deep and dreadful must be driving the ghost, and we have not yet found the key."

"No wonder you lie awake at night. You have it all reasoned out."

"I wish I did. But are you willing to be our bait, if we can think of a way to set it all up?"

"Let the blackguard come on!"

"Then we shall move ahead. I had intended to cross-question Jamie Hatton and Darnley again, perhaps Chris too at Hatfield, but I believe we shall just summon them here tomorrow. So you must send someone posthaste for pavilions from St. Alban's, those I recall from their summer fair."

"You believe it's Darnley, do you not, Your Grace?" he asked suddenly, almost hopefully.

"He's at the top of the list," she admitted as they rowed around another bend. The hedges were indeed thorny, and she gathered her skirts to keep them from being snagged. She peered down into the water to note the weighted barrels from which the thick bushes grew. They were spaced about three feet apart and filled with stone ballast above the soil. The swell of rainwater had raised the surface level to lap at the tops of the barrels. But with a swish of oar, water would splash in and rock the hedges as if they were an upside-down reflection of the disturbed water. By the height of the barrels here, she judged the depth to be about four feet, near that of the pond at Hatfield where she and Meg had ventured out. But she'd tell Cecil that part later.

"These hedge paths wind ever tighter with several false turns," Cecil said as he rowed farther in. "There is no goal per se, but only a wider opening in the very heart of it."

"This must be an eerie place at night."

"At night? Surely, you are not thinking——"

"Lit by a single lantern from your boat in the goal, waiting for our prey, who believes you are his prey. Our ghost will hardly come out here in sunlight or a blaze of torches. Which reminds me, my lord, you keep shifting the subject and have not yet answered my question about the ghost of the manor. Tell me all you know of him."

"Of her."

"Indeed? A woman ghost? I shall not take that as an omen."

"A unique ghost, the former owner told me. It—or she—

drips water on the floor and leaves her bare footsteps and the marks of her sopping petticoat hems dragged through it."

"A female ghost bold enough to swim is one after my own heart," Elizabeth boasted, though gooseflesh prickled her arms.

"It's said," Cecil admitted, grudgingly, she could tell, "that it's the ghost of a woman who drowned in this very maze."

Chapter the Sixteenth

 THE PAIN WAS NEARLY UNBEARABLE. EACH JOLT OF THE horse's hooves on the road ripped through Jenks, but he fought blessed oblivion. He had to stay awake to guide the horse. He had to get to Hatfield, but not too close, call to someone to fetch help, to tell Her Grace from a distance what he'd learned in London . . . before he died . . . because he was sure he would, from pain if not plague. He tried to picture Elizabeth Tudor and Meg Milligrew standing together at his grave, looking so alike, both mourning his loss.

He'd managed to walk to Whitehall Palace; his appearance had shocked the two grooms left behind to care for the injured horses. At first light, he'd taken a mount which was healing from deep cuts, a young stallion he recalled Lord Darnley had abused at Hampton Court, which must have been sent to

Whitehall. Its limp had long healed, and he'd ridden it as hard as he'd dared today.

Now he turned the nervous horse off the road as he approached Hatfield. He cut through the fringe of forest until he could see the house. Though he slowed the big beast to a walk, he flushed both deer and woodcock. Hanging on its neck, he prayed he didn't faint and fall off or a hunt party might discover only his bones someday. He could barely hold on to this horse or his own pain one moment more....

He woke on the ground with the horse standing nearby, cropping grass. The slant of the sun showed it was early afternoon. The trees above him spun and whirled. And then he heard what he knew could save him, if he wasn't just dreaming again.

"Don't you rogues bring those sheep anywhere near my knot garden. If they eat these yew hedges, they'll be dead in a trice! Keep them on the larger lawn, or I'll run them off myself!"

Meg. He had to get to Meg. This was no yearning dream, not with that anger in her voice.

With great difficulty, he rolled to his side, then to his belly. Somehow he got his knees under him and began to crawl. When he collapsed, he dragged himself. The edge of the clearing where the lawns began...where he could see Meg's red head as she bent over her knot garden...seemed as far away as she did from his grasp and love.

"M——m," he tried to call her name and was appalled no word came out. He tried to clear his dry throat. On all fours, he leaned his shoulder against a tree trunk and managed to lift one filthy, shaking hand to his mouth. He whistled shrilly, the way he did to summon horses he had trained.

He saw her stop hoeing—or was she just using the hoe to

search for something? She turned toward the road and lifted a hand to shade her eyes.

Again, he forced his hand to his mouth and drew in a deep breath that seemed to rip each broken rib. Somehow he found the strength to whistle again.

She turned toward him. She began to walk, then run, across the gravel lane toward the trees. Once she was in the shade of forest she'd see him certain. Only, as desperately as he needed her help, as much as he wanted to cling to her, he couldn't let her near him.

"Stop!" he wanted to shout, but it came out a mere croak.

"Jenks? Jenks, is that you? Mercy, what happened?"

"Stay—stay," he tried to tell her but it came out a hiss.

"Oh, dear heavens, you're hurt," she cried, gripping her hands to her breasts and coming closer. "Robbers on the road? Oh, Jenks . . ."

"Yes—thieves," he finally managed to say. But as she came nearer, he summoned the strength to cry, "No!"

She stopped ten feet from him. She was sweating, she looked dirty and confused and appalled, but she'd never looked better.

"I've been—in London," he croaked out.

"In London? But the pl—"

"Listen to me. Tell Her Grace I couldn't find Bettina."

"Bettina's dead, too. I found her in the knot garden laid out and stone cold the morning after you left. I was just looking through every inch of the shrubs for other clues since the local authorities who took her body just asked if there were witnesses, but didn't look around themselves."

Jenks fought to focus his scattered thoughts. With Bettina dead too, the queen could be next. "Listen—to me. I went to

Gray's Inn. Her Grace—she can't trust Chris Hatton. And Cecil's hiding something. I'll—I'll write it if you bring me paper."

"As if you could hold a pen," she said, shuffling closer, her eyes narrowed as she looked him over. "I've nursed folks through many a disease before and not been sick myself. You—you think you've caught it?"

"Don't know. No signs—yet."

"We'll have to ask permission for you to be in the vicinity. You'll have to stay out in the woods, but I'm going to take care of you."

If he had not been so sapped by pain, he would have rejoiced. "At least go tell Her Grace what I said," he gritted out. "Then bring me some paper soaked in vinegar, then dried."

"But she's gone on to Theobalds. All of us are to go there first thing on the morrow, but I'm to ride over today."

"Then you tell her—go now."

"And leave you here to die of those injuries? You're black and blue, and I'll bet you've got a broken bone or two. At least they didn't take your horse. Jenks, Her Grace would want me to tend you—and I want to. I'm going to go in and write what you said and send it to her by Ned, then I'll be right back."

Damn, he thought through the mist of pain. Her Grace had left Ned behind with Meg. But she was coming back to him . . . to tend him.

"But what about Cecil?" Meg asked, still shuffling closer. "What about Cecil?"

"Just tell her to trust no one."

"Nonsense. She's always trusted you and she can trust me with her life. Swear to me you'll be here when I get back, or else I'm coming over there to examine you right now. Swear it to me on——on Her Grace's honor."

She walked close by but passed him and took his horse's reins, perhaps so he wouldn't ride away while she was gone.

"I swear," he said with a sigh that was the last of his strength.

William Cecil looked out of breath as he was admitted to the queen's wing of three small rooms at the manorhouse. "What is it, Your Grace?" he cried. "Lady Rosie said you were nearly beside yourself when you received a note from Hatfield."

"From Meg Milligrew via Ned Topside, whom I've sent directly back with orders," she said, flourishing a letter. "Jenks returned to Hatfield beaten by thieves, but he's been all the way into London."

"London? No wonder you're distraught. You'll have to isolate him for a time and——"

"Yes, Meg wants to tend him even if he should become ill. But the thing is, he actually went to Gray's Inn and found information somehow. She says she'll know more to tell us when they arrive tomorrow, as I told her to bring him here but that they must use one of your garden buildings to avoid everyone. Cecil, she writes that Chris Hatton is not to be trusted."

"Aha. Perhaps we won't have to spring our elaborate snare then, if Jenks has something specific on Hatton. I believe either one of us could trip up Chris Hatton under questioning if we could get him away from Jamie Barstow."

"Don't rejoice that we have our murderer yet," she said, sinking in a puff of huge skirts on a bench under a narrow window.

"For, you see, this same missive also says you're hiding something."

"What?" he asked, and she passed him the note to read. She noted how he snatched it up nervously.

"But," she went on, even as he skimmed it, "it is the *post scriptum* that interests me most. Strange how one agonizes and strains to find clues to probe the murderer's twisted mind, and they just fall in one's lap. Read that part aloud to me, my lord."

Still frowning, he cleared his throat. " 'I was thinking, Your Grace, I must keep the stupid sheep out of my knot garden, because the yew leaves there are poison. But Bettina was found dead in that very knot of yew. Chewing the leaves or a distillation of yew in her wine would kill her quick with no outward marks. Medicinally it must be given in small, measured doses, like what I've been doling out in Jamie Barstow's tonic to cure his weak kidneys. But the point is, could Bettina have been placed in yew because she was poisoned with yew?' "

"She's got a point there," Cecil said. "If Bettina were poisoned, it could have been with yew plucked from the maze at Hampton Court or Hatfield—or from an overdose of Jamie Barstow's medicine."

"Medicine which both he and Chris had access to, no doubt, but she says here she's been doling it out to him. *My* point is, we must be on our continual guard and suspect the worst if Bettina was indeed poisoned, for perhaps our versatile, opportunistic killer has now taken a fancy to that method of murder. Jamie and Chris live together and both have had sudden and suspicious internal ailments which no one else has shared. In short," she said, getting up to pace, "the murderer could be slowly poisoning both Chris and Jamie as his next victims."

"You can't mean Meg!"

"No, for Meg is a healer and would do nothing amiss to be sent from court or accused of any wrongdoing as she was before. But that doesn't mean someone else can't be poisoning Chris and Jamie's wine or food. If so, you must admit that would eliminate them from suspicion."

"And greatly narrow our field of suspects."

"I have, however, ordered Meg to dose Chris and Jamie with antidotes and purgatives at once. But she is *not* to tell them why, only say it is to get their systems back in alignment with their humors. If Meg can't cure them, I may have to summon doctors of the Royal College of Physicians from wherever they've fled in the wretched plague. The murderer will not claim another victim!"

"But could two men be slipped the same poison, and one get the gripes and one a sort of dysentery?"

"Who says it has to be the same poison, or perhaps the dose has been slight so far, and they are just reacting differently." She sat down again, putting her hands to her head as if to hold her thoughts together. "The maze ghost still has us on the run, I fear," she admitted. "I try not to, but I live in terror of what is around the next corner."

"So you are going to cancel the gathering here?"

"No. Setting the snare in your water maze is the best thing to do, though not without risk. We could try watching Chris and Jamie's food from garden to kitchen to their mouths, but that would be tedious and overly obvious—and it's just one more theory."

"At least I don't fear poisoning here at Theobalds. Mildred always oversees..." he said before his voice trailed off.

"And Kat still insists she taste my food first as she has for years. When I eat alone, she occasionally seasons it the way she knows I like, too. Cecil, I believe I am about to go mad," she declared, jumping up again. She covered her eyes with the palms of her hands. "Whoever is tormenting me is winning if he—or she—always has me looking over my shoulder. And, despite the fact it *appears* this may clear Chris and Jamie, I'm still not sure we have one damned, solid clue to place someone above the others on our list of possible culprits. It may be simply my prejudices for or against individuals that makes me suspect someone more."

Her voice broke, and she turned to look out the window so he would not see the tears in her eyes.

"Your Grace, when I was sore afraid as a boy, my father used to say, 'For God hath not given us a spirit of fear; but of power, and of love, and of a sound mind.' "

"A sound mind—that's a good one lately. Yet I prefer that Bible quote to the threatening one nailed on my ascension oak."

"You have the power to solve this, Your Grace."

"Sometimes 'might does not make right.' As for love, Cecil, I can only pray that the person behind all this is not someone I—or you—dearly love and would loathe to lose."

At high noon the next day, the courtiers and servants the queen had left behind at Hatfield came in procession to Theobalds, even as Cecil's meager staff hastily pounded the final tent poles in the ground. To lull their prey into relaxing his or her guard, the queen had sent for more than gaily striped pavilions. Two trumpeters greeted the party, and imported ale and food were laid outdoors upon a board table covered with a bright green cloth.

"My lord," Elizabeth greeted Chris as he dismounted, "you look much improved."

"No longer under the weather, as the rain has cleared at last," he jested. "That soothing peppermint concoction your herb mistress said you recommended did me an immediate service, Your Grace," he went on, going down on one knee in the grass and kissing her beringed hand. "My stomach's better and my breath sweeter, even without cloves, which Mistress Milligrew noted could be souring my system, too. Jamie's also better," he added, turning to smile at his friend, who dismounted right behind him.

"In short, Your Gracious Majesty," Jamie said with a laugh and went down on his knee too, as if he and his friend were a matched set of andirons, "I will not be darting off into the bushes."

Though the queen had been prepared to force a good mood, she laughed from the heart, seeing the two of them at her feet like fond swains come courting. She noted too how Rosie, blushing just to be near Jamie again, looked relieved at his return to robust health.

"Your Majesty," Jamie went on, "should the kingdom's treasuries ever shrink, you will not need to have Secretary Cecil petition stingy Parliament, but merely decree that anyone who is ill must pay the royal treasury for your clever herb girl's services."

Others standing close, including Darnley and his mother Margaret, chortled as if Jamie had made the wildest joke. Yet Elizabeth was grateful to him and Chris for elevating the mood from plague and murder. Earlier this morning, the queen had received the report from the Hatfield bailiff assuring her that Bettina had been properly buried. The authorities had also ruled that "suspicious but unnamed causes" had brought about Bettina Sutton's "sudden and unfortunate death, for no signs of assault or disease were discovered upon said body."

In short, the queen thought, there had been and would be no help from the authorities at Hampton Court and Hatfield— but that which she and Cecil would fabricate soon to set their plan in motion.

To her surprise, Robin belatedly joined Chris and Jamie's jest, kneeling and kissing her hand, then Lord Darnley, though she'd have liked to kicked him back on his bum. Her cousin Margaret remained while the men finally rose to their feet and, with the others, traipsed after Cecil and Mildred as they began to give a tour of the house and immediate grounds.

Elizabeth overheard Cecil tell everyone as planned, "After all of you partake of some dinner, I shall show you the fantastical water maze. Six rowboats will take any of you through it at any time. It's a challenge, I tell you that. And it's my solace and thinking spot, and the most privy place I have here or anywhere. As for tonight, Her Majesty's principal player, Ned Topside, has adapted some sage or lighthearted speeches. . . ."

"Some of those sage speeches by her Gracious Majesty, I hope," Margaret said at her elbow.

Though Elizabeth saw her Tudor cousin was drinking sugared malmsey, it obviously was not sweet enough to mellow her usual bitter tone, even when she might be trying to be pleasant.

"I trust the ride over did not tire you, Margaret," the queen said as the countess dipped her a curtsy.

"Now that the rain has stopped, it is lovely to be out. Hatfield, all cheek-by-jowl with courtiers and servants, is rather cramped quarters compared to what I'm used to. Not to mention that ubiquitous guard Clifford in the hall," she added portentously. "Yet I see this manor is an even smaller retreat. Does the size of your realm seem to be shrinking lately?" she said and chuckled.

The queen smiled stiffly at that subtle jab. She had noted that Clifford rode in directly behind the Stewarts. She hated to do it, but she would have to call off his vigil of watchdogging Margaret and Darnley to free them up to do their worst tonight.

"I thought," Margaret went on with a sweeping gesture toward the array of tents and tables, "that you had eschewed all pleasantries during plague time and with the unfortunate deaths of the Suttons. If I were you—"

"You are not me, and will never be, Margaret. Yet perhaps you still harbor hopes that the Tudor blood in your son's veins will make him someone's choice to sit a throne."

Margaret looked appalled, as if she'd never considered such a thought. "Indeed, I hope for nothing of the kind, Your Majesty, however much I see my son's many virtues, as does any good mother—such as Lady Cecil here."

Elizabeth spun, amazed to see how close Mildred had approached unheard behind her. But it was noisy now, as some milled about the grounds and servants climbed out of the cumbersome carts of baggage and goods which had brought up the rear of the procession.

"I believe, countess," Mildred said, her voice cold as steel as she bobbed her betters a curtsy, "you refer to my stepson, Tom, as my son Robert is still in leading strings, and hardly glowing with virtues yet, as is your son and heir."

And then, over the women's shoulders, Elizabeth saw what she'd been waiting for. Still far back, separate from the other carts, Meg Milligrew drove one heaped with straw.

Jenks, the queen thought. It must hold poor Jenks. She was so anxious to know how he was and to hear of his journey into London she would have liked to sprint to greet him. Granted he had disobeyed her orders to avoid that city, but he had done it for his queen and at great risk to his own person.

But sadly, she must carefully keep her distance from him. Paying scant attention to her companions, though she occasionally took part in their stilted conversation, Elizabeth noted an exhausted-looking horse tied to the back of Meg's cart. Her long-honed eye for horse flesh made her certain it was the same one that Lord Darnley had abused back at Hampton Court.

"I trust Lady Cecil will show you to your quarters in the manor, just down the hall from mine," Elizabeth told Margaret. "I hope your dear, devoted son won't mind sleeping out under the stars."

"It looks to be an awfully small manorhouse," Margaret whined, taking up that tack again. "But yes, please show me to my rooms, Lady Cecil."

"Room," the queen corrected pointedly, vexed at Margaret and Darnley, however much she'd steeled herself not to let on. "I have three, and you have one. I will see you later this afternoon, dear cousin."

With Ned and Clifford trailing a good ways behind her, the queen slipped around the manorhouse and down the path toward the small dairy barn where Meg had pulled off the road. The ramshackle garden sheds stood beyond.

But when the queen turned away from the barn and headed deeper into the forest, she heard Ned's low whistle, so distinct from the sharp ones Jenks often used to call his mounts. She turned back and saw Darnley had followed her out here—and that, he, too, was surprised to see that he was being followed. He was obviously startled as Ned and Clifford came quickly up behind him. Surely he had not intended to make an assault on her person here.

"What is it, my lord?" the queen called to Darnley who, now discovered, came a bit closer, then swept her a graceful bow.

"Forgive me, Your Majesty, but I thought my mother had come out here—with you. I saw you speaking."

"She went into the house. Come, walk with me, as I was just about to circle around to the lane," she said, drawing him away from Meg and Jenks, though she figured if word leaked out that Jenks was here and had been to London, no one would go near him anyway. In so many ways, she felt she was sitting on a barrel full of fireworks.

Though she turned back to be certain her guards were still walking behind, the queen kept up the pretense of being calm, chatting to Darnley to allay any suspicions he might have about being suspect. She asked him about the weather and their journey from Hatfield and requested he play some lute music later, though not after supper, so he could be at leisure as night fell.

Returning on the lane, they passed Meg's cart with the horse still tied behind it. Elizabeth realized then why Meg must have brought the poor beast. For some reason, Jenks could have ridden from London on it, and Meg had probably promised him she would try to heal it, too. That would be just like Jenks and Meg.

"Look," Darnley interrupted her thoughts with a snicker. "Some jolthead's put the cart before the horse, an ill-kept one at that."

He meant it as a jest, but it was the last straw with this man she did not trust and could not abide. Darnley and her cousin Margaret were no doubt behind all that had happened ill since she'd refused to let them go off to Scotland to foment their Papist plots. But as she spun to give the wretch what-for, he made the mistake of smacking the poor horse on the rump.

The animal snorted and jerked his reins free of the cart's back rail. Elizabeth thought the stallion recognized Darnley and would run. But it charged, nipping him—head and shoulder—and bumping him so hard Darnley went to his knees and covered his head with both arms. Though his shoulder padding and hat had taken the worst of the attack, when Darnley yelped and scrambled to his feet, the queen saw his forehead was bleeding.

"Damned, mangy beast!" he cried and whipped out his sword as if he'd run the horse through.

"No drawn weapons in the queen's presence!" Elizabeth commanded. "Stand away from me!"

Clifford and Ned exploded at him to wrench his sword away. Glaring at the horse and her servants, Darnley brushed himself off. When he realized he was bleeding, he dabbed his forehead with a narrow silk and gauze scarf he produced from his doublet.

For drawing a sword near her person, the queen could have banished him from court or even imprisoned him, but he must be kept free to fall into her trap tonight. Now, even more, she could believe it was he who tried to strangle her, who struck poor Templar from behind with a brick, then cleverly poisoned Bettina, perhaps even Chris and Jamie.

"I recognize that maggot-eaten beast," Darnley clipped out, not daring to retrieve his sword, which no one proffered him. "The damned horse is one which I tangled with at Hampton Court."

"He recognized you, too, my lord," Elizabeth declared, boldly seizing the animal's reins and patting his neck to steady herself as much as to quiet him. "Be grateful he didn't take his hoofs to you as you took your whip to him. Never forget that those harmed, lowest to highest in the land, may rightfully strike back!"

He dared to glare at her, hatred naked on his face before he masked his feelings again. And then she realized that the scarf with which he blotted the blood from his forehead was identical to the garters she'd been choked with. Since Kat had given those out in droves, it didn't prove he was the strangler, but he'd certainly kept them in remembrance of something when she hadn't seen their like about for days.

More disdainful than dismayed, with a stiff bow, the black-guard strode away without his sword. He would probably assure his mother that, as soon as they rid themselves of the English queen, either they or Mary, Queen of Scots would be next in line to sit on the English throne. If Elizabeth were betting on who was the murderer in her mazes, she'd pick her own kin, the Scots-loving Stewarts, hands down. And she'd even wager, especially after this incident, she herself was, once again, the next intended victim.

Chapter the Seventeenth

 AS THE LATE SUMMER'S DUSK SETTLED OVER THEO-
balds, their plan began to unfold.

Torches flamed from metal stanchions. Food and
drink flowed freely. Under a nearly full moon,
guests mingled and walked the grounds, hearing numerous lectures from the proud host about how such and such a vista
would look when they returned in several years. With planks
laid on sawhorses, Ned built his trestle platform just outside
the moat. Elizabeth and Cecil had also set the stage for the
murderer—night, a crowd, a maze.

"Someday we will be able to house all of you in great comfort," the queen overheard Mildred assure her guests more than
once. She was their only suspect who had not visited the water
maze today, though she could know it well from her time here
before the others arrived. With growing trepidation, Elizabeth

had seen that even Kat had seemed fascinated by a rowboat tour of the watery twists and turns.

Darnley, the queen had been informed by Clifford, had gone through the maze with Chris Hatton at first light and again with his mother. Jamie had rowed Rosie through it while Kat took a nap in the house.

"I can tell Jamie is going to ask for my hand, Your Grace," Rosie had whispered to her royal mistress earlier. "But I never want to desert you, and how can a queen's maid of honor wed one of his rank—or lack thereof?"

"You know very well how," the queen had told her with an affectionate squeeze of her arm. "The queen elevates her dear maid of honor's betrothed and turns her maid to lady of the bedchamber once she's wed. With Kat ailing I cannot do without you. But Jamie will be dependent on me to prosper, so you shall both live at court in my service."

Rosie had vowed eternal loyalty, but Elizabeth knew how husbands could change things. With a sigh, she went about her duties, helping Cecil weave their web.

As much as the queen had wanted to see Jenks from afar and call out some questions to him, the press of people had kept her from trying to visit him again. Meg said he was resting comfortably and showed no signs of the plague.

"Since Jenks can be left alone now," Elizabeth had told her, "I want you to secretly hie yourself into the manorhouse as soon as Ned begins his presentation this evening. I shall come inside, disrobe, and you shall don my clothing."

"So we will exchange garments as we have before, and you'll row into the maze in mine?"

"No. You will be sitting in my gown in my window overlooking the guests—supposedly with the headache I shall develop on cue," Elizabeth explained. "But I will not be wearing your skirts or any others—nor be rowing."

"But you will have guards with you?"

"Counting Cecil, I shall have two, but simplicity and surprise are essential. Do not worry for me, as everything is arranged. You'd best return to Jenks for a while. And how do things stand between the two of you?"

"I was stunned to hear what he had done," Meg admitted, wringing her hands, "though he's always risked a great deal to help you. But he said he risked his life this time because he despaired I didn't care a fig for him. Even now, he doesn't make a murmur in all his pain. And to think he's been suffering over loving me in silence all these years." She shook her head and pressed her clasped hands between her breasts. "It's a stronger aphrodisiac than any herb I could name."

"And have you told him so?"

"I think he knows."

"The more I've seen the Cecils' dilemma, the more I believe assuming such is not enough, my Meg. If you care for Jenks, you must tell him now, but," Elizabeth added on her way back to join her courtiers, "be on time the moment Ned begins to speak!"

Elizabeth had written her steward at Hatfield that her yeoman Stackpole was not to come to Theobalds with the guards accompanying her courtiers. At least the man would be useful for one thing before she replaced him. Just after supper, while Darnley played the lute and guests sang madrigals on the lawn outside the moat, Stackpole made his entrance. He rode hard toward the manor, though he had no idea he was part of their plot, delivering a message Cecil himself had written and sent back to Hatfield.

Cecil was ready, standing with Mildred, on the old drawbridge over the moat, as if it were the gallery in this *al fresco* theater. Cecil made a great fuss of stopping Stackpole and taking the note from him. He carried it to the queen through the press of people as Darnley strummed his last chords and the singing trailed off.

Such silence fell that the queen could hear a night owl nearby in the trees. The breeze lifted her tresses off her flushed face.

"A note from Hampton Court via Hatfield," Cecil informed the queen loudly enough that everyone could hear.

"From whom?" she demanded, turning her profile to their audience.

"The coroner admits he forgot to inform us that he turned up something on Templar's corpse, a note which reveals—"

"My lord, not here, not now," she scolded. "I cannot bear to have this lovely evening ruined by having to fret about my lack-brain legal authorities again. Keep that note but do not bring it up to me before tomorrow morn. I will have some merriment this eve in these dour times, I swear I shall, and you will not gainsay me!"

She even threw her fan, which Rosie retrieved for her. Cecil pretended to try to reason with her again, then, when she dismissed him, he stomped off toward the maze, folding and placing the note in his flat hat. As if wishing for a diversion, Elizabeth motioned for Ned's histrionics to begin.

"And now," he called out in his clearest voice as he mounted the platform, "I shall present a few speeches to promote frivolity and to honor gaiety."

In the front row, for they were all groundlings of necessity this evening, Elizabeth began to hang her head and stroke her brow as if her head pained her.

"And to the person who laughs and applauds the loudest, a rare prize," Ned went on, "a decent mattress to replace the straw-stuffed ones in the pavilions!"

Laughter. Elizabeth waited until it passed and sighed. Kat came over. "One of your headaches coming on, Your Grace?" she inquired, as if she knew the script.

" 'S blood, I'm afraid so. It was that row with Cecil set it off," she said, rubbing her temples harder under her plumed hat. "One can't countenance a thing that rustic coroner says, and Cecil's in a stir as if it were state business. I believe I will go upstairs and sit in my window to listen to Ned from there."

"I'll come along, too," Rosie declared, "and Kat can stay out here with Lady Cecil." Elizabeth saw that Jamie was standing near his beloved, even as Chris Hatton had been hovering, watching his queen most of the evening with apparently adoring eyes. She could hear whispers in the crowd as others spread the news that Her Majesty was feeling indisposed.

"No," Elizabeth told Rosie, "you both stay here. I want everyone to have a good time, and I shall sit up in that very window to be sure you do." She pointed to her chamber window above the moat, directly behind Ned's little stage. "Consider it a royal command. Mildred," the queen told Lady Cecil, for it seemed she suddenly huddled nearby, too, "I need to go inside for a bit. All of you, carry on."

Trying not to rush through her exit, she made her way over the moat bridge and entered the courtyard, then went into the manor and up the central staircase to her small suite of rooms.

Meg, bless her, was already there, stripping off her skirts and sleeves.

"Here, Your Grace, I can help unlace you."

"And now," Ned's voice carried through the window, "I shall commence the evening's enjoyments with a speech from the new and fashionable Italian comedy, *The Potion of Pleasure*. Close your eyes and dream you are in sunny Italy and have found such a magic liquor there as to make anyone who drinks it either fall in love with you or die poisoned by rue and regret...."

"He's overdoing it," Elizabeth muttered as Meg unlaced the back of her gown, "especially since I think our murderer's been brewing poison of late."

"Overdoing it, that's Ned. Just think, this is our own tiring house behind his stage. But what are you going to wear then? I don't see a th—"

"In the coffer on top—Ned's riding clothes."

"You didn't tell me that part of it."

"I said I wasn't wearing skirts. Just hurry!" the queen commanded, untying and yanking the loosened bodice over her own head. She untied her heavy petticoats herself and let them fall into a pool she stepped out of so that Meg could step in. "Lace yourself as best you can," Elizabeth told her, "because I must get out to the maze posthaste. Your hair looks right but, even in here, wear my hat, and do not fidget!"

It had taken Elizabeth longer than she'd planned to walk far around the crowd on the front lawn. Despite the warmth of the weather, even fully clothed and booted, she found the water colder than she'd expected. She was shivering already. Bucking the current, she made her way toward the maze into which Cecil had rowed nearly a quarter hour ago.

She saw some sort of twisted bunting hanging over the entrance. Draperies or some swag of heraldic decoration? Part was of muted color, but part was stark white with scalloped edges. Why had Cecil suddenly put that here?

Then Elizabeth realized that she was looking at the hacked off skirts and petticoats of the murdered Bettina.

She almost screamed to Cecil and Clifford to come and look. Had the killer ferreted out their plan and thrown down his version of a gauntlet? Did it imply, *Keep out* or *I dare you to come in*? Elizabeth wished she'd put an individual watch on each of her suspects, but she was afraid that would scare the guilty one away.

She almost fled in fear, but this trap was the best chance they had to stop this madness. Suddenly furious at such diabolical defiance, she yanked the material down. Entering the maze, she jammed it inside the first interior wall to hide it, though the thorns scratched her hands and wrists.

Steeling herself, forcing each slow step, she made her way toward the dead end where she would hide, just one wall away from the heart of the maze where Cecil waited. From there, she would be able to overhear whoever approached him and, hopefully, glimpse him or her rowing past.

She partly pulled herself along farther by holding on to the barrels in which the thorn maze was planted. Each booted step took her through water which lapped nearly to her shoulders. She felt again for the dagger in its scabbard she'd strapped on so that it rode between her breasts. Clifford, hidden just behind the maze, ready to duck through a single opening he'd hacked in it to reach Cecil, had a dagger and a sword—Darnley's, for it pleased her to think of him being captured with his own weapon.

But even before Elizabeth could get herself in place, she heard a boat behind her. It could be nothing, but it could be everything, and here she yet stood in the main path. She pulled herself toward the barrels on her left, turned sideways, and ducked under the maze wall so she got soaked up to her chin.

Though thorns snagged her man's cap and pinned-up hair and scratched her forehead, she was out of the main channel. Yet she had no way from here to see who was in the boat which rocked the water as it passed. She hoisted herself up a bit by the edges of the barrels. After that harrowing experience underwater in the pond at Hatfield, feeling as if her breath were choked from her, she had no intention of so much as getting her mouth under, let alone her nose.

When the water quieted, she went back out into the main path, moving stealthily toward her position near the goal. Whoever had gone by was no doubt nearing Cecil already.

William Cecil sat in the goal of the maze with his boat rocking slightly. A breeze had sprung up, disturbing the water even more than did the rain-swollen current. The hedges walling him in seemed to shift and sigh. Somewhere an owl hooted its haunted cry.

He used an oar to keep out of the shrubs so the thudding *bump, bump* of boat against a barrel would not drive him to distraction or frighten anyone away. Moonlight or not, the single, small lantern set in the bow of the boat seemed so meager now. He was getting tired of pretending to strain to read the note from his hat. This wasn't going to work. The ghostly murderer of the royal mazes would never come here to this one he owned, despite the fact they were tempting him or her with a grand prize.

He wondered if the queen and Clifford had waded in yet, Clifford from the back of the maze, the queen from near the rowboats. They had pored over the maze pattern he'd drawn for them, as well as showed them in person. Now, for some reason, he kept picturing that wooden maze game Templar Sutton had brought for a gift on the day of his daughter's christening. Its little ball had click-clicked through the turns to the *E* for Elizabeth in its very center.

He sat bolt upright. What if, from the first, Elizabeth had been the target of the maze murderer? When the attempt to strangle her failed because Bettina approached, to cloak the assassination plot, the traitor had dispatched the Suttons as a diversionary tactic. This elaborate sham they'd planned tonight could play directly into the mastermind's scheme to kill the queen while Cecil, more or less, treaded water.

He almost called out to Elizabeth to be certain she was safe, even at the risk of ruining their plan. But then he heard the muted, rhythmic *swish, swish* of oars in water. An oarlock creaked. His stomach knotted as his deepest fear was realized.

"Mildred?" he croaked out when he saw who rowed the boat. "Mildred!"

It could not be her behind all this, he told himself, gaping as her drawn white face emerged from shadow and her boat bumped his.

"I was worried about you, my lord. Whatever is in that letter?"

"You should not have left our guests," he said, sounding inane to himself, but he was so frightened of what she might say or do next. The queen, he knew, was listening.

"They're entranced with Ned Topside, so they won't miss me. I'll go right back, but I had to settle something once and for all between us. I have something to confess—about another night in the maze at Hampton Court."

He blinked back tears. He tried to speak but nothing came out.

"My lord," she went on, her voice greatly agitated, "I eavesdropped on you and the queen that night and heard her warn you to keep a watch out for a piece of black cloth torn from the garment of one who had assaulted her. So I hid a skirt of mine which had a tear, the one Bettina was later buried in. But I swear to you, I did not harm anyone."

Yet to Cecil's utter horror, she leaned into her boat and lifted a brick from beneath her skirts, holding it in both hands as if prepared to heave it at him. He felt sick to his soul. She'd killed Templar to cover her attempt to strangle the queen, and if that were true, Bettina—and now . . .

"I want this brick to be in the foundation of Theobalds we will build together for Robert and our family," she said, holding it out to him. "I sent for it from your ancestral home and believe it should be the cornerstone of our home here—the sign we will start over together."

He almost fell into the water in relief.

"Mildred, I know I've been so busy, so distracted—"

"I knew when I wed you that you'd bedded Bettina and how

disappointed you must have been in yourself. I believed then and now that rash, random transgression and your ill-conceived first marriage would make you work hard at our union."

"Not hard enough. Forgive me."

"I have finally decided to. But I must tell you, my—my behavior since Robert's birth was not all my own doing, that is, I've suffered from some dread mental or spiritual disease over which I had no control. But I think I'm better now. Her Grace tells me that you love me, and I believe her. You spend enough time with the woman that she should know. I should not have left our guests to tell you all this now, but who knows what time you will be to bed tonight—and I wanted to lift from your heart the despair I've caused you."

Tears blurred his vision. He had longed to do that very thing for her and failed, for she—and the queen—had somehow healed her. They rocked their boats as they reached for each other and kissed.

"I love you with both my heart and mind, my Mildred," he whispered. "But you must return to our guests and quickly. I can't tell you why, but please—"

"Oh, I see," she said, looking calm and wise like the Mildred he used to know. "You're not really here because you are vexed at the queen or want to be alone. She has sent you to catch whoever has been using her royal mazes for murder. Please, Will, have a care for your safety as well as hers."

"Go now, and pray no one else is quite as clever as you," Cecil whispered and helped her turn the prow of her boat outward. Their hands clasped before she bent to her oars.

Elizabeth overheard most of the exchange between the Cecils. She was relieved for them, but their untimely reconciliation could cause the murderer to bolt. After Mildred rowed away— the queen could see her silhouette as the boat flashed by the dead end in which she was hidden—she almost called to Cecil to be sure he knew she was in place. The silence stretched on and on, broken only by the persistent hoot of an owl and the occasional, distant sound of laughter from the manor grounds.

As water dripped off her chin, she thought of the female ghost who had supposedly drowned herself in this maze and now left barefooted prints and a trail of water in the house at night. Nonsense, she told herself. As her father had said, ghosts were merely someone's guilty conscience, so no wonder England was full of them. But she began to tremble even more.

She stood still as a statue when as she heard the *swish, swish* of water again. So smooth was the passage of a boat slipping past she could not glimpse more than a dark form bent over the oars. But she could tell one thing: this person was stronger than Mildred, who had thrashed the water more. At least it could not be Kat; this must be a man. And so much for musings about a ghost. This rower was sinewy flesh and blood.

Elizabeth pressed her ear to the prickly leaves which grew so thick here Cecil's lantern did not penetrate. If it hadn't been for the wan moonlight, the darkness would be a wall of its own. The hedge grew lower here, too, so to reach him directly she would need to put her whole head underwater. Since she refused to risk that, she would instead go around the end of this cul-de-sac to get to him. Slowly, she edged in that direction.

"Who goes there?" Cecil cried out to the rower. "Unmask!"

Unmask? Elizabeth thought. Someone was trying to hide an identity until the moment of murder?

"I'm not masked, Secretary Cecil." A man's voice. "It's just this bandage on my forehead flapped over my face—see? A whoreson wild horse bit me today."

Darnley's voice. She should have known it was Darnley from the first.

"Ah, Lord Darnley," Cecil said, quite loudly, "it is you." Elizabeth could hear his voice shaking as he too must realize Darnley was indeed their murderer. She drew her dagger, hoping Clifford was ready to rush in at the first cry of Cecil's warning words, *You amaze me!* But Darnley must give himself away verbally or physically before they did surprise him.

"I apologize for interrupting your solitude, my lord," Darnley said, "but I have a privy favor to ask and the court seems full of spies lately, spies hostile to me."

"Then what do you have to say no one else dare hear?"

"I realize the queen has every right to change her mind—most women seem to, and she above all. But I petition you, my lord, as you have her ear which even outsiders suddenly brought to court have had more so than even I or my mother despite our shared royal blood with Her Grace. . . ."

"Outsiders like Templar and Bettina Sutton?" Cecil interrupted Darnley's nervous rambling.

"Yes, if you must know. Privy tours and meetings, invitations to the widow to go to Hatfield when the household was much reduced even of nobles. But what I am imploring you, my lord, is that you reason with Her Majesty to allow me to join my father in Scotland."

That was the first thing the blackguard had said which made Elizabeth waver on the certainty of his guilt. If he'd come to kill Cecil—to strike down another she obviously heeded and trusted more than she did her own Stewart kin—why waste time with petitions? Unless, that is, it was just to get Cecil to lower his guard.

Every muscle in the queen's body tensed, and a pain cramped her left calf. Gritting her teeth, trying to listen, she lifted her leg and pulled her toes up with her hand not holding the dagger. Leaning against a barrel, she fiercely kneaded her muscle, even through the damned stiff boot.

"Lord Cecil, I swear to you, it will behoove you to have me in your debt, for I intend to rise high in Scotland, one way or the other, since it seems I never shall here."

Since Darnley was talking as loudly as Cecil, he could surely not be a murderer who relied on stealth. But if the murderer wasn't Darnley . . .

" 'One way or the other?' " Cecil repeated Darnley's words. "Hell's gates, that sounds more than opportunistic—quite ruthless to me, my lord."

"You do realize, Cecil, it is to your and the queen's advantage to have me in Edinburgh to keep a good eye on her cousin, the Scots queen, and on my honor, I will."

Your honor? Elizabeth nearly shouted. Still hobbled by the cramp, she moved slowly toward the opening of the dead end, straining to hear what else Darnley would say. So far he had not attacked Cecil in any way and had actually made sense, though she'd trust him about as much as she'd trust herself swimming the entire length of this cold, wretched maze.

She was not certain whether she felt thrilled or thwarted

when Darnley thanked Cecil for any help he could give, and, with a cheery good night, began to row again.

Elizabeth moved back as he passed her and evidently rowed out of the maze. She resheathed her dagger in relief, though she felt like crying. This continued push and pull of deep, dark water might as well be a stream of her own fears. She had failed and had better wade out of here before she caught the ague or a cold. Though she supposed Mildred, at least, had cleared herself of suspicion, she wasn't entirely sure about Darnley. He might yet be simply toying with them. The nightmare was not over but rolled on.

The queen waited for a few more agonizing minutes, then admitted to herself that the maze murderer had called her bluff and beaten her again. She must summon Cecil to pick her up and order Clifford to wade his way out. But as she opened her mouth, she heard again the distant creak of oars and felt the water roil.

Chapter the Eighteenth

THE THIRD TIME'S A CHARM, THE OLD SUPERSTITION danced through Elizabeth's head while she waited to catch a glimpse of this boat as it went by. But the sounds and sway of water stopped.

She held her breath. Surely she had not imagined it, a ghost boat in the maze. She should have asked Cecil if the woman who drowned here had rowed herself out or waded in.

Then she heard a muffled cry, a thud, a splash, but not, thank God, from Cecil's direction. She started out of her hiding place to see what had happened, but the plop and creak of oars began again. What could have been dropped in the moat? It had been a big splash that now rocked her and the maze walls.

A boat with a single hunched figure rowed swiftly past the opening of her hiding place, as if he or she knew to avoid each false and fruitless turn. Perhaps it was someone else, simply here for innocent reasons, like Mildred and Darnley. Elizabeth was certain she heard low voices coming from the maze goal, so Cecil must know the boatman. He could have summoned an additional guard to keep them doubly safe. Obviously, he knew the rower or he would have called out or at least spoken up as he did with Darnley.

Elizabeth strained to hear and cursed the fact she couldn't catch a glimpse of them without leaving her lair, so she began to slowly make her way out of her cul-de-sac again. She gasped to see a floating body, facedown in the water, snagged in her path.

She nearly screamed for Cecil, but what if this too was part of a trap? Worse, what if this *was* Cecil, but she could hear him talking, couldn't she? The set of the body's broad shoulders, the head of hair were so familiar. No, thank God, it wasn't Cecil.

Fearing this might be a ruse in which the floater would come to life to pull her under, she poked at the man's shoulder. He didn't budge. Fighting to steady herself in the constant current, she rolled him over and sensed, as well as saw, who it was.

Chris Hatton! Had Chris's body been the splash she'd heard? Not Chris dead, too. The snare had been sprung and not by her and Cecil.

"You amaze me!" Elizabeth shouted their signal for help. When no one answered, she cried, "Cecil! Chris Hatton's here, hurt or dead! Call Clifford!"

She breathed easier as she heard Cecil begin to row toward her. His prow, then the hulk of his boat entered her hiding place to push her back, holding the floating body, against the three-sided hedge walls.

"Cecil, someone's tried to kill Chris. He'll be heavy, but let's get him in your boat. Who else rowed in?"

"Just like your dear, departed Sir Chris, Secretary Cecil is indisposed, so I've borrowed his lantern," the man in the boat said and lifted it, nearly blinding her.

The distinct scent of gillyflowers floated to her. She knew that voice. Jamie? Jamie Barstow! But he could not have hurt his dear friend. Jamie had everything to win by befriending, not betraying her and Cecil, didn't he?

"I'm so pleased you called out," he went on, "because I was becoming bored with whispering to myself as if Cecil were simply chatting with someone. I needed to be sure he bled a bit more, shall we say, before I made my exit. And, lo, it is Her High and Mighty Majesty herself on guard."

"I'll summon my other guards—"

"If you mean Clifford, whom you've had watching me at Hatfield all week—and then at the back of this maze tonight—he's incapacitated too, though I do regret hitting him over the head and hog-tying him. He's a servant like myself, one not likely to ever be recognized or rewarded at court."

Though she wanted to scream, she forced herself to deal calmly with this clever man. "Clifford was watching the Countess of Lennox and Lord Darnley," she corrected, pleased her voice was steady, for she was trembling terribly.

"So, after all I've done, you didn't think me worthy of a watchdog. But here you are watching me privily. Really," he went on, his tone mocking, "we must stop meeting for trysts in mazes, my queen."

"It was you who listened at Mary Sidney's keyhole when I

agreed to meet Robin Dudley, you who forged that first note and left the one nailed on my ascension oak."

"I'll leave another nailed to your coffin, something else from the Bible, I think, such as, 'I have broken down all her hedges. I have brought her strongholds to ruin.'"

"You've misquoted that, but then the devil can cite Scripture for his own purpose."

"I knew I would enjoy debating you in person as much as I have from a distance, High-and-Mighty."

As they spoke, she wedged Chris's shoulders between two barrels to keep his head above water, though he gave no sign of life. "Your assumption that we are alone is wrong," she brazened, "and I'll summon my other guards if you don't let me pass."

When Jamie snickered at her bravado, she knew for certain he meant to kill her. Otherwise, he would not risk being so scornful and insulting.

"You do realize," he went on, "what I've netted myself in one fell swoop tonight?" To her rising terror, she noted his teeth gleamed white in lantern light. The murderous traitor was grinning.

"Finally, I'm rid of my lord and master, *Sir* Christopher Hatton," he boasted when she did not deign to answer, "who but pretended to be my friend and has ever looked down on me as a servant."

"I've never seen him treat you that wa—"

"Despite the times I've protected and saved him with my wit—my soul—he reaped all the benefits."

"You went to Gray's Inn with him, then to court, and live far above your station."

"But I was not allowed to stay at Gray's long enough to be called to the bar, was I?" he ranted, suddenly losing control. "No, at your whim and for 'Handsome Hatton's' face and form, I was pulled out of Gray's, which could have been my salvation. I could have become a lawyer, not dependent on him as my father's been at his father's beck and call all these years. How do you think I felt to be reprimanded by Master Sutton for leaving Gray's early, when I had no choice? Truth be told, Chris's father agreed to send me to Gray's as his son's servant. If I hadn't had to tutor the numbskull, who knows if I would have been allowed to so much as read a book or set forth an argument there!"

"I regret all that, for you have a sharp mind, however much perverted it has become of late. But you had no right to—"

"I have the right to hate Chris and you—and to find a way to bring you to justice. Isn't it terribly tragic," he plunged on, his voice mocking again, "that poor Handsome Hatton must have been fooling around in a boat after drinking too much wine tonight and hit his head on a barrel, then fell in and drowned? It was a long fall from his lofty station in life— though not so lofty and long a fall as for you. Everyone thinks you are inside the manor, but here you are, meeting Sir Christopher Hatton for an assignation just as you went out to your trysting spot with Robert Dudley in a maze. But tonight, you've sadly—perhaps when Chris tried to press himself upon you and Cecil intervened—you've all somehow drowned in the altercation."

"And Clifford somehow tied himself up and knocked himself unconscious? It won't work, Jamie. Best give it all up."

"I'm grateful for the reminder to haul him out into the forest and bury him somewhere. No, Your High and Mighty Majesty, it will work and I will win, for I take opportunity where I find it. There will be such chaos at the loss of England's young, popular queen that no one will notice I have left the court, grief-stricken, of course."

He lifted a tennis ball–sized piece of ballast from a barrel and cocked his arm as if he'd stone her as she stood, trapped. Her thoughts darted as he went on, "Now about Cecil, who no doubt never thought you should have brought me to court with Chris in the first pl—"

"That's not true. Cecil, like I, values brains, and you have those in spades." She had to get to Cecil soon. She feared this demon had already used ballast stones instead of bricks for attempting a murder on this night.

"Too late for compliments," Jamie insisted with a snicker. "You know, your brilliant principal secretary actually fell just now for my news that your Lady Ashley had attacked my beloved Lady Rosie and called her Anne Boleyn. I came directly to him, I claimed, to avoid vexing you with your vile headache."

She just gaped at him, fearing she was indeed bested in this life and death duel. He'd been wily enough to play on Cecil with Kat's dementia. Then she might indeed be doomed.

"You have heard of Anne Boleyn, High-and-Mighty?" he goaded. "Cecil and you, like the Suttons, underestimated me."

"You are in error about that. You cleverly poisoned Bettina, didn't you?" she countered, trying to stroke his sick pride. "You did not take your yew tonic, even though you were truly ill and Meg Milligrew doled it out to you. You saved it and poisoned Bettina. And endeavored to do the same to Chris."

"How clever of you, in turn, but, once again, you are dealing in half truths, and even wily lawyers always get caught for that," he said with another chuckle, as if they yet played some sort of game. "You've guessed right about Bettina but wrong about Chris."

He began tossing and catching the rock in one hand over and over. "You see, Bettina drank a goblet of my medicine I'd been saving, mixed with wine, to make all her troubles go away, I promised. But I had only a dram left for Chris, so I soaked his favorite breath cloves in it, just enough to make him suffer before I hoped to increase the dosage. We poor lackeys who are sent on errands to fetch cloves for our betters chew the cheaper gillyflowers, Your High-and-Mighty, but our breath is just as sweet. Since you've never taken to dancing with me or hanging on me as you do Chris or Robert Dudley, you would not know that."

She forced herself to ignore that barb. "So Chris was saved by Mistress Milligrew's purgatives only to be attacked in this maze by the man he most trusted and relied on?" she asked.

"He recovered so quickly that he was in fine fettle tonight, wanted to row the maze with me, so I let him come along. But, as for you and me, our battle of wits is no longer amusing. I regret to inform you the game is ended, and I have won."

"Jamie, I admire your attention to detail and could use an informant such as you in my employ."

"You're dismissing me for a dolthead again!" he cried and heaved the stone at her. She tried to dodge it, but, only slightly slowed by the water, it hit her left wrist. He immediately picked up another, bigger stone from a barrel.

"Then you don't love Rosie?" Elizabeth challenged, her voice sounding panicked now. "I told her earlier today I would raise you high to wed her——"

"It wouldn't change a thing since I was never noble or even gentry to begin with, no matter if you would bestow a title or some court sinecure. But do I love her? I was regretful I would have to disappoint her until she told me flat a few minutes ago that if it was a choice between serving you and wedding me, her loyalty lay with you. No one——*no one* recognizes the worth and genius of the rural servant's boy!" he roared. "And so, I'm taking a letter north with me to Mary, Queen of Scots, informing her that, when she's asked to come and take your throne, she'll owe it all to me."

When he named her nemesis, Elizabeth was so stunned at the magnitude of his betrayal she stood momentarily speechless.

"I've played up to Lord Darnley, too," Jamie went on, "at a dear price——a *dear* price to that sodomite, I tell you, but if he prospers with Queen Mary, I'll need him. As for now, I must tidy up here and be going."

He was going to stone her, to drown her. She found her voice again. "It was you who tried to strangle me in the maze at Hampton Court," she accused. "Why didn't you finish the deed then, Master Barstow?"

"Ah, *Master* Barstow now, is it? You look down on anyone not——ah, at least to the manor born."

"No, I look down on a tormentor and murderer and betrayer, whom God will judge and punish, whether or not someone else does first."

"A bold speech, but then, you are good at that. I didn't finish strangling you because that would not have made the game so pleasant. I wanted the challenge of proving I could demand your utmost attention, then still beat you, Templar, and Cecil in a convoluted lawyer's chess match, and I have done so—royally."

He gathered yet more stones and laid them on his knees.

"Tell me about you and Bettina," Elizabeth demanded. "I see you draped her skirts across the opening of the maze this night."

"Are you the one who ripped them down? The wielder of those garden clippers was the one who used to help his father shear both sheep and trim hedges on the Hattons' estate—and to long for so much more. A clue to my identity left right between the whore's spread legs, and you didn't credit me for even that."

"Nor was it to your credit that you must have had—not an *affaire de coeur*, for you have no heart—but an affair of lust with Bettina at Gray's." She was gambling she could get him angry enough to make a mistake, even to miss her when he threw that growing pile of stones.

"She was, shall we say, more than willing," he said smugly. "We were very careful in those years, but I was annoyed she might divulge our liaison when she came to court."

"She did not betray your confidence."

"She betrayed me!" he shouted. "Like you, like everyone, she favored Chris over me. But I'm the one who enjoyed her charms, and I'm going to enjoy this. Like the others, you are about to become just another piece of the puzzle that is my maze masterpiece. And I shall live to outfox another queen and her minions when Mary of Scots comes here to take your throne."

Jamie cocked his arm, then set his lantern down in the prow to pick up yet another stone from the barrel of ballast. Elizabeth saw but one way out, the path she dreaded and had vowed never to take again. Sucking in a breath, even as he hurled a stone, she ducked beneath the surface of the water.

This was better than before, she thought, shoving herself between two barrels, grateful no skirts weighed her down. She felt her way through the cold current, forcing herself to hold her breath. When her lungs were nearly bursting, she exploded upward one path over from Jamie in his boat.

He evidently heard her; the oarlocks creaked as he beat the water and shoved at hedges to come out of the dead end and after her.

Cat and mouse in the maze, she thought, trying to picture Cecil's sketch of it. As Jamie's boat blocked the end of the path she'd emerged in, she took another breath and went another row over, then another. Temporary salvation, for this third passage could not be accessed from the main one on which he found himself. Let him try to outwit her in this maze. She could eventually work her way out of the entire labyrinth, but that would put her in a stretch of open water where he could catch her, so the game was not done yet.

Concentrating despite the stinging in her eyes and nose, the queen retraced her steps backwards. She could hear her pursuer breathing hard, coming closer each time her ears emptied of water, or could that be her own ragged breath?

She pictured the watery paths he would have to take to come after her again, and lay in wait. Rowing desperately now, he bounced the corners of hedges, splashing. Elizabeth had finally gone deadly calm inside, desperate but determined.

She could tell he came closer, only one thorny wall away. Taking a breath, she went under and popped up next to his boat as he passed, just missing the thrust of his oar.

Her lungs bursting, Elizabeth surfaced and gasped for air. "I win!" she screamed.

Startled, Jamie slammed his oars in the water to halt and half stood, lifting an oar to strike her. She rocked his boat toward, then away from her hard enough to throw him out, headlong into the hedge on the other side.

His face raked through the thorns, and he splashed into the water. A dull thud resounded as his head hit a barrel. She braced herself, then turned his boat and rammed the prow into him, once, twice when he came up, flailing, choking. If she could but pin him against a barrel . . .

Elizabeth held her breath again and went under two rows away to wait. She heard and felt nothing but roiling water which slowly stilled. No sound from him unless he too would carry on the game to lay yet another trap, or he walked through the water to come stealthily after her. Still, nothing.

But then she heard a boat, this one, thank the Lord, from outside, coming toward, then into the maze. It shot quickly past her position in the first false turn, but she saw Rosie rowed with Kat in the stern.

"Rosie, help me! There's a man after me in the water," she shouted, deciding not to spring his identity on her yet.

"Your Grace? I thought you were in the manorhouse!"

"Be careful near that drifting boat. Row back toward the maze. Lord Cecil is back there and needs help and Chris is—"

"But here comes Lord Cecil. Oh no, with a bloody head and someone—Chris Hatton, hurt too—in his boat."

Cecil and Chris alive, the queen rejoiced, even as Rosie's voice rang out again, "But where's Jamie? I thought he came out here, and I need to talk to him."

Despite the shock poor Rosie had coming, Elizabeth felt warmed by salvation's victory. Behind Rosie's boat came Cecil's craft, floating in the current while he dazedly held his bleeding head with both hands. But he'd somehow brought Chris with him, for his big body sprawled over the side of the boat as he coughed up water.

"I told you not to fall in again, lovey!" Kat cried as if nothing were amiss with Cecil or Chris. "If you get hurt, you'll never live long enough to become queen."

"Don't fuss over this single bruise of mine, but tend to the others," Elizabeth ordered as Meg and Mildred bustled from one sick bed to the other. "If you can get them through the night, we'll fetch the doctor from St. Alban's in the morning."

Jenks was out in the garden shed fast asleep, but Cecil had lost a lot of blood and had a blinding headache. Yet each time Mildred bathed his bruised forehead, he smiled.

Clifford had been knocked out and tied up on solid ground, without seeing who or what had hit him, so perhaps Jamie had felt some affinity for a fellow servant. Chris Hatton had a concussion and water in the lungs, but his grief that his best friend had so deluded everyone seemed to pain him as much.

Regretful that a person of such promise in her kingdom could have been so embittered and gone so bad, the queen had ordered Jamie Barstow guarded in death as she had not in life. His body lay on the lawn, covered by a sheet to await burial after his unfortunate "accident" in the maze, which had set the guests all agog. The potentially brilliant lawyer Jamie Barstow would have no day of trial or punishment in court but before

God's judgment throne, she thought sadly. But however slighted he had felt, however overlooked, it gave him no excuse for making murder a rule in his demented games.

Despite the fact that daylight was yet hours away, the queen's courtiers had been told that he had confessed to Lord Cecil in the water maze that he had murdered Templar and Bettina Sutton. Then, the public story went, the guilt-ridden killer had drowned himself, though Cecil and Chris had tried to save him.

Clifford had agreed to swallow his pride to say he had merely backed into a tree limb in the dark. Elizabeth would reward both him and Rosie well, not only with preferments but with seats on her Privy Plot Council, should there ever—God forbid—be the need for it to be assembled again.

"I can't believe it of him—his doing all of that," Rosie sobbed into the queen's handkerchief since she had already soaked her own. They sat in a small chamber down the narrow, first-floor hall from the one in which the injured men were being tended.

"I thought it best to tell you the truth," Elizabeth explained to her friend. "It's painful but, in the end, will make us wiser and stronger, too."

The queen had donned a robe Kat had fetched, but her hair was still wet and she'd taken off Ned's water-logged boots to go barefooted.

"Yes, I'm grateful to have this clear sign," Rosie managed, blowing her nose again. "I shall remain as I was—a virgin serving you, Your Grace."

"Do not think we will live unhappily," Elizabeth promised, rising and patting her shoulder. "I warrant there won't be one dull moment, though I wish for such at times."

Rosie nodded, but began to cry again. Kat, ever more adept at consoling others, sat beside the young woman and pulled her into her arms.

Elizabeth stood watching, cherishing the memories of Kat comforting her in her youth. Let her tend to Rosie now, for Elizabeth must continue to find strength elsewhere for the days ahead.

Aching and exhausted, the queen heaved a sigh and leaned against the door one moment more, then headed down the hall to see how the injured men were faring. The maze murderer had been wrong that she did not admire men of common or yeoman stock like Clifford or her dear Jenks, even Templar. Though educated, titled men like Cecil, Chris, and Robin were the bones on which she'd build her kingdom, commoners would be the very flesh and blood of it.

Tomorrow, she thought, she would send Darnley to Scotland with greetings to her dangerous cousin Mary, yet hold Margaret Stewart here. It was good to keep one's friends close, but to reign and rule, one must keep enemies even closer. Soon she would make grand plans with Cecil to visit the university town of Cambridge, and she would return to her beloved, beleaguered London as soon as it was safe. She no longer felt like the ghost of herself, for the queen that she could be had much to do.

Hearing someone behind her, she glanced back, but saw no one there. Yet distant lantern light reflected in wet footprints and a trail of dripped water on the floor. Whether they were hers or not, the queen, she thought, must not be ruled by fear, so she just kept going.

AUTHOR'S NOTE

Kat Ashley died the next year, "much lamented." It was the same year in which Henry Stewart, Lord Darnley, wed Mary Queen of Scots. Some scholars have claimed they cannot understand why the wily, brilliant queen miscalculated to allow Darnley to go to Scotland, while publicly promoting Robert Dudley to Mary as her choice for Mary's husband. I believe Elizabeth Tudor hardly ever miscalculated, though I don't believe she could have foreseen the catastrophe—in keeping with the times, a violent murder, of course—that resulted.

Mary "Rosie" Radcliffe remained Elizabeth's loyal companion for forty years, never wedding despite her beauty and popularity. Sir Christopher Hatton also never married, but remained a favorite of the queen, holding many offices until his death in 1591. Hatton, like Robert Dudley, built a grand home to entertain the queen, but none could rival Cecil's Theobalds, which, unfortunately, does not stand today, though its grounds are a lovely public park.

Elizabeth visited Theobalds on her summer progresses at least twelve times, and Cecil wrote in his usual understated style that the creation of Theobalds was "not without some partial direction from Her Majesty." Cecil and Mildred's son Robert inherited both Theobalds and his father's brilliance to become Elizabeth's chief advisor in the mature years of her reign.

Robert Cecil also served Elizabeth's successor, King James I (the son of Mary, Queen of Scots, and Lord Darnley) who fell in love with beautiful Theobalds. Robert Cecil agreed to trade King James Theobalds for Hatfield House; Theobalds Palace became a favorite royal home where the king died in 1625. Although many Elizabethan houses boasted fine mazes, the one at Theobalds was unique. A visitor to the grounds the year of Cecil's death wrote of "the pleasure of going in a boat and rowing between the shrubs."

I have always found mazes fascinating and have been lost twice in the current one at Hampton Court, planted for William of Orange and Queen Mary Stuart nearly a century after Elizabeth's death. The Tudor maze was probably on a different site from the trapezoidal one that can be visited today.

Excellent books on British mazes include *Labyrinth: Solving the Riddle of the Maze* and *The British Maze Guide*, both by Adrian Fisher. *Mazes and Labyrinths: Their History and Development* by W. H. Matthews is also fascinating. Mazes and knot gardens are making a comeback today in gardening and religion as is highlighted in many current periodicals, including "A-maze-ing labyrinths wind up in backyards: Ancient tradition can be a modern refuge," by Shawn Sell in *USA Today*, October 12, 2001.

Although it seems in the story that both the rural authorities slighted the murder investigations of Templar's and Bettina's deaths, such practice is authentic for those times, in major cities as well as the countryside. Autopsies were not yet permitted. The innocent or guilty verdict was based on "common knowledge" (what people saw), not on what we would call proof or evidence. If a murder case did go to trial, it was over in a matter of minutes and, though juries decided the outcome, little defense was offered. Our justice system may be based on English common law, but we have come a long way since.

As for other points of interest in Tudor life, it is not true that Queen Elizabeth took a bath "at least once a month whether she needed it or not." In the Tudor palace of Whitehall, Elizabeth's father had ordered built a sunken tub in a small, windowless room with a heated tile stove; this early "Turkish bath" was excavated in 1939. Elizabeth bathed often and had a keen sense of smell—perhaps not a boon in those times.

According to authorities today, Queen Catherine Howard's ghost does haunt Hampton Court. Researchers from the University of Hertfordshire were allowed to spend ten days in the palace, seeking evidence for reported murmurs, patches of cold air, and the sound of footsteps to track her presence in the "Haunted Gallery." The "wet woman" at Theobalds manorhouse is based upon the dripping female ghost at Scotney Castle in Kent.

At Windsor Castle, the ghost of Elizabeth herself has supposedly been seen, once by the current Queen Elizabeth's sister, the Princess Margaret. The sight of the Virgin Queen is often accompanied by the smell of rosewater, one of her favorite fragrances. Princess Margaret said she followed the queen's ghost to the door of the library, where she disappeared. (After all, no self-respecting manor or castle in the British Isles should be without its own ghost.)

And lastly, the clove-scented gillyflowers are our modern-day pinks, related to carnations. The word *pink* is of later origin than the Tudor era; they were probably eventually called pinks for their ragged or pinked edges. Although the origin of the word *pink* is unknown, it could have come from the pale, rose-hued gillyflowers.

One thing I did change to suit the story is that, unlike William Cecil, Christopher Hatton attended not Gray's Inn but Inner Temple, where Elizabeth saw him and brought him to court.

How "Rosie" Radcliffe came to court as a Yuletide gift to the queen and the customs and foods of the Tudor holiday season—as well as a mysterious murder during the traditional Yuletide hanging of ivy, mistletoe, and holly—will occupy Her Majesty in the next Elizabeth I Mystery: *The Queene's Christmas.*

Karen Harper
December 2001

TO MAKE A KISSING BUNCH

The size depends upon the span of the two hoops, one thrust through the other, which form the skeleton of the hanging. Wrap the hoops in ribbon, lace, or silk strips. Garland the hoops with holly, ivy, or sprigs of other greens, even apples or oranges. If at court, for a certain, string green and white paper Tudor roses from the hoops. Lastly, a sprig or two of mistletoe must needs be centered in the bunch for all to see. In the spirit of the season, hang the bunch where folks, high and low, may kiss beneath. Include enough mistletoe that men who kiss under its greenery and claim a berry for each kiss do not denude the bunch and ruin all the fine preparations.

DECEMBER 24, 1564
WHITEHALL PALACE, LONDON

"NOTHING BETTER THAN A YULETIDE HANGING," MEG MILLI-grew, Elizabeth's Strewing Herb Mistress and court herbalist, said as she came into the queen's privy chamber with a basket of white-berried mistletoe.

"The decking of halls is not to begin until the afternoon," the queen remarked, looking up from her reading. "I want to be there to see it, mayhap to help."

"It is to be later, but your maids were trying to snatch these to make a kissing bunch when I need them for Kat's new medicine."

In the slant of morning light, Elizabeth sat at the small table before a Thames-side window, frowning over documents Cecil had given her to read. She could hardly discipline herself to heed her duties, for the palace was already astir with plans and preparations. This evening began the special Twelve Days of Christmas celebration she had promised her people, Kat, and herself, though December 25th itself was always counted as the first day.

"Kat seems to do well with that mistletoe powder in her wine," the queen observed, sanding her signature. "Using it has been worth the risk, and, heavens knows, the royal physicians haven't come up with anything better."

"I'll never forget the look on your face, Your Grace, when I told you that taking too much of it is poison. But just enough has calmed the heat of Kat's heart's furnace and given her new life."

"I knew to trust your knowledge on it, and pray I will always know whom to trust," Elizabeth said as if to herself. She rose and turned to the window. Scratching the frost off a pane with her fingernails, she gazed out. Though a small stream of open water still flowed at the center, the broad Thames was freezing over from both banks. She took that for a fortuitous sign that a Frost Fair on that vast expanse was a good possibility.

As the queen returned to her work, the mistress of the herbs worked quietly away and the mistress of the realm was content to have her there. Since before she was queen, Elizabeth had gathered about her several servants as well as courtiers she could trust. She and Meg Milligrew had been through tough times together, and Meg was a member of what the queen dubbed her Privy Plot Council. Should some sort of crime or plot threaten the queen's court or person, Her Majesty assembled her covert coterie to look into it and work directly with her to solve the problem.

Meg greatly resembled the slender, red-haired, pale queen and so could stand in for her, at least at a distance, if need be. Kat Ashley had been a valued member of the secret group before her faculties began to fade, and the brilliant, wily Cecil had ever served his queen, as well privily as publicly. Stephen Jenks, Meg's betrothed and a fine horseman, had been the queen's personal body-guard in her days of exile and now was in the Earl of Leicester's retinue, though ever at the royal beck and call.

The queen's cousin Henry Carey, Baron Hunsdon, a courtier she relied on, had served in her Privy Plot Council too. Edward Thompson, alias Ned Topside, a former itinerant actor and her Master of Revels at court, was invaluable whether working overtly or covertly. Ned, the handsome rogue, was a man of many faces, voices, and personae, and rather full of himself at times. But however witty and charming the blackguard could be, she would scold him roundly for being late this morning.

The queen had sent for Ned to hear of his preparations for the holiday traditions and tomfooleries. For the six years she had been queen, Ned had served as Lord of Misrule, the one who planned and oversaw all Yuletide entertainments, both decorous and raucous. She wondered if Meg had appeared because

Ned was coming. Elizabeth knew well that the girl might be betrothed to the quiet, stalwart Jenks, but had long yearned for the mercurial, alluring Ned.

"It's a good thing for you," the queen clipped out the moment Ned was admitted, "that the Lord of Misrule's whims can gainsay all rules and regulations in these coming days, for your presence here is long overdue, and I must leave soon."

Ned swept the queen a deep, graceful bow. "Your Most Gracious Majesty," he began with a grand flourish of both arms, "I will be brief."

"That will be a novelty. Instead, write out what merriments we shall see each night, for I want no surprises. As penance for my own frivolity, I must meet with the Bishop of London's aide, Martin Bane," she added with a dramatic sigh that would have done well in a scene from the fond romances or grand tragedies Ned staged for the court.

"That Puritan's presence here these next days will be enough to throw a pall over it all!" Ned protested.

"Keep your impertinence for the banquet tonight, or I will put a lighted taper in your mouth to keep you quiet," she retorted, but they exchanged smiles and Meg giggled. Ned's eyes darted to the girl; it was evidently the first he had noted her here.

"Ah, but that's only for the roasted peacock," he recovered his aplomb, "and I intend to skewer with barbs and roast with jests everyone else. But there is one thing, Your Grace, a boon I would ask which will enhance, I vow, the entertainments for the court."

"Say on. Some new juggler or more plans for that mummers' morality play?" she asked, moving toward the door.

"To put it succinctly, my former troupe of actors is in town. Lord Hunsdon, patron of the arts that he is, tells me The Queen's Country Players are performing at the Rose and Crown on the Strand. I'm surprised they have not sought a family reunion yet. Of course, compared to my work here at court, theirs is no doubt rustic and provincial, but I thought," he went on, pursing his lips and shrugging, "if I went to see them, we could arrange a special surprise for Twelfth Night or some such—"

"A fine idea," she cut off his rambling. "Is your uncle still at their helm and that other popinjay, ah . . ."

"Randall Greene, Your Grace. I know not, but will inform you as soon as I know the current state of their affairs."

"But don't be gone long to fetch them. You're needed here, is he not, Meg?"

"Oh, yes, Your Grace," came from the coffer's depths where it seemed Meg hid her head as if to keep Ned from seeing her. "For all the responsibilities on his shoulders for the Twelve Days, that is," she added.

Elizabeth pointed to her writing table, and Ned hastened to take a piece of parchment. He dipped one of the quills in her ink pot, though he dared not plop himself in her chair, at least, not until he began his reign as Lord of Misrule. That so-called King of Mockery could get by with anything, however much he was the butt of jokes in return for his own wit.

"At least you didn't say you'd stuff an apple in my mouth as if I were the roast boar," Ned mumbled without looking up, as his pen scratched away. "I'd much prefer the lighted taper."

She had to laugh. However full of bombast, Ned always made her laugh.

———

Meg hoped Ned didn't realize she was watching every grand and graceful move he made.

"What are you doing in her coffer?" Ned asked her when the queen left the room. "You seem as busy as I truly am." He didn't even look up from his scribbling, though, when the door closed behind the queen, he scooted his paper before her chair and sat. The man, Meg fumed silently, was always busy at something or other, including chasing women, but never her. Yet there had always been something between them. Ninnyhammer that she was, Meg scolded herself, now that she was wedding Jenks sometime this winter, she'd never know what it was.

"Just hiding some mistletoe," she told him. "It's for Kat's potent medicine and not for the kissing bunches. Her Grace's ladies are making them now."

"Fancy fripperies. But, you know, one thing I remember about my mother," he said with a sigh, "is that she'd always hang little cloth figures of Mary, Joseph, and the Christ child in the hoops, so she'd never let my father kiss or pinch her under them, mistletoe or no. She'd have made a good Puritan, eh?"

"Unlike her son," Meg bantered, always striving with Ned to give as good as she got.

"Maybe you should make a kissing bunch just for Jenks."

She looked across the chamber at him when she had been trying not to and, silent for once, Ned glanced up at that moment. Their gazes snagged. Silence reigned but for the crackle of hearth flames and the howl of river wind outside.

"I hope you're happy, my Meg, and make him happy."

"I intend to be and do so. And I'm not your Meg. Not now and never was."

"As prickly as holly, aren't you? Who taught you to read and walk and talk to emulate Her Grace, eh?"

"You did because she commanded it. And who used to chide me all the time that I was clumsy and slow?"

"Hell's teeth, not anymore. You've grown up in every way."

"But," she said, her voice tremulous, "I will make a kissing bunch for Jenks, a special one with sweet-smelling herbs like dried heartsease and forget-me-not, lovers' herbs."

"Alas and alack the day," he murmured, his heavily-lashed, green eyes still on her. He started to put his hand over his heart and hang his head most mockingly—she could tell that was what was coming—but he stopped himself. Instead, he gave one sharp sniff and went back to his writing.

"Always jesting, even when you're not the Lord of Misrule!" she scolded, surprised at her sharp tone after sounding so breathless a moment ago.

Ned had always been the Lord of Misrule in her life. He'd turned her emotions topside more than once, but she was certain, she told herself, that she was right to accept Jenks's suit. Now *there* was a man to be trusted.

"I've much to do and can't be wasting time with you," she added and threw a stray mistletoe berry at Ned as she slammed the coffer closed and hurried from the room.

The queen found Secretary Cecil and the Bishop of London's aide Vicar Martin Bane awaiting her in the presence chamber. At age forty-three, Cecil looked thin, pale, and careworn, but even compared to that, Ned was right: Martin could cool a room quicker than anyone she knew.

"You requested a brief audience, Vicar Bane," she said when both men rose from their bows. "How does Bishop Grindal at this most important time of the Christian calendar?"

"It's of that I've been sent to speak, Your Most Gracious Majesty," Bane began, gripping his hawklike hands around what appeared to be a prayer book. Ordained in his own right, Bane served as liaison to her court from Lambeth Palace across the Thames, the traditional home of the Bishops of London, both in Catholic times and this Protestant era. Yet in the winter months, when Grindal was often in residence at his house on the grounds of St. Paul's Cathedral in the city itself, Bane spent more time in here at the palace.

Despite his somber black garb, the man was good-looking with classical features and a full head of graying blond hair to match his neatly trimmed beard. But he was of stringy build and always seemed to be shrinking within his clothes. His cheeks were hollow, as if something inside his head sucked in his face and sank his icy blue eyes beneath his jutted brows.

"You see," he went on in a clear, clipped voice when she nodded he might continue, "there is some concern with all this coming merriment. The Bishop and I did not at first realize you meant to flout your own family's statutes."

The queen felt her dander rise. "You refer, I assume," she clipped out, "to the Unlawful Games Act of 1541, banning sporting activity on the twenty-fifth day of December and The Holy Days and Fasting Days Act of 1551, prohibiting transport and merriment, laws enacted in my father and my brother's reigns."

At that rapid recitation, Bane's adam's apple bobbed, perhaps endangered of also being sucked inside the dark void of the man. Did he not think she had a brain in her female head? She knew full well that both Bishop Edmund Grindal and his right arm, Vicar Martin Bane, favored the rising Puritan element in her country. They were men who saw the Catholic church as nearly satanic but also viewed the Church of England, of which their queen was head, as dangerously liberal and in need of severe reform.

"I did not know you would be so ..." he stumbled for a word, "current on those laws, especially seeing that your promise to your people on Michaelmas, in effect, Your Majesty, appears to have rescinded said laws—"

"Suspended them for this year alone, after which they will be assessed anew," she interrupted, her voice as commanding as his was cold. "The Tudor kings allowed such statues to be enacted for specific reasons which are not pertinent now, in *my* reign, Vicar Bane."

"Yes, of course, I see," he said, his voice noticeably quailing as he shuffled a wary step back. He glanced askance at Cecil, only to find no help from that quarter. "Perhaps, I was a bit wide of the mark," he added, "but we of the bishopric of the great city of London believe that even snowballing is a profane pastime, and if you encourage a Frost Fair on the Thames after all these years, London's citizens will be buying and selling on holy days, let alone running hither and yon on the ice."

"But we are leaving that all up to the Lord God, are we not?" Elizabeth inquired sweetly. "If the Thames freezes over by His will, when it has not in ages, I shall take it as His most gracious sign that my housebound and hardworking people may truly enjoy this holy season by holding a fair on the river. I myself recall earlier Frost Fairs with great fondness, after not having seen one whit of profane behavior."

"But do you not live a rather sheltered life, Your Majesty? And we must consider your reinstituting of mummings. The earlier laws were partly passed because crime rose so severely when everyone was going hither and yon masked in play acting of sundry sorts."

"Yet my father himself, who cast off the excesses of the Catholic Church, loved masques and mummings at court and more than once played Lord of Misrule himself. I repeat, the decrees are for this one year, Vicar Bane, to see how things go. I assure you the precious, holy aspects of Christmas will be made dearer if they are not stifled by poor, plain rituals. We must have joy in this season of the year, for the Lord's gift to us and even for our gifts to each other. I am certain you will convey my words to Bishop Grindal and bid him come to court to-morrow to lead us all in prayer at the morning service. And you, of course, are welcome always to increase our happiness here."

When Bane saw he was beaten and bowed his way out, Cecil's stern face split in a grin. "The man doesn't know what hit him, but I warrant it feels like a jousting steed at full tilt," he told her, rubbing his hands in glee. For once those capable hands were not filled with writs or decrees, so perhaps even the diligent Cecil was ready to slacken up a bit at Christmas.

"He'll be back, lurking in corners," Elizabeth said, "but I refuse to let him or anyone else overthrow my hopes for these holidays. My most important tasks of the day are to present the new livery to my household staffs and to oversee the hanging of garlands and greens—and, the Earl of Sussex has asked for some time, no doubt to warn me against listening to Leicester again."

A sharp knock on the door startled them both. At her nod, Cecil went to open it. Two yeomen guards blocked the way of the agitated-looking Scot, Simon MacNair, brandishing a letter. Behind him, looking even more distressed was Robin Dudley, whom everyone now, except the queen in private, addressed as Leicester.

"Your Gracious Majesty," MacNair clipped out, "forgive my intrusion, but I have a message of utmost import."

"What import, man?" Cecil demanded, plucking the letter from his hand as the guards let both men enter and they bowed.

"From Edinburgh, I see," Elizabeth said, noting well the familiar, large, crimson wax seal the Queen of Scots employed.

"From your royal cousin to you, Your Grace," Cecil said. She saw him skim the letter even as he handed it over.

"Tell me what it says, Sir Simon," Elizabeth told MacNair. "Or, by the look on your face, Leicester, should you tell me?"

"Very well," Robin said. "The Scots queen has flat refused my suit for her royal hand."

"*Your* suit? *Mine* rather!" Elizabeth cried. She hoped that MacNair not only thought she was shocked and distressed but would report it forthwith to his royal mistress. Mary Stuart had taken the bait, though she was not yet hooked. If she rejected the Earl of Leicester, as Elizabeth had hoped, she might bite all the quicker and harder on the tasty Henry Stewart, Lord Darnley, whom Elizabeth intended to dangle before her.

Both royal Tudor and Stuart blood—for *Stewart* was the Scots' version of Queen Mary's Frenchified *Stuart*—ran in Darnley's veins. At the prompting of his parents and without Elizabeth's permission, the comely, twenty-year-old Darnley had courted the newly widowed Queen Mary in France, before she returned to Edinburgh. Distantly related to Elizabeth, Darnley was a dissolute weakling. If he were king, he would sap the power Mary of Scots would need for any bid to seize her rival Elizabeth's crown and kingdom.

Elizabeth lowered her voice and tried to look morose. "I am deeply grieved the Scots Queen, my dear cousin, does not think to take that which I have so lovingly offered and advised."

"How could she, Your Majesty," MacNair put in, "when the earl wrote privily to her he was not worthy of her?"

"What?" she demanded. "I have made him worthy of her, said he is worthy of her!" She felt her skin flush hot. Over anyone else, friend or foe, she could remain calm, but not over this freebooting blackguard she had long loved. And now Robin had defied her again when she had told him to keep clear of this business and she and Cecil would handle it. But no, he had gainsayed her and jumped in with both feet as if he were bidden to make royal decisions here.

"You wrote her privily, in effect warding off her affections?" she cried, striding to Robin and hitting his shoulder with her balled fist. The wretch stood his ground.

"I was surprised, too, Your Grace," MacNair went smoothly on, "since it has long been noised about that the earl has a curtained painting of Mary Stuart he dotes on. I hear 'tis in his privy rooms at Kenilworth, near the corridor on which hangs a smaller one of Your Most Gracious Majesty."

Elizabeth was so furious her blood rang in her ears, thumping with the beat of her heart. She steadied herself as she had countless times ere this and said in a well-modulated voice, "Thank you, Sir Simon, for delivering this letter and for your additional information. I assure you I shall read most carefully my cousin's thoughts and respond to her in kind. Farewell for now. Leicester, you may stay."

When the door closed on the Scot and the queen heard her yeomen guards move back into their positions outside, she said calmly to Cecil, "Please ask Ned Topside to join us for a moment, my lord." He nodded and complied instantly, going out the back way by which she had entered.

"Topside?" Robin said, fidgeting and holding his ground by the other door as if he too would flee. "What has he to do with any of this?"

"I won't even ask you about the portrait of *her* you have hanging in your rooms while the smaller one of *me* is in the corridor. I am wearied to death with your caperings, to put it prettily, my lord. I give you an earldom but you presume to play king."

"Hell's gates, Your Grace," he exploded, "you've been using me as a pawn to be taken by a foreign and enemy queen, so I thought I'd at least ascertain what the woman looked like. It's a poor portrait of her, especially next to any of you, including this one!" he cried and yanked a locket on a chain out of his doublet. He tried to pry it open with some difficulty.

"Nevermind trying to make amends," Elizabeth insisted. "It's probably rusted shut from disuse if it hides my likeness!"

"If it is rusted shut, it is from my tears you no longer love me as you once did—at least said you did!"

"And now I want nothing but silence from you! You were to keep to the side in my dealings with Mary Stuart, not get your sticky, greedy fingers into the Christmas pie like Jack Horner in the corner," she told him, wagging her finger as Cecil knocked once and entered with Ned.

"You called for me, Your Grace?" Ned said. He and Cecil looked almost as nervous as Robin.

"Master Topside, I regret to inform you that there is someone else I must appoint as Lord of Misrule this year, one who believes he can go his own way, so he will be perfect for the part. And you shall be his aide."

Ned looked confused, hurt, then angry. "But I—things are already greatly planned, Your Grace, and I was just about to visit my former colleagues, the Queen's Players, at the Rose and Crown, as you said I might."

"You may still do so, but you will be assisting the new Lord of Misrule, especially at the Feast of Fools, where he will rule indeed."

She glanced at Robin, then away. He had gone from deathly white to ruby red. And he had not yet learned when to keep his mouth shut.

"You first raise me to the earldom, then offer me to your cousin queen, then make a laughing stock of me?" he demanded.

"When people remark that I keep my friends so close, Cecil," she said, turning to him, "I merely smile and nod, but the unspoken truth is, of necessity, I keep my enemies even closer. Ned, you may fetch your players, but be certain, if you stage a play, that the Earl of Leicester as the new Lord of Misrule takes the part of buffoon—or villain!"

"*Holly and ivy, box and bay, put in the house for Christmas day,*" the queen's maids of honor and ladies in waiting chanted the old rhyme as they decked the halls, where kissing balls hung from rafters and lintels. *Falalalalas* echoed in the vast public rooms of the palace. But the queen's mood was still soured as she watched all the frivolity. Truth be told, she'd like to feed both Martin Bane and Robin Dudley a big bowl of mistletoe berries.

"It's not really true, is it?" Rosie's voice pierced the queen's thoughts. Four of her maids were standing close, looking at her on the first landing of the newly garlanded staircase.

"What was that again?"

"It's only a superstition about the holly berries, isn't it?" Rosie prompted.

Anne Carey, wife of Elizabeth's cousin Baron Hunsdon, came to the queen's aid. "Obviously," Anne said, "it's pure folk custom that these more pointed holly leaves are male and the more rounded ones female." It was custom to count whether more sharp-leafed or smooth had been gathered each year; whichever kind was in the majority supposedly decided whether the man or wife of the house ruled the roost in the coming year.

"I shan't leave to chance," Elizabeth said, "who commands this dwelling or any other palace for the entire year. I don't give a fig how many sharp leaves of holly are hauled in here, a woman rules."

She basked in their smiles and laughter. They made her feel better, and she was greatly looking forward to the rewarding of the new liveries to the kitchen staff. Finally, she began to buck up a bit.

With her main officers of her palaces, the queen processed

toward the vast kitchen block. Behind her came the four chief household officials—the Lord Chamberlain, Lord Steward, Treasurer, and Comptroller—with some of their aides, laden down with piles of new clothes. She had sent for her former groom and favorite horseman, Stephen Jenks, because anytime she chose to leave her yeomen guards behind, she felt better with him in tow.

The royal kitchens of the Tudor palaces actually held three staffs that occupied separate areas: the hall kitchen served minor courtiers and household servants who ate in the Great Hall; the lord's kitchen provided for the nobles who sat on the dais in the Great Hall; and the privy kitchen fed the queen and whomever she chose to have dine with her. This particular set of liveries was going to her privy kitchen staff.

The mere aroma from the open hearths and brick ovens pulled the queen fully back into the mood for Christmas. The bubbling sauces, spitted roasts, and plump pillows of rising dough being kneaded for pastries and pies made her nose twitch. In a long line stood her staff, Master Cook Roger Stout to lowest scullery maid and spit boy. The fancy livery was for those of the highest echelons and those who served at table, but everyone would receive at least a piece of cloth or a coin. Most gifts were given on New Year's Day, but the household staffs needed their new garments now to look their best these coming Twelve Days.

Elizabeth went down the line from pastry cooks, to larders, confectioners, boilers, and spicers, giving a quick smile and word of praise to each with the varied gifts. "Is that everyone?" she asked the beaming Stout as he sent his staff back to their tasks. "I see there's a doublet left."

"I reckon it's for Hodge Thatcher, Your Most Gracious Majesty, as I noticed him missing. If he's nodded off, I'll have his skin."

"More like poor Master Hodge is busy putting the skin and feathers back on the peacock for tonight," Elizabeth countered.

Hodge Thatcher was Dresser of the Queen's Privy Kitchens, which meant he "dressed" or ornately arranged the fancy dishes for the feasts. It was no mean task to garnish and decorate soups, meats, and pies. For entertaining foreign ambassadors, he'd turned out many a finely refeathered, roasted swan with the traditional, tiny crown upon its head. For this evening, he must re-affix the roasted peacock's iridescent coat and prop up the fan of feathers. Once, years ago, she'd seen Hodge at that task when he first came to serve in her father's kitchens. She glanced over at the hatches through which Master Hodge must inspect all food before it was carried upstairs to her table, whether she was eating in public or in private.

"His workroom is by the back door to the street, is it not?" she asked and took the items down the crooked corridor herself while Stout and her entourage hurried along.

"Ah, yes, what a fine memory you have, Your Majesty," he cried, sounding out of breath, "for his is the last door before passing through to the porter's gate and so outside the walls. Allow me to ascertain if he is within and announce you," he added, but the door was narrow and the queen poked her head in ahead of the others.

"He's not here," she declared at first glance into the dim

room, lit by a single lantern on the cluttered work table. She saw the small area served also for storage: pots and kettles, spits and gridirons hung aloft on hooks and hoisting chains.

Then, amidst all that, the queen saw bare feet dangling head high. She gasped as she gazed up at a bizarre body, a corpse, part bird, part man.